The Best Western Stories of
LES SAVAGE, JR.

The Best Western Stories of LES SAVAGE, JR.

Edited by
Bill Pronzini
and
Martin H. Greenberg

Thorndike Press • Chivers Press
Thorndike, Maine USA   Bath, Avon, England

This Large Print edition is published by Thorndike Press, USA and by Chivers Press, England.

Published in 1996 in the U.S. by arrangement with Golden West Literary Agency.

Published in 1996 in the U.K. by arrangement with Ohio University Press.

U.S. Hardcover 0-7862-0585-7 (Western Series Edition)
U.K. Hardcover 0-7451-3916-7 (Chivers Large Print)
U.K. Softcover 0-7451-3922-1 (Camden Large Print)

Thorndike Large Print ® Western Series.

The text of this Large Print edition is unabridged.
Other aspects of the book may vary from the original edition.

Set in 16 pt. News Plantin.

Printed in Great Britain on permanent paper.

British Library Cataloguing in Publication Data available

Library of Congress Cataloging in Publication Data

Savage, Les.
    [Short stories. Selections]
    The best western stories of Les Savage, Jr. / edited by
Bill Pronzini and Martin H. Greenberg.
        p.   cm.
    ISBN 0-7862-0585-7 (lg. print : hc)
    1. West (U.S.) — Social life and customs — Fiction.
2. Western stories. 3. Large type books. I. Pronzini, Bill.
II. Greenberg, Martin Harry. III. Title.
[PS3569.A826A6 1995b]
813'.54—dc20   95-42201

Contents

Contents

Acknowledgments

"Introduction: Innovative Writer, Remarkable Man," by Jon Tuska. Copyright © 1991 by Jon Tuska.

"King of the Buckskin Breed" in *.44 Western*. Copyright © 1951 by Popular Publications, Inc. Copyright © renewed 1979 by Marian R. Savage.

"Silver and Shells for General Kearny" in *Dime Western*. Copyright © 1943 by Popular Publications, Inc. Copyright © renewed 1971 by Marian R. Savage.

"Dangerous Orders" in *Zane Grey's Western Magazine*. Copyright © 1951 by The Hawley Publications, Inc. Copyright © renewed 1979 by Marian R. Savage.

"Six-Gun Bride of the Teton Bunch" in *Lariat Story Magazine*. Copyright © 1947 by Real Adventures Publishing Co., Inc. Copyright © renewed 1975 by Marian R. Savage.

"Lunatic Patrol" in *Argosy*. Copyright © 1945 by Popular Publications, Inc. Copyright ©

Introduction

Innovative Writer, Remarkable Man: Les Savage, Jr.
BY JON TUSKA

We remember always, I think, how we first discovered those authors who come to mean the most to us in our lives. For me, I came to Les Savage, Jr., only recently. I had been adviser on the first edition of *Twentieth Century Western Writers* (1982) and co-editor-in-chief of the *Encyclopedia of Frontier and Western Fiction* (1983) when Dale L. Walker, then editor of *The Roundup*, the house organ of the Western Writers of America, sent me a copy of a letter about Savage's omission in those books by a man he described as "one of WWA's faithful fans," a Mr. Bernie Nalaboff. This was followed not many days later by an urgent letter from T. V. Olsen, who admitted a tremendous debt to Savage's influence on his own Western fiction and enclosed a bibliography of Savage's novels.

I located a used copy of *Return to Warbow* (1955), and that was all it took! Savage's omission in both of the reference books with which I have been associated has been rectified in their respective second editions.

Les Savage died early, at the age of thirty-five, from complications arising out of hereditary diabetes and elevated cholesterol. He seems to have known that he did not have long and in what little time he had he produced a most remarkable body of work, at least eighty stories and novelettes and twenty-four completed novels. He was born 10 October 1922 in Alhambra, California. At the time his mother was a silent screen actress and his father's career remained that of a Hollywood still photographer. Growing up, Les was certain he wanted to be an artist. Then, at nineteen, he wrote his first story and sold it. That changed the course of his life permanently. Already by the end of 1943 his name was well established in the Western pulp magazines of the day and over the next several years he could be relied upon, whenever his name appeared on the contents page, to tell a riveting story, highly atmospheric, assiduously accurate as to period, and vividly evoked. He was meticulous about plot and he invariably had a detailed outline before him prior to setting the first word on paper. In writing pulp novelettes (stories between 20,000 and 45,000 words), Savage would write the first and last chapters and then fill in the rest. When he began writing book-length novels, he used the same method. He was inventive, innovative, and he loved to experiment, all characteristics that got him into any number of battles with editors and which also kept him effectively in the pulps. Former pulp writers from Frederick Faust (Max Brand) to Fred Glidden (Luke Short) have gone on record that writing for slick magazines such as *Collier's* and *The Saturday Evening Post* was a matter of ideas and attitudes. There was also a more rigid adherence to formulae than in the pulps. For those editors who loved Savage's work, especially Malcolm Reiss of Fiction House (*Action Stories, Frontier Stories, Lariat Story Magazine*) and Don Ward of *Zane Grey's Western Magazine*, he gave them more often than not the very best he had.

His painstaking research is apparent in virtually all that he wrote, his intimate grasp of the terrain wherever a story would be set, his vital familiarity with the characteristics of flora in the changing seasons, and the ways of horses, mules, and men. He did this in an entirely natural and graceful way, displaying only covertly specialized learning in a dozen disciplines from mining, geology, and period furniture to dress, anthropology, and firearms. He might have been a poet because of the striking images he could conjure. In "The Brand of Señorita Scorpion" in the Summer 1944, issue of *Action Stories*, he generated a truly sinister mood when the heroine, Elgera Douglas, entered an area near a recently dead volcano. She "recognized cottonwoods and aspens and a scattering of juniper, but none of the trees had foliage. Their branches reached out naked and grey, like malignant clawing hands. When a slight wind sighed down from the rimrock, they rattled in hollow, mocking echo." It was rare to find this kind of writing in any pulp magazine. Moreover, even his most memorable descriptions of nature were usually reflective of human emotions, as this sunset in *The Wild Horse* (1950): "The timber was bunched in dense patches here, and beyond its tangled mat a sentinel peak had speared a falling ball of fire. Light spread in a crimson tide from this impaled sun as if it were flooding the world with its life blood, to form ruddy pools on the open glades and cover the forest floor with a sanguine dappling. The foliage of the poplars caught it up thirstily, till each slick olive-green leaf gave off a brazen glitter. It made a tawny illusion of the shadows, to close about Rockwall like a dark mist whenever he left the patches of light."

Following Savage's death, his correspondence, manuscripts, notes, and file copies of his pulp stories were destroyed by fire. What this has meant is years of digging through copies of pulp magazines to locate and authenticate all that he did write other than his novels. In point of fact, Les wrote very few short stories. He preferred the novelette. After all, Fiction House paid him 1½¢ a word which meant that he was paid between $225 and $450 for each novelette he might write. It was also a form with which he seems to have been most at ease since it gave him ample opportunity to develop his characters and to experiment even iconoclastically with the formulary patterns of Western narratives, to provide stories that had a variety of alternative endings to the usual romance between the protagonist and the heroine.

Another aspect of his work which also kept him in the pulps was that when he did end a story with a romance, the heroines were frequently mixed bloods or full-blooded Indians or Mexicans. This was not done at the time in slick magazines or in Western films. Nor was Les oblivious to this difference. Many of his early book-length works based on the plots of pulp novelettes published earlier altered the race of the heroine and when he did not do this, as in *The White Squaw* (1952), when he was hired to write the subsequent screen version, he was expected to change the plot so that the white protagonist does *not* end up with the Indian maiden as he does in the book. In "The Lone Star Camel Corps," Corporal Eddie Carnahan ends up committed to the Syrian woman, Lidea Kerem. When he incorporated this novelette into his later book-length novel, *Once a Fighter* (1956), Lidea Kerem is rejected by the white protagonist in favor of the Anglo-American heroine, Vickie Becknell.

At times, Savage might allow himself to be guided by such restrictions, but at others he would defy them. In *Savage Stronghold* (1953), the heroine is raped and it is up to the protagonist to help her through this difficult time and to reassure her that his love for her is as great as it ever was. In *Doniphan's Ride*, Nate Hatcher seeks out Inez Torréon who had been married to his Uncle Kirby and who is now pregnant with Kirby's child and tries to persuade her that he still loves her. It is ambiguous whether she will come and live with Nate. In subsequent decades, of course, this kind of ending to a Western story became more acceptable, but Les Savage, Jr. was writing this way when it definitely was not what was expected by the reading public.

As early as "Señorita Scorpion" in the Spring 1944, issue of *Action Stories*, Savage created a heroine who would be loved by more than one man but who would marry none of them. She would be his first series character, and also his last. Malcolm Reiss at Fiction House demanded of those who wrote for the magazines he edited that they stress the physically violent and brutal. It wasn't so much a matter of killing as it was bloody and vicious fights in which the protagonist was often severely injured in the process of pursuing his goal. Les Savage, Jr. fit in so well not because he adapted his stories to include such episodes but because he was in his element in creating such scenes. This characteristic can be found in numerous novelettes he did not write for Fiction House as, for example, "Water Rights — Bought in Hell!" which appeared in 1944 in *Star Western*, a Popular Publications pulp. This story contains a gripping, even chilling, fight between the protagonist and a blacksmith, the former armed with only a small hoof hammer, the blacksmith with a sledge ham-

15

mer. The fight is so vivid that every painful blow registers. Yet, Savage usually would leaven even the most harrowing episodes with humor. The blacksmith is so badly beaten that he holds his head, moaning softly. " 'Next time,' sobbed Dirk hoarsely, 'use a bigger hammer.' "

Savage fashioned a compelling setting for the first four Señorita Scorpion stories. Don Simeon Santiago discovered the Santiago Mine in 1681. He was accompanied by a slave, a captured English freebooter named George Douglas, a huge, yellow-haired man who had previous experience in a tin mine in Cornwall before going to sea. In digging out the mine tunnel, the hundred peons helped virtual prisoners working the mine dig through a mountain and find an enclosed valley, an idyllic area bounded on all sides by the Dead Horse mountains. An attack on the mine by Apaches and Comanches leaves the tunnel collapsed and only George Douglas and a peon woman alive. For two hundred years, in this sequestered place called Santiago Valley, the Douglas line continues, living in the great hacienda that Don Simeon had built, prospering from the bounties of nature and the breeding of longhorns which were also sealed off at the time of the mine's collapse. In the first story, Chisos Owens is

16

summoned by Anse Hawkman to the Texas border town of Boquillos. Hawkman is a range hog who four years before took possession of Owens' Smoky Blue ranch. He offers Owens a thousand dollars to capture Señorita Scorpion, dead or alive. She has been mercilessly preying upon all his holdings and, following each depredation, she disappears into the Dead Horse mountains. " 'She's a devil,' " Hawkman tells Owens. " 'They say she's lightning with a knife or a whip or a gun. Tall, blonde, rides like a fury.' " Owens sees her for the first time in the main street of Boquillos after looting Hawkman's gambling den there. "The tall roundness of her body was accentuated by her tight yellow blouse caught in a broad red sash and her clinging leggins of buckskin with bright flowers sewn down the seams. At the sound of Chisos' pounding boots, she turned her head sharply, and he could see a flash of blue eyes behind a narrow black mask, and her long blonde hair cascaded around, shimmering in the sun, stunning and unbelievable against the high color of her face." After decades of digging, those in the Santiago Valley have finally been able to penetrate again through the collapsed tunnel. While the basic conception owes more than a little, perhaps, to Zane Grey's *Riders of the Purple Sage* (1912), everything else about these stories is strikingly original. Of course, Owens does not capture Elgera Douglas. Instead, predictably, he falls in love with her, but a final reckoning with Anse Hawkman has to await "The Brand of Señorita Scorpion." In the Winter 1944, issue of *Action Stories*, in the third Señorita Scorpion story, Savage introduced Johnny Hager, sheriff of Brewster County, to the saga. This story was titled "Secret of Santiago" and it was followed in the very next issue, Spring 1945, by "Curse of Montezuma," perhaps the most memorable of the first four stories for its powerful imagery surrounding the appearance of a man claiming to be the reincarnation of Montezuma and its evocation of Aztec rituals and dress.

I have said that Señorita Scorpion was the first and last of Savage's series characters. However, she was not his only attempt at creating one. In "Señor Black-Mask — Dead or Alive!" in the Winter 1946, issue of *Action Stories* he introduced a figure clearly a clone from Johnston McCulley's popular Zorro stories which were still making frequent appearances in pulps published by Standard Magazines. This black-clad figure with a black mask fighting for the freedom of the peons apparently did not exert the fascination with readers that Señorita Scorpion had. At least four more Señorita Scorpion stories appeared in the pages of *Action Stories* between Winter 1945, and Winter 1949, one of them, "Gun-Witch of Hoodoo Range," from Winter 1948, written not by Savage but by Emmet McDowell, another frequent contributor to Fiction House pulps. Whatever the case, to this day copies of *Action Stories* with a Señorita Scorpion story in them sell at a premium price to collectors and she has been the subject of research being done on pulp magazines by such authorities in the field as Nick Carr and Robert Sampson.

In the late 1940s, Savage's life underwent significant changes. He published his first novel in 1947, *Treasure of the Brasada,* one of his best, set in the Texas border region he knew so well, and the next year he married. Marian brought to this marriage her young son, John, who was called Butch, and Savage adopted him and later dedicated his novel, *Land of the Lawless* (1951), to him: "To Butch, My Son, and I could search the world and never find a better one." Savage continued to write stories for the pulp magazines but from this point on all of his attention and vital energy were directed at producing book-length fiction.

Both Les and Marian loved the beach and

enjoyed breakwater swimming so they combined their savings and bought a modest home on Linnie Canal in Venice, California. It was a single-story, frame structure with one bedroom and a large, glass-enclosed sun porch *and* an attic. The sun porch was fashioned into a bedroom for Butch. A ship's ladder was constructed that ran up the bedroom wall into the attic. This space, about seven-by-nine, was high enough to permit standing upright. Flooring and a three-by-three skylight were added. Electrical wiring was installed so that the room was well illumined both day and night. A trap door was placed over the ceiling entrance. Thus Les had complete privacy and it was understood that unless you were specifically invited to come up, he was to be left alone. After breakfast, Les would climb the ladder and go to work. He worked four or five hours in the morning and usually another hour or longer at night. He was consistent with this schedule for five days of the week but, when inspiration moved him, he might also be heard up there on weekends, pounding away on his typewriter.

Les Savage, Jr., had an outgoing personality and a robust sense of humor, according to Frank Castle, one of his close friends and a fellow Western writer. Yet, he often preferred listening to talking. He seldom discussed his work except at meetings of the Fictioneers, a group of writers located in Southern California who would gather to discuss royalties, rights, agents, and the mechanics of their profession.

In making the transition from pulp writer to novelist, Les made what would prove a portentous decision for him. Rather than reprinting his pulp novelettes in paperback story collections as, for example, Frank O'Rourke and Thomas Thompson did, he chose to develop many of them into book-length novels. I use the word "develop" rather than the word "expand" because in the truest sense they are not expansions in the way that, for instance, Louis L'Amour later added padding, extraneous scenes, and superfluous characters to get the needed length from his pulp novelettes to produce book-length paperbacks. Les would completely redraft the original story. He might retain many of the same characters, even by name, but he would totally change the roles they had to play, reprising only what he felt were the best scenes from the novelette. Frequently, this would mean that the whole thrust and form of the narrative would be altered so significantly that the finished product bore only the loosest relationship to the novelette which inspired it. Some of these were more successful than others, but in all cases the differences remain greater than the similarities, so that reading the later novel is never the same experience as reading the novelette.

His second novel, *The Doctor at Coffin Gap* (1949), was published by Doubleday and the publisher considered Savage a welcome addition to its stable of writers producing regular entries for its on-going Double D Western series. The novel was developed from a novelette which had appeared first in 1947 in *Lariat Story Magazine* and Malcolm Reiss at Fiction House bought it for inclusion in *Two Western Books* where it appeared in the Fall 1949, issue under the title "Doctor Gunswift." Confronted with the burgeoning paperback reprints that were flooding the market, Fiction House hoped to compete by offering *two* book-length Western novels under one cover for twenty-five cents, not only in *Two Western Books* but also in companion pulps, *Two Western Romances* and *Two Western Action Books*.

It was Les' idea to publish his best novels in cloth editions with Doubleday with the hope of having them appear also in pulp publications and, eventually, in paperback reprints. Les' agent was August Lenniger who represented a number of Western writers. One of them was D. B. Newton. Newton's pulp novelette, "Gunhawk's Kid," first appeared in the December 1947, issue of *Western Novels and Short Stories*. Newton expanded it to book length and sent it to Lenniger, suggesting that he place it with Phoenix Press, a lending library hardbound publisher. Instead, Lenniger sent the book to Pocket Books which accepted it as the first Pocket Book original Western. When hardbound publishers saw a paperback house publishing original paperbacks and not reprints they were furious and, for a time, Pocket Books backed off, fearful that hardbound publishers would withhold reprint rights on titles it wanted to reprint, offering them instead to a competitor. Fawcett Books was not so timorous. It decided to specialize in original paperback fiction and not concern itself with reprints. Les developed a recent pulp novelette, "Lure of the Boothill Siren," which had appeared in *Lariat Story Magazine* in May 1949, into a novel he titled *The Wild Horse* and it was published in 1950 as a Fawcett Gold Medal Original novel with Les' byline. When Doubleday found out about it, the firm claimed to Lenniger that Les Savage, Jr., was a Doubleday Double D author and that Doubleday alone had rights to book-length fiction published under that name. Henceforth, the seven Gold Medal Originals that Les would publish under the Fawcett imprint appeared only under pseudonyms, six by Logan Stewart and one by Larabie Sutter (as Les explained it to Butch, the secret was in the initials: L. S.). By the time that the Doubleday subsidiary, Hanover House, published Les' first major historical novel, *Silver Street Woman* (1954), he had got back the right to use his name and he resumed publishing paperback originals as by Les Savage, Jr.

Savage was more fortunate when it came to motion picture rights. Gene Autry's Flying A Productions at Columbia Pictures purchased *The Doctor at Coffin Gap*, although the film that was made, an Autry opus titled *Hills of Utah*, bore little relationship to the novel. Universal-International bought screen rights to *The Wild Horse* and filmed it under the title *Black Horse Canyon* (Universal-International, 1954). As a tie-in with the release of the motion picture, Fawcett for the first and only time reprinted a Savage Gold Medal Original, retitling it *Black Horse Canyon* for its reissue in June, 1954. To help market the reissue, Joel McCrea was quoted on the back cover as saying that "it is my favorite Western and I got a real thrill out of playing the part of Rock in the Universal-International picture made from a book that I will never forget." Space forbids me to say more about *The Wild Horse* except this: the parallel in the pulp novelette between a wild horse that cannot be broken and a frontier woman for whom no man will ever be enough makes it, I believe, a far more interesting and gripping story than Les' development of it into a novel in which the woman and the protagonist end up in a formulary ranch romance at the end — more interesting and more gripping, perhaps, to contemporary readers but *not* more saleable to motion pictures in the early 1950s! It was a better ending for that time.

After 1950, Savage wrote very little for the pulp market, in part because he was busy with his novels but also because he had made an even more profitable connection with Don Ward of *Zane Grey's Western Magazine* than had previously existed between him and any editor at any magazine. Don Ward appreciated Les' unique and imposing talent and, following publication of the Zane Grey Award-winning story, "Saddlemates," in 1949, Ward accepted whatever Les sent him, be it a short story, a self-contained extrapolation of a novel in progress (*Last of the Breed*, a Dell Books original paperback of 1954, had first appeared in the magazine in

1951 in a shortened form; "Danger Rides the River," from the March 1953, issue was an excerpt from *Silver Street Woman*), and even condensed or complete versions of his book-lengths which were to be published by Doubleday. *The Hide Rustlers* (1950), *Shadow Riders of the Yellowstone* (1951), *Land of the Lawless*, and *Outlaw Thickets* (1952), all published in hardcover by Doubleday, appeared in *Zane Grey's Western Magazine* and, of course, all were reprinted by Pocket Books.

Savage developed *The White Squaw* from an earlier Fiction House novelette and it was bought for the screen by Columbia Pictures. Les was hired to produce the screenplay. He did a second stint at Columbia as a screenwriter, adapting his novel *Return to Warbow* which was released in Technicolor in early 1958. It was the last of Les' novels to be made into a film and, already as he was working on it, the health problems which would soon claim his life were eating into his time and his industry.

As Bill Pronzini wrote in his brief foreword to a Les Savage, Jr. story in his anthology, *Wild Westerns: Stories from the Grand Old Pulps* (1986), technically *Zane Grey's Western Magazine* "was not a pulp; it was a digest-size magazine. But in its aim, its contents, and even the paper on which it was printed, it was indeed a pulp. . . ." The last issue of *ZGWM* appeared in January 1954, and with its passing, Savage's last haven in the magazines passed as well. Lee E. Wells, whose name often shared a contents page with Savage in Fiction House publications and who would eventually turn to writing book-length Westerns when the pulp market faded, was a member of the Fictioneers as well as a fellow member of the WWA along with Les. He recalled in the obituary he wrote for *The Roundup* how, even when pressed, Savage would seldom complain too loudly but would resort instead to quiet understatement. When the folding of a paperback newsstand distributor was brought up at a Fictioneers meeting, Les characteristically said, "Things *are* a little rough." "He had his problems, his worries, professional and personal," Wells wrote, "but he never mentioned them, as too many of us do."

Surely one of Les' greatest disappointments was the lackluster reception accorded his major historical novels which were among the finest books of their kind. *Silver Street Woman* was reprinted by Pocket Books in a Cardinal edition. His *magnum opus, The Royal City* (Hanover House, 1956), set in New Mexico during the Pueblo Revolt of 1680, was not purchased for reprint although now it is the only one of his twenty-four novels currently in print, from the Museum of New Mexico Press. Doubleday, under its own imprint, issued his last major historical novel, *Doniphan's Ride*, which appeared posthumously.

At the time of his death — on 26 May 1958, at St. John's Hospital in Santa Monica, California — Savage was at work on his twenty-fifth novel. August Lenniger engaged Dudley Dean McGaughey to complete it and it was published in 1959 under the title *Gun Shy* and the joint byline of Les Savage, Jr. and Dudley Dean. Because McGaughey continued to produce original Western novels for Fawcett, this would be the only Savage book other than *The Wild Horse* that was reissued in a second printing.

D. B. Newton was a friend of Savage's during the last decade of his life. "He was a remarkable person," Newton recalled in a letter to me. "Physically ill-favored, but you quickly forgot about his odd appearance when you discovered that the man behind it had one of the sweetest natures of anyone you were apt to meet. I never heard him make a derogatory remark about another writer — something pretty unique in itself. He seldom talked much about his own accomplishments, but he was always interested in hearing what others were doing. (He did tell me that his first attempt at fiction was a submarine story, researched out of an encyclopedia. I don't know when he began selling but he must have been in his teens, and he was soon the top star at Fiction House.) Even during my years at Los Angeles we didn't see each other too often, because he lived in Santa Monica and I was out in the Valley. He and his pretty wife (whose name for him was 'Pappy') did come to dinner once, but mostly I saw him at gatherings of a scruffy group of freelancers who called themselves the 'Fictioneers,' and met at the Cafe de Paris in Hollywood once a month.

"Because of the perilous state of his health, his friends all knew he probably wouldn't be with us long. An item in one of the trade papers, stating that Les Savage had gone into the hospital, upset us all — but he showed up at the monthly dinner to assure us that it wasn't he but his father. When, at last, Bill Cox phoned to tell me that Les had just died, it was no less shocking for being expected at almost any time. It was a very quiet bunch of us that turned up for a memorial service.

"Les never stopped growing, even though he was working against time. His stuff for

Fiction House was sometimes pretty wild, with fantastic characters and bizarre action scenes (like the hero riding through a valley with rattlesnakes leaping at him from every direction). But as he got deeper into novel writing he settled down, and his big historical novel, *The Royal City*, was certainly a solid piece of work."

This collection of some of the best of Les Savage, Jr.'s short fiction opens with "King of the Buckskin Breed," which appeared in the November 1951, issue of *.44 Western*. It is late Savage, at least as far as his pulp contributions are concerned, and a story in which a man must not only prove that what he has said is true but also a story in which a man must come to terms with himself and his essential nature. He must then make a choice, between a white woman with whom he has been in love for some time and a mixed blood who represents freedom and a life in the wilderness.

"Silver and Shells for General Kearny," which appeared in *Dime Western* in December 1943, is early Savage and it amply demonstrates how, even at this stage in his career, he had a firm grasp of the complex social and economic fabric in New Mexico in general and Santa Fe in particular. This time period and this place would engage Savage's attention again and again, in "Traitor Town," a short story published in *Zane Grey's Western Magazine* and in *Doniphan's Ride.* Although set in an earlier period, New Mexico is also the setting for *The Royal City.*

Also set in the period of the Mexican War, although in Arizona rather than New Mexico, "Dangerous Orders" was published in *Zane Grey's Western Magazine* in April 1951, and reprinted by Bill Pronzini in his anthology, *Wild Westerns: Stories from the Grand Old Pulps.* It is an example of Savage's talent for the short story form at its finest, compact, succinct, with sharply etched characters who definitely belong to the period in which it is set. Savage was hired to do the adaptation for television of this story and it ran as an episode of *Dick Powell's Zane Grey Theatre.*

At a time when most heroines were virgins, Savage frequently featured heroines who were married, only adding to the tension. That is the case in "Six-Gun Bride of the Teton Bunch" which appeared in the July 1947, number of *Lariat Story Magazine.* The complexity of human motivation in this story, combined with the vivid evocation of Old Faithful, leaves a lasting impression.

"Lunatic Patrol" dates from that period

when Savage was experimenting with first-person narratives. It appeared in *Argosy* in May 1945. It is, I believe, his most successful first-person narrative and more satisfying in this regard than other such efforts, as for example "The Man Who Tamed Tombstone" in *Mammoth Western*, or "Lash of the Six-Gun Queen," a Señorita Scorpion story which appeared in *Action Stories*. In its compactness, Savage was able to make the weather a very real character and through an adroit use of delayed revelation to tell a compelling narrative. Surely, the narrative is more ambiguous than most instances of a Royal Mounted Policeman from this period, and more human.

"Chuck-Wagon Warrior," from *Zane Grey's Western Magazine* in January 1951, provides an ornery protagonist in the person of a camp cook. Les could draw this kind of character with amazing skill, as he did in another story of a camp cook, "The Last Ride of Pothook Marrs," a *Lariat Story Magazine* novelette which he developed into his Logan Stewart novel, *The Trail* (1951). This story is especially notable for the succinctness with which the characters are introduced, the dynamics of their interrelationships, and the penchant, so typical of the frontier, to resort to hyperbolic windies at every available opportunity.

Les developed "The Devil's Keyhole," which appeared in *Zane Grey's Western Magazine* in November 1949, into his late novel, *Hangtown* (Ballantine, 1956). In the novel, Anders *is* responsible for faulty engineering projects and he is a drunk because of his yearning after his wife who has left him. The short story is more circumscribed but the engineering expertise of bridge-building is only one more exceptional instance of how easily and naturally Savage could integrate complex technology into a fast-moving narrative.

Finally, "Saddlemates," which appeared in *Zane Grey's Western Magazine* in April 1949, and which was reprinted in *Zane Grey Western Award Stories* (Dell Books, 1951) was Savage's first contribution to the magazine and the one which established him so well in Don Ward's esteem. The opening sentences again demonstrate how Savage would use nature to reflect human emotions. It is also an oblique reference to his own relationship with Butch, the importance of a son to a man no longer young, and the fortitude and wisdom which were so much a part of Les Savage, Jr.'s character and personality.

Perhaps, once you finish reading this collection, your sympathies will be, as are mine, in accord with what Lee E. Wells wrote of Les in his eulogy. "An old cowboy saying goes, 'Success is the size of the hole a man leaves when he dies.' The writing profession, WWA, and his friends are much aware of the big hole that Les Savage left." Might I presume also to add: his readers?

King of the Buckskin Breed

"I'LL WAIT IN THE HILLS. . . ."

In the spring of 1840, Fort Union had stood at the confluence of the Yellowstone and the Missouri for eleven years. And in that same spring, Victor Garrit came down out of the mountains for the first time in three years. He came down on a Mandan pony, still shedding its winter coat, with his long Jake Hawkins rifle held across the pommel of the buffalo saddle. Those years of running the forest alone had changed his youthful handsomeness, had hollowed his face beneath its prominent cheekbones, had settled his black eyes deep in their sockets. It gave his face the sharp edge of a honed blade, and made a thin slice of his mouth which might have left him without humor but for the quirk which came and went at one tip. He stopped twenty feet out from the huge double-leaved gate in the palisaded wall, calling to the guard.

The small door in one of the leaves opened and John Farrier stepped through. Chief factor of Fort Union since 1832, his square and beefy figure in its three-point blanket coat and black boots was known from New Orleans to the Canadian Territories. He greeted Garrit with a broad grin.

"We saw you coming in, Vic."

"Your Indian runner found me in Jackson Hole last month," Garrit said. "He said you were in trouble, and would give me amnesty if I came."

"You've got my protection, as long as you're here," Farrier told him. He scratched thoughtfully at his curly red beard. "You know Yellowstone Fur is in a hole, Vic. The Blackfoot trouble has kept my company trappers from working their lines for two years. If we don't get any fur this year we go under. The free trappers have been operating over beyond the Blackfoot country. They'll have their rendezvous in Pierre's Hole this year. If we can get a train of trade goods through and get their furs, we'll be in business again."

Garrit's eyes had never been still, roving from point to point along the palisaded wall in the suspicious restlessness of some wild thing. "And you want me to take the pack train through?"

"You're the only man can do it, Vic. I can't get any of these mangy lard-eaters around the post to take the chance, not even for double wages and a bonus. The trader's here, but he had to get all of his crew from St. Looey." The factor put a freckled hand on Garrit's knee. "Yellowstone might forget a lot of what happened in the past, if you saved the day for them, Vic."

Garrit's black eyes never seemed to lose their gleam, in their shadowed sockets, and it only added to the wildness of his gaunt face. "You'd go under if the company went under, wouldn't you, John?" he asked.

Defeat pinched at Farrier's eyes, making him look old. "You know I plan on retiring soon. I couldn't do it without Yellowstone's pension."

The quirk at the tip of Garrit's lips became a fleeting grin. "You've been my only friend up here, John. I don't think I'd be alive today without you. Where's the trader?"

A broad smile spread Farrier's beard, he slapped Garrit affectionately on the knee, turned to lead him back inside. There were a dozen company trappers and *engagés* gathered on the inside of the door, gaping at Garrit as he rode through. He followed Farrier past the great fur press in the middle of the compound to the hitchrack before the neat factor's house. He dismounted, still carrying his Jake Hawkins, and followed Farrier through the door. Then he halted, shock filling his face with a bloodless, putty hue.

Enid Nelson sat in a chair by the crude desk, rising slowly to her feet with sight of Garrit. And beside her, John Bruce took a sharp step forward, staring at Garrit with red anger filling his heavy-jawed face.

"Damn you, Farrier," he half-shouted. "You didn't tell me it would be Garrit. What are you trying to do?"

Farrier dropped his hand on Garrit's tense shoulder. "I gave him my word he'd have my protection, Bruce."

"Protection, hell!" Bruce stormed. "As an officer of Yellowstone Fur, I order you to put this man under arrest immediately."

"John — " Enid wheeled toward him, her voice sharp. "You can't ask Farrier to go back on his word!"

Bruce glared at Garrit, breathing heavily, held by Enid's angry eyes for a moment. Three years of soft living had put a little weight around his belly, but he still bore a heavy-shouldered handsomeness, in the buffalo coat and cowhide breeches of a trader. Garrit was not looking at him, however. Since he had first entered, his eyes had been on Enid. She was a tall girl, auburn-haired, with a strong beauty to her wide-set eyes, her full lips. The Palatine cloak with its pointed hood, the tight bodice holding the swell of her mature figure, the skirt of India muslin — all brought the past to Garrit with poignant impact.

Bruce finally made a disgusted sound. "I'd rather go alone than be guided by a wanted man."

"You'd never make it ten miles alone," Farrier said. "The trader for Hudson's Bay tried it last year. The Blackfeet caught him. He lost his whole pack train. He was lucky to get his men back alive."

"Those weren't Blackfeet," Garrit said thinly.

Bruce stared at him blankly a moment, then a derisive smile curled on his lips. "Don't tell me you're still harping on that Anne Corday fable."

Garrit's head lifted sharply. He turned to pace restlessly across the room, glancing at the walls, like some animal suspicious of a cage. "It's no fable," he said. His voice had lost its accustomed softness. "Anne Corday was with those Indians that got the Hudson's Bay trade goods last year. The same woman that got my pack train down on the Platte."

Farrier stopped John Bruce's angry retort with an upheld hand. "There may be something to it, Bruce. The few trappers of ours that have gotten through haven't been able to keep any pelts on their lines. Their traps have been cleaned out more systematically than any Indians would ever do it."

Enid turned to Bruce, catching his arm. "John, if Garrit's the only one who can get you through, let him do it."

"And let him take another five thousand dollars' worth of trade goods whenever he feels like it?" Bruce said. "I'm not that foolish, Enid. And you have no right to give him amnesty, Farrier. When the company hears about this, there's liable to be a new factor at Fort Union."

He turned and stamped out the other door, leaving an empty silence in the room. But Farrier winked at Garrit.

"They sent Bruce up here to learn the ropes so he could take over when I retire. But he can hardly be factor if there ain't any Yellowstone Fur, can he? And there won't be any Yellowstone Fur if he don't get through to the rendezvous. And he won't get through unless you take him. When he cools off, he'll see how simple it is."

With a sly grin he followed Bruce out. Slowly, reluctantly, Garrit looked back to

Enid. His weather-darkened face appeared even more gaunt. When he finally spoke, his voice had lowered to a husky murmur.

"It's funny. I've dreamed of seeing you again, for three years. And when it comes . . . I don't know what to say."

A smile came hesitantly to her soft lips. She moved toward him, reached out a hand shyly, impulsively, to touch his mouth.

"That quirk's still there, isn't it?"

The touch of her hand was like satin, bringing the past back so painfully that it made him pull away, turn from her, start to pace again.

"It's the only thing that hasn't changed, in you," she said. "I don't think I'd have recognized you, at a distance. You must have lost twenty pounds. You're dark as an Indian. And so restless, Vic. Like some animal."

"The woods do that to a man, I guess," he said. "You got to be half animal to stay alive in the Blackfoot country." His deepset eyes filled with that restive gleam as he glanced around the walls. "I never saw such a small room."

She shook her head from side to side, staring at him with hurt, troubled eyes. "Was it worth it?"

He turned sharply to her. "Would you

spend five years in jail for something you didn't do?"

"Don't you want to come back, Vic?"

"Come back." He looked at her an instant, the pain naked in his eyes. Then he turned away stiffly, voice low and tight. "More than anything else in the world, Enid. It's the only thing that keeps me going."

"Things have changed, Vic."

The gaunt hollows beneath his prominent cheekbones deepened, as he realized what she meant. "You . . . and Bruce?"

"I tried to wait, Vic." She turned her face away, as if unable to meet his eyes. "You have no idea how hard it was." Then she wheeled back, catching at his arm, the words tumbling out. "You've got to understand. I did wait, you've got to believe me, but it was so long, not hearing from you, then someone brought word you were dead — "

"It's all right, Enid. I understand. I had no right to ask that you wait." He paused, then brought the rest out with great effort. "I suppose you and John plan to be married after he makes good on this trip?"

"Oh, Vic — " It was torn from her, and she wheeled around, face in her hands, shoulders shaking with sobs. He stared at her, helplessly. He wanted to go to her, to take her in his arms, more than anything else he'd wanted in these three years. He started to, then his hands dropped, and he stopped again, as he realized he had no right. She was tortured enough, in her dilemma. Even though she knew he was alive now, it did not change things. He had no more to offer her than he'd had three years ago, when he fled. Finally, in a barely audible voice, he said:

"For your sake, and for Farrier's, I hope Bruce decides to let me take him through. Tell them I'll wait in the hills to the west. These walls are getting too tight."

HELL-CAT'S BREW

John Bruce's pack train left Fort Union on the twelfth of April, following the Yellowstone River south. There were ten men and thirty mules, loaded with the tobacco, Du Pont powder, Missouri lead, knives, traps, flints, vermilion, bridles, spurs, needles and thread for which the free trappers and Indians at Pierre's Hole would trade their furs.

The cavalcade toiled through the rolling grasslands south of the Missouri, forded countless creeks swollen and chocolate with spring. They passed the mouth of the Powder

River where the sand lay black and fine as Du Pont on the sloping banks, and fighting their way through clay flats turned viscid as glue by the rains, finally gained the mountains.

There had not been too much talk between John Bruce and Garrit during the days in the lowlands. But now, as they pulled to the first ridge ahead of the toiling mules, and halted their horses among the pines, Bruce let out a relieved sigh.

"Thank the Lord we're through that clay. I thought I'd go crazy. I never saw such country."

Garrit sat staring off westward at the undulant sea of hoary ridges and valleys, rolling away as far as he could see. "It's a good country. You've just got to get used to it," he said. His broad chest swelled as he drew a deep breath of air, syrupy with the perfumes of pine and wild roses. "Take a whiff of that. Like wine."

Bruce frowned closely at him. "Don't tell me you actually like it — running like an animal all these years in this wilderness."

Garrit tilted his narrow, dark head to one side. "It's funny," he said. "A man doesn't think about liking it, or not liking it. He just lives it. Maybe he should stop to appreciate it more often."

"I used to see those mountain men come into St. Looey," Bruce said. "I never could understand what made them come back here, year after year, till some blizzard got them, or some Indian."

Garrit glanced at him, the humor leaving his face. "No," he said. "You wouldn't understand."

Surprise widened Bruce's sullen eyes. Then his lips clamped shut, and the antipathy dropped between them again. "You want to be careful, Garrit," he said. "I still think I should turn you in."

A sardonic light gleamed in Garrit's eyes. "But not till I've brought you through safe with the furs that'll make you chief factor of Fort Union."

Bruce's face grew ruddy, and he started to jerk his reins up and pull his horse over against the mountain man's. But a rider came laboring up the slope behind them, stopping Bruce's movement. It was Frenchie, a burly man in a cinnamon bear coat and elkhide leggings, a red scarf tied about his shaggy black hair, immense brass earrings dangling against his cheeks. He drew to a halt beside them, blowing like a horse.

"Now for the climbing, *hein?*" he grinned. "Looks like we go through that pass ahead."

"Not by a longshot," Garrit said. "How

long you been in this country?"

"Jus' come north to work at Fort Union this spring," the Frenchman said. "Man don't have to know the country to see that pass is the easiest way through."

"Exactly why we don't take it," Garrit said. "The Blackfeet have caught three pack trains in there the last two years. They don't think there's any other way through Buffalo Ridge. But I know a trail over that hogback to the south."

"These mules are already worn down from that clay," Bruce said angrily. "I'm not taking them ten miles out of our way to climb over a peak when there's a perfect pass through — "

"Farrier sent me along to keep your hair on your head," Garrit said thinly. There was no quirk left at the tip of his lips. "Any time you want to go on alone, just say so."

Bruce grew rigid in the saddle, his eyes drew almost shut. For a moment, there was no sound but the stertorous breathing of the animals, standing in a long line behind them. Finally Bruce settled into the saddle.

"All right," he said, sullenly. "What do we do?"

"It's getting late. I'll scout ahead. I want to be sure what we're going into. If I'm not back by the time you reach that river in the valley below us, make camp there."

Garrit heeled his horse down off the crest and into timber. As the men disappeared behind, the only sound that broke the immense stillness was the sardonic crackle of pine cones underfoot. He could not help his usual grin at the sound. There was something sly and chuckling about it, like the forest having its own private little joke on him. It always brought him close to the mountains, the solitude, and it made him realize what a contrast his present sense of freedom was to the restive confinement he had felt in the fort.

But thought of Fort Union brought the picture of Enid back to him, and his exhilaration faded. Through all these years he had carried with him constantly the painful desire to return to her, to the life they had known. Seeing her at Fort Union had been a knife twisted in the wound. He still felt a great, hollow sickness when he thought of her being promised to Bruce. Could she be mistaken in her feelings? He had seen something in her eyes, something she had been afraid to put in words. If he cleared his name, so he could go back to her, would she realize —

He shook his head, trying to blot out the thoughts. He realized he had climbed halfway up to the next ridge without looking for sign. A man was a fool to dream in this country. His head began to move from side to side in the old, wolfish way, eyes picking up every little infraction of the normal rule of things.

It was near dusk when he found the sign. He was five or six miles beyond the pack train, emerging from a fringe of quaking aspen along a stream in the bottom of a canyon, and he caught sight of the early berry bush ahead. A few of the red-black berries were scattered on the ground, and half a dozen of the limbs had been sliced cleanly near the root. As he approached, a magpie began scolding far up the slope. It was another of the forest sounds that invariably turned the quirk at the tip of his lips to a grin. There was something irrepressibly clownish about the raucous chatter. *Just keep talking, you joker,* he thought. *Long as you jabber I'm safe.*

He got down to study the moccasin tracks about the early berry bushes. They were only a few hours old, for the grass they had pressed down had not yet risen straight again. As he stood up, the magpie's scolding broke off abruptly. It made his narrow head snap around. The weather seams deepened around his eyes, squinting them almost shut, as he searched the shadowy timber. Then he hitched his horse and headed for the trees. An animal look was in his face now and he ran with a wolfish economy of motion. He reached a dense mat of buckbrush and dropped into it and became completely motionless. He could still see his horse. It had begun to browse peacefully. The timber was utterly still.

After a long space, he began to load his gun. He measured a double load of DuPont into his charge cup and dumped it down the barrel of his Jake Hawkins. He slid aside the brass plate in the stock, revealing the cavity filled with bear grease. He wiped a linen patch across this, and stuck it to his half-ounce ball of Galena. He rammed the lead home, and then settled down to wait.

For ten minutes he was utterly motionless. His eyes had grown hooded, the quirk had left his lips. The fanwise sinews of his fingers gleamed through the darker flesh of his hands, as they lay so softly, almost caressingly, against the long gun.

Then the man appeared, coming carefully down through the timber. He saw the horse and stopped. The brass pan of his Springfield glittered dully in the twilight. Garrit knew the conflict that was going on within him.

But finally, as Garrit knew it would be, the temptation was too great, and the horse decoyed him out.

He approached the animal, frowning at it. At last he began to unhitch it.

"Don't do that, Frenchie," Garrit said.

The burly Frenchman wheeled toward the sound of his voice. Surprise dug deep lines into his greasy jowls.

"By gar," he whispered. "You are an Indian."

Garrit's voice was silken with speculation. "I thought you were the Indian."

"Ho-ho!" The man's laugh boomed through the trees. "That is the joke. He thought I was Indian. And I find his horse and think the Indian take his scalp."

"Shut up," Garrit said sharply. "Don't you know better'n to make that much noise out here? I found sign down by the creek. Some Blackfeet had cut early berry branches for arrows."

Frenchie sobered. "We better go then, *hein?* My horse she's up on the ridge. Bruce he got worry about you and sent me to look." Garrit unhitched his horse and began the climb beside the man. Frenchie sent him an oblique glance. "You really belong to the woods, don't you?"

"How do you mean?"

"I was five feet from you and never see you. Like you was part tree or something."

"A man learns that or doesn't stay alive."

"Is more than that. Some men belong, some don't. Them that do will never be happy any place else."

It touched something in Garrit that he could not define. "Maybe so," he shrugged.

"For w'y you guide Bruce through like this? You hate him."

"It's for Farrier," Garrit said. "He's been my only friend up here. He'll go down with the company if they don't get any pelts this year."

"And for Anne Corday?"

Garrit glanced at him sharply. "What do you know about her?"

Frenchie shook his head. "Nothing. Except this is the first trade goods to go through mountains this year. Is like honey to bear. Five thousand dollar worth of honey. You have been hunting three year for Anne Corday without the success. Wouldn't it be nice if you were along when she show up to get these pack train?"

Garrit was looking straight ahead, his dark face somber and withdrawn. He would not admit it to Frenchie, but the man had struck the truth. Part of his motive in taking the train through had been his debt to Farrier.

But another part was his realization of what a strong lure this train would be to the men with Anne Corday. If he could catch them in the act, with John Bruce as witness. . . .

"It's funny you should talk that way," Garrit said. "Most men won't admit Anne Corday exists."

"I only know the stories I hear. You were youngest man ever trusted with Yellowstone Fur's trade goods for the rendezvous. Engaged to Enid Nelson in St. Looey. Big future ahead with the company." He sent Garrit that oblique look. "How did it really happen? I hear different story every time."

Garrit's eyes lost their focus, looking back through the years. "We had brought the trade goods by boat to the mouth of the Platte. Gervais Corday was camped there. He said he'd been a free trapper till Yellowstone Fur squeezed him out. He'd fought them and some Yellowstone man had shot him. They had to take his arm off. It made him bitter as hell toward the company."

"I would be bitter too," Frenchie said softly.

Garrit hardly heard him. "Anne Corday was his daughter. He'd married a Blackfoot squaw and kept Anne up there with the Indians. We were the first white men to see her. I guess no white man has ever really

52

seen her since. It was raining. The Cordays invited us into their shelter. There was whiskey. You don't pay attention to how much you're drinking, with a girl like that around. She danced with me, I remember that. She got us so drunk we didn't know what was going on. And her pa and his men got away with our goods."

"But why were you accused of taking the furs?"

"Cheyennes caught us before we got back to St. Looey. My crew was wiped out. I was the only one left alive. I had to get back the rest of the way on foot. It took me months. Nobody would believe my story. Too many traders had worked that dodge on Yellowstone, and had taken the trade goods themselves. If there had been witnesses, or someone had known of the Cordays, or had seen them, it would have been different. But I was completely without proof."

"And nobody has seen Anne Corday since," Frenchie mused. "She mus' have been very beautiful woman."

Garrit nodded slowly. "I can still see her — "

He broke off, as he became aware of the expression on Frenchie's face. The man tried to hide it. But Garrit had seen the sly curl of the lips. Hot anger wheeled Garrit into Frenchie, bunching his hand in the filthy pelt of the cinnamon bear coat and yanking the man off-balance.

"Damn you. You don't believe a word I'm saying. You were just leading me on — "

For a moment they stood with their faces not an inch apart. Garrit's lips were drawn thin, his high cheekbones gleamed against the taut flesh. Finally the Frenchman let his weight settle back against Garrit's fist, chuckling deep in his chest.

"Do not be mad with Frenchie for making the joke, *M'sieu*."

Garrit shoved him away with a disgusted sound, trying to read what lay in those sly, pouched eyes. "Don't make another mistake like that," he said thinly. "It's no joke with me."

It was full night when they got back to camp. The mules were out in timber on the picket line, grazing on the buffalo grass and cottonwood bark, indifferently guarded by a pair of buffalo-coated men. The pack saddles were lined up on one side of a roaring fire. Garrit came in at a trot, calling to the trader.

"Bruce, don't you know better'n to build a fire like that in Indian country? Get those mules and saddle up. We can't stay here now — "

He broke off as the men about the fire

parted. There was a horse near the blaze, with two willow poles hooked in a V over its back. From this *travois* the men had just lifted the woman, putting her on a buffalo pallet by the fire. Before they closed in around her again, Garrit caught a glimpse of the Indian sitting on the ground beside the pallet, head in his arms. Bruce pushed his way free, a flat keg of Monongahela in one hand.

"We can't move now, Garrit. The woman is sick. Our interpreter's been talking with them. Game has been scarce this spring. She's so weak she can hardly talk. The man had tied himself to the horse to stay on."

"That's an old dodge," Garrit said. "They've probably got a hundred red devils waiting, now, out in the trees, to jump you."

"Wouldn't you have run into them on your way back?"

Garrit shook his head darkly. "You just got to learn the hard way, don't you? If she's hungry, that whiskey won't help."

"I was just giving the men a drink. I thought a shot might revive her."

"You were what?"

"Giving the men some," Bruce said irritably. "Now don't tell me I can't do that. Farrier said he gave his men a drink every other night."

"I suppose you had some too?"

"I did. How else can a man keep his sanity out in this Godforsaken country?"

Garrit shook his head disgustedly, glancing at the laughing, joking, red-faced men. "From the looks of them they've had more than their share. If you want to get anywhere tomorrow, cork that keg up right now."

He turned to walk over to the group and push his way through, to stare down at the woman. She was in an elkhide dress with openwork sleeves, whitened by bleaching, a stripe of vermilion paint was in the part of her black hair, and more was blotched on her cheeks. She lay with her head thrown back, eyes closed, breathing shallowly.

He felt the blood begin to pound in his temples. He felt shock spread its thin sickness through his belly. Suddenly, he found himself on his knees beside her, his hand grasping her arm, jerking at her.

"Open your eyes; you're no more starving than I am. Get up — "

The Indian man raised his head from his arms, calling weakly to Garrit, "*Kola, kola* — "

"Friend, hell," Garrit said savagely. "*Ma yan leci kuwa na* — "

Bruce shoved his way through, grabbing at him. "Garrit, what are you doing?"

"I'm telling him to come over here," Garrit said hotly. "He isn't weak, and this isn't

56

any Indian. It's Anne Corday."

"Let her go," Bruce said roughly. "You're crazy. You can't treat a sick woman that way."

"She isn't sick, damn you, she's Anne Corday — "

Bruce pulled him back so hard he sat down. He jumped to his feet like a cat, whirling on Bruce, so enraged he started to hit him. Then he became aware of the men, sitting down around the campfire. Only one was still standing, and he was rubbing at his eyes, a stupid look on his face. The others were dropping their heads onto their arms, or lying back in their buffalo robes. A couple were beginning to snore stertorously. Even Bruce's eyes had a heavy-lidded look to them.

"What's the matter?" Garrit said.

"Nothing." Bruce shook his head. "Just sleepy."

"How much of that whiskey did you drink?"

Bruce yawned heavily. "Maybe a little more'n I should. But it wouldn't do this. Just been a long day."

"Long day, hell." Garrit spotted the keg of whiskey, walked savagely over to it. He picked it up, uncorked it, sniffed. "She did this," he said, wheeling on Bruce. "That's laudanum, she's put laudanum in the whiskey — "

Then he stopped. Bruce had sat down against one of the saddles, arms supported on his knees, and his heavy head had fallen onto those arms. Garrit's eyes flashed back around the men. Frenchie was not among them. He realized he had been too intent on the whiskey. It was too late. Even as he started to wheel, with the heavy grunt in his ears, the blow struck his head.

THE FIGHT

He regained consciousness to the sense of throbbing pain at the base of his skull. Someone was shaking him gently.

More pain dug new seams about his eyes, as he opened them.

"I thought you'd never come around," John Bruce was telling him. "It's lucky that Frenchman didn't split your head open."

He helped Garrit sit up. It was dawn, with the timber drenched in a pearl-gray mist all about them. The men were gathered around him, grimacing, rubbing their eyes, staring stupidly at each other. One of them was feeding a spitting fire, another was at

58

the edge of camp, retching.

"We came out of it a couple of hours ago," Bruce said. "Been trying ever since to revive you."

Garrit shook his head again, winced at the pain. "How could they have got that laudanum in the whiskey?"

"When I gave her a drink, she tried to hold the keg," Bruce said. "She dropped it, spilled some. The Indian picked it up. There was a little confusion for a minute, there, when they could have put it in. I never would have believed laudanum would do that."

"If you drink enough," Garrit muttered. "Farrier used it at Fort Union once. The Indians got so drunk they were going to start a massacre. He spiked their whiskey with laudanum and it knocked them out." He sent a dismal glance to where the pack saddles had stood, beyond the fire. "Did they get everything?"

"Even the animals," Bruce said. "We're stranded."

"Did you send that Frenchman after me?"

"No. He just disappeared."

"I guess he was trying to keep me from coming back," Garrit mused. Then he looked up at Bruce, wide-eyed. "Now will you believe me?"

59

The man shook his dark head. "I've thought Anne Corday was a myth for so long, it's hard to accept it, even now. I might as well join you in the mountains. This will finish me with Yellowstone Fur."

"It will finish Yellowstone Fur, if we don't get that pack train back."

Bruce's black brows rose in surprise. "What chance have we got? They have a night's start on us, and they're riding. We'll be lucky to get back to Fort Union on foot, as it is."

"A crowd like this will never make it back through that Blackfoot country on foot," Garrit told him. "Your best bet is to hole up while I go after our horses. If you can hold these men here till I get back you still might get a chance to stay with Yellowstone Fur."

Bruce protested, but Garrit finally convinced him it was their only chance. He drew a map in the earth. There was a creek in the next valley that ran ten miles northward into a canyon so narrow and tortuous it could not be reached by horses. Bruce was to do his hunting now, try to get enough meat to last the men several weeks, and then walk in the water of the creek to its head. This would leave ten miles of his back-trail covered, and in such an inaccessible place, he would be comparatively safe from Indians, if he did not move around.

Bruce finally agreed, and Garrit made up a pack of smoked buffalo meat and dried corn, rolled it in one three-point blanket, and took up the trail.

They had not bothered to hide their tracks. They led northwest from the Yellowstone, toward the heart of the Blackfoot country. It convinced him more than ever that he had not been mistaken. Only someone with connections in the tribe would have dared head so boldly into their land. And Anne Corday's mother had been a Blackfoot.

He left the mountains for a while, and hit the high plains, rolling endlessly away from him, so devoid of timber in most places that he could not travel much during the day for fear of being seen. On the third day he reached the Little Belts. After the endless plains, it was like coming home. He plunged gratefully into the shadowed timber on the first of the rolling slopes.

Now it was the real running. It brought out all the animal attributes bred in him these last years. There was an intense wolfishness to his unremitting dog-trot, long body slack, head down and turning incessantly from side to side, eyes gleaming balefully in their shadowed sockets, not missing a sign. He ran on their trail till he could run no more and then crawled into a thicket and lay in stupified sleep and then woke and ran again.

He began to see tepee rings, circles of rocks in parks or open meadows that marked the campsite of an Indian band. It made him even more watchful. On the fourth day he sighted the first Indians. He was climbing a slope, with a magpie scolding in the firs. Despite his aching weariness, he could not help his faint grin at the sound. *Just keep talking, you joker.*

His moccasins crushed resiliently into the mat of pine needles, and for another hundred yards he climbed steadily. Then the magpie broke off sharply. He stopped, staring up the slope, and wheeled and darted for a dense clump of chokecherry.

He was on his belly, hidden in the brush, when the Indians appeared. They passed within fifty yards of him and never knew he was there, a part of Blackfeet on the move, with their pack horses, their wives, their children. The scent of their tobacco floated to him, and it was not willow-bark *kinnikinnik,* but the rank plug cut the traders used. There were new axes on their saddles, and new iron bridles on their horses. They had been trading their furs with Anne Corday.

The band of spare horses made his mouth water. But he could not try for one in broad daylight, and since they were heading in the wrong direction, he did not want to lose half a day by following them south to their night camp. So he ran on.

On the fifth day he ran out of food and was afraid to shoot game for fear he would be heard. But he knew the Indian tricks. He found *tinipsila* roots and ate them raw and later on came across some bulrushes by a stream and ate the white part like celery. And farther up the stream were wild strawberries and a few service berries that only an Indian could swallow with a straight face. It gave him enough nourishment to keep running.

That night he found three more tepee rings in a shallow valley. The grass had not begun to grow up around the circled rocks, so he knew they had been planted recently. The horse droppings leading north were fresh enough to have been left that morning. It was the way he wanted it.

He followed the trail by moonlight, his lank figure fluttering through the shadow-black timber like a lost animal. He found the new camp near dawn. Three tepees formed pale cones in the center of a clearing, with the horses grazing on picket ropes.

Under ordinary circumstances, he would have moved more slowly, but the squaws would be rising soon, and he wanted to get away before that. So he had to approach the horses directly, not giving them time to get used to him. He picked out a pinto with lots of wind in its heavy throttle. Before he could reach it, however, one of the animals spooked and whinnied.

This brought the dogs from where they had been sleeping near the embers of last night's fire, and their baying raised the camp. They circled him in a pack, snapping at his legs and yapping crazily. Kicking them off, he pulled the pinto's picket pin and ran down the rope to the plunging horse. The first Indian to jump through the door flap had a clumsy London fusil.

He saw that he couldn't get it loaded in time, and started to run for Garrit. The mountain man threw all his weight onto the picket rope, pulling the pinto down so he could throw the loose end around its fluttering snout in a war-bridle. He did not have time to unknot the other end from about its neck. He pulled his Green River knife and slashed it.

The Indian reached him then, leaping through the pack of dogs to swing viciously with his clubbed fusil. Garrit ducked and the butt of the gun thumped against the pinto's flank. Holding the plunging horse with one hand, he threw his Green River, blade first, with the other. There was but a foot between them, and he saw it sink to the hilt in the man's shoulder.

The Indian staggered back, face contorted with pain. Garrit scooped up the rifle he had been forced to drop and threw himself aboard the horse, kicking its flanks. He raced out of camp with the dogs yapping at his heels and the other Indians stopping halfway between the tepees and the herd to load their fusils and fire after him. The short-range London guns would not reach him, however, and he plunged unhurt into timber.

He knew they would follow and ran the horse for the first creek. He went south in the water, for they knew all the tricks too. After two miles of riding the shallows he went out on shore and left sign they would be sure to follow and made them a false trail leading on south till he found a talus bench that led into another creek. The pony was unshod and would not even leave shoe scars on the rocky bench. In the water he turned north again. When he could travel north no longer in the water he left it once more. He was far enough above the Indian camp to start hunting for the Cordays' sign now. It took him several hours to pick it up.

They were pushing twenty-five pack horses, and he could travel at three times their speed if he drove hard. And he drove hard. All day, with only time out to water the horse and shoot a buck whose haunch he roasted over a fire and ate as he rode. He gave the horse an hour's rest at sundown and then went on.

By dawn the horse was beaten down but Garrit knew he was near his quarry for all the signs were not many hours old. His belly sucked at him with its hunger and his face, covered with a week's growth of scraggly beard, had the haggard, driven look of some animal. It took all his grim purpose and the bitterness of three years' exile to push him those last miles. Then, in the late afternoon, he topped a ridge and saw the line of pack horses standing in the park below him.

He left the horse and dropped down through the trees on foot. Closing in on the camp, he became a shadow, flitting from tree to tree. Finally he bellied down and crawled like a snake through buckwheat and chokecherry bushes till he could see the whole camp.

They had evidently just finished trading

with more Indians, for there was a pile of unbaled pelts heaped to one side of a campfire, and a pack saddle next to them, with some trade goods still lying on the ground. The Blackfoot who had come to Bruce's camp with the woman was busily loading another pack saddle onto one of the horses lined up near the trees. The other three were at the fire. Frenchie was on his hunkers, still wearing his immense cinnamon bear coat, sorting out the pelts they had just gotten. Gervais Corday stood above him, tall, bitter-eyed, one-armed. And Anne Corday was feeding new wood to the fire.

The weather seams deepened about Garrit's eyes, as he stared at her, giving his face an expression close to pain. This was the woman he had hunted for three years. Hers was the face he had seen in a thousand dreams. And now it was before him. Her blue-black hair no longer had the vermilion in its part. It was blown wild by the wind, and made a tousled frame for the piquant oval of her face, with its black eyes, its ripe lips. She had discarded the Indian dress for a shirt made from a red Hudson's Bay blanket, and a skirt of white doeskin with fringes that softly caressed her coppery calves. Even in his bitter triumph, he could not deny her striking, young beauty.

"Ho-ho," Frenchie chortled. "There are over twenty prime beaver here. Another year or so like this and we'll be rich."

Gervais frowned down at him. "You said this would finish Yellowstone Fur."

"Is true." The Frenchman grinned. "They don't turn this pack train into furs, they go under. But why stop? There is still American Fur, Rocky Mountain Fur. Even Hudson's Bay."

"Did they take my arm?" Gervais' voice was acid. He began to pace back and forth, slapping at his elkhide leggins with his good hand. "Did they ruin me? What do I care about Rocky Mountain or Hudson's Bay? They didn't smash my life. It is Yellowstone Fur who will pay." His voice began to shake. "They can't take a man's life and toss it away like a puff of smoke. Ruin everything he worked for so long. Cast him and his daughter upon the wilderness — "

The girl caught his arm, her voice low and placating. "Father, please, don't get excited again — "

"Excited!" He turned on her with blazing eyes. "How can you talk that way? You were ruined too. All my plans for you. Instead of a great lady you're nothing but a wild animal running the forest with me."

"One fur company is just as bad as the

next," Frenchie said. "You saw how American Fur pushed Lestrade off his rightful lines. If you'd fought them, I'm sure they'd have taken your arm just as quickly."

"Frenchie," the girl said sharply. "Don't start him off again. You're just twisting things around. Maybe he had reason to fight Yellowstone, but — "

"I don't know — " Gervais pulled away from his daughter, pacing again. "Perhaps Frenchie is right."

"Of course I'm right," the big Frenchman said. "What good would it do to stop now? If you take what we've made and try to start again, some other big fur company will only pinch you off again. We've got to ruin them all, Gervais. Only then will it be safe for honest men out here again. They take your arm this time; they're liable to kill you next time — "

"They won't get the chance, Frenchie," Garrit said, rising from the chokecherry bushes.

The three in the clearing and the Indian by the horses all turned in surprise. Garrit walked toward them, his Jake Hawkins held across one hip. Gervais finally let out a pent breath, speaking in a voice thin with shock.

"I thought you said you took all the horses."

"I did," Frenchie said. "The man's inhuman." Then he let out his bellowing laugh. "*Sacré bleu,* I should have kill you. The only man in the world who could have catch us on foot, and I let him live."

At that moment a quick movement from the Indian spun Garrit toward him. The man had tried to jump behind one of the horses and scoop up a loaded rifle and fire, all at the same time. His gun boomed simultaneously with Garrit's but he had tried to do too much at once. His bullet dug into the ground a foot from Garrit, while Garrit's bullet struck him in the chest, knocking him backward like a heavy blow.

But it gave Frenchie his chance. He reached Garrit before the mountain man could wheel back, with Gervais Corday rushing right in behind. Garrit was off-balance when the Frenchman grabbed his rifle. It was his first true sense of the man's bearlike strength. He felt as though his hands had been torn off with the rifle when Frenchie wrenched it free.

The big Frenchman swung it wide, clubbed, and brought it back in a vicious circle. It would have broken Garrit's head open. All he could do was drop to his knees. The heavy gun whistled over his head and smashed Gervais right in the face as he came rushing in on Frenchie's flank.

The one-armed man made a choked sound and dropped like a poled ox. Garrit came up off his knees into Frenchie, locking the rifle between them. It knocked the Frenchman back off his feet and he rolled to the ground with Garrit on top, fighting like a cat.

The quarters were too close for the rifle and the Frenchman let it go to pull his knife. Garrit tried to grasp the wrist but the Frenchman spraddled out for leverage and rolled atop Garrit.

The mountain man saw the flash of a blade and jerked his whole body aside. The knife drove into the ground. Frenchie yanked it out, but Garrit got hold of the knife-wrist with both hands and twisted it inward as he lunged upward with his whole body.

It drove the knife hilt-deep into the Frenchman. He let out a great shout of pain and flopped off Garrit. As the mountain man rolled over and came to his feet he saw Anne Corday on her knees beside her father, fumbling the pistol from his belt. Garrit ran at her, reaching her just as she raised the weapon. He kicked it out of her hand.

She threw herself up at him, clawing like an enraged cat. He caught both hands, spun aside, used her own momentum to throw her. She hit on her back so hard it stunned her, and she made no attempt to roll over or rise.

Garrit wheeled back in time to see Frenchie staggering into the trees, one hand gripped over his bloody side. Garrit got the loaded pistol and ran after the man. But by the time he reached timber, Frenchie was out of sight. Garrit heard Anne Corday groan and roll over. He didn't know how much time it would take him to find Frenchie. He couldn't risk it, he couldn't take that chance of losing the pack train again, with the girl and her father still in the clearing.

Reluctantly, he turned back to Anne Corday. The anger was gone from her face. Grief and shock rendered it blank. She was staring at her father, as if just realizing how crazily his head was twisted. Garrit knew, then, what she must have known. The blow of the rifle butt had broken Gervais Corday's neck.

"SHE'LL ALWAYS BE CALLING. . . ."

It was two days before the girl would talk to Garrit. He buried her father and the Indian up there in the Little Belts and took the

72

pack train and started back to Bruce.

The second night he made camp on the white beach of a creek in a narrow gorge that rose a hundred feet above them and would hide the light of their fire. The girl sat on a heap of buffalo robes, watching him draw a spark with his flint and steel. When he had the blaze started, her voice came softly out of the night.

"You love this country, don't you?"

He was silent awhile, staring into the flames. "I guess you're right. The country gets into a man without him even knowing it." He paused, then slowly turned to look at her. "You don't hate me?"

"I've been mixed up these last two days." She spoke in a low, strained voice. "For a while I thought you were to blame for my father's death. But the Frenchman killed my father." She shook her head slowly. "Something like this was bound to happen sooner or later. Father was changing so. I thought he was bitter enough, at first. But he was getting even worse. He was becoming a fanatic. Actually, you have as much reason to hate me. We ruined you, didn't we?"

He turned and walked to where she sat, towering above her, his face narrow and dark with thought as he gazed down at her. "I should hate you. I've tried to. But what I saw in that clearing changed a lot of things. Don't you realize how Frenchie was using your father?"

She stared at the sand, her lips still pinched and white with grief. "I realize now. The Frenchman didn't show his true colors till that afternoon. We thought he was a friend, another man who had been ruined by Yellowstone Fur. But he was nothing more than a thief, using my father's bitterness against Yellowstone to further his own ends."

"And your bitterness?"

Her face turned up to him defiantly. "Were we wrong? Wouldn't you despise the people who ruined your father?"

He dropped beside her, caught her hands. "It wasn't Yellowstone Fur itself, Anne. Has your father so filled you with his bitterness that you can't see that? There are decent men in Yellowstone. There's a man named Farrier down at Fort Union who could have turned me in, but he gave me a break."

"They sent a man out to kill my father — "

"Did your father really convince you of that? I saw a copy of the Yellowstone man's orders. He was sent to try and negotiate a new deal with your father for his territory. It was your father who started the fight. The Yellowstone man was only defending himself."

She jumped to her feet, eyes flashing. "Now you're trying to twist it up. I forgave you my father's death. Isn't that enough?" She wheeled away from him, walking to the end of the sandspit. She locked her hands, staring out into the night for a long time. Finally she said, thinly, "You think you'll take me in. You think you'll show me to all those men who don't believe Anne Corday exists, and it will clear your name."

"It's what I've been working toward for three years," he said, in a low voice.

"You'll never even get me back to Bruce," she said.

"Where would you go, if you escaped?" he said, gently.

"My mother is still with the tribe, up near Flathead Lake," Anne said. "I would be safe with any band of Blackfeet I met. But I don't need that. Don't you know who is following us?"

He felt his head lift in surprise, as he realized what she meant. "How could he, with a wound like that?"

"I know him," she said. "When he sets out to do something, nothing can stop him. You could stab him a dozen times and he could still walk a hundred miles. Frenchie is following us, Garrit, and he will catch us. You will never take me in."

★ ★ ★

Garrit did not sleep much that night. He tied Anne Corday's hands and spent most of the time scouting the gorge. It rained the next day, a spring thunderstorm that made the creeks overflow their banks and wiped out the trail of the pack train. Garrit pushed hard, knowing there was little chance of meeting Indians in the storm. But thought of the Frenchman hung more heavily upon him than any danger of Indians. If Anne Corday was right, the man would be a constant threat, hanging over them till they reached Bruce. It made Garrit jumpy, imbuing him with more than his normal restlessness.

They made a miserable camp in a cave, both of them soaking wet, and he hung a three-point for Anne to undress behind and then she wrapped the blanket around her and huddled over the fire.

"Do you remember how it was raining the first night we met, down on the Platte?" she said.

"And you took us into your shelters and let us dry our clothes and drink your whiskey and we got drunk as Indians on ration day."

"I had been drunk before. It was more than that. It's bothered me ever since."

"It has bothered me, too," she said, softly.

He stared down at her, trying to fathom

the strange look in her eyes, to untangle the mixed emotions in himself. Her lips, so red, so ripe, seemed to rise toward him, until they were touching his, with her body in his arms.

After a long while, he backed away, staring down at her. There was a twisted look to her face, a shining confusion in her eyes. Then, for an instant, the expression in her face changed. Her eyes seemed to focus on something behind him. When they swung back to his face, she reached up to pull his lips down to hers once more.

Only senses developed through three years of living like an animal would have detected it. Some sound, unidentifiable in that instant, reached him. He tried to tear himself loose and twist around. He shifted far enough aside so that the knife went into his arm instead of his back.

The girl scrambled away from him, lunging for the rifle he had kept loaded at all times, these last days. Sick with pain, he tried to wheel on around and rise. He had a dim view of the Frenchman above him, the pelt of his coat matted with dried blood, a murderous light in his eyes.

Then his fist smashed Garrit across the face, knocking him back against the wall of the cave, and his other hand pulled the knife free of Garrit's upper arm. Garrit rolled over, dazed by the blow. His eyes were open, but he could barely see the Frenchman, lunging up above him, raising the knife for the kill. He tried to rise, but his stunned nerves would not answer his will. Anne Corday stood on the other side of the cave, the loaded Jake Hawkins in her hands. There was a wide-eyed vindication on her face.

The Frenchman straddled Garrit with a triumphant bellow, and the uplifted knife flashed in the firelight as it started to come down.

Then the shot boomed out, rocking the cave with its thunder. As if from a heavy blow, the Frenchman was slammed off Garrit and carried clear up against the wall of the cave. He hung there a moment, and then toppled back, to sprawl limply on the ground. Garrit stared blankly at him, until he finally realized what had happened. A Jake Hawkins packed that much punch, close up.

Slowly he turned his head, to see the girl, still holding the gun, smoke curling from its muzzle. Her face was blank, as if she was surprised at what she had done. Then that same confusion widened her eyes. With a small cry, she dropped the rifle, wheeled, and ran out of the cave. He got to his feet and tried to follow, but almost fell again at the mouth and had to stop there. He heard a whinney, then the drumming of hoofs. He stared out into the dripping timber, knowing he was too weak to follow her. The knowledge turned his face bleak and empty.

John Bruce's pack train returned to Fort Union on the first day of September. The trade goods were gone from the packs, now. They were bulging with dark brown beaver pelts and buffalo robes. The saddle-galled horses filed soddenly in through the great double-leaved gates, met by cheers and greetings of the *engagés* and hunters and trappers of the post.

Farrier took Bruce and Garrit to his office. Enid was there, in a wine dress, a pale expectancy in her face. Bruce grasped her arms, a boyish eagerness lighting his heavy features momentarily. Garrit thought the presence of himself and Farrier must have restrained them from an expression of their true feelings, for after looking into her eyes a long moment, Bruce turned to Farrier, telling him of Anne Corday. When he was finished, Farrier turned in amazement to Garrit.

"And what happened to the girl?"

Garrit stared around at the walls, feeling that constriction again. He rubbed at his arm, still sore from the knife wound Frenchie had given him. "She got away," he said, curtly. "I couldn't help it."

"Your name will be cleared anyway," Farrier said. "Bruce's whole crew is witness to what happened. You've saved Yellowstone Fur, Garrit, and they'll certainly reinstate you with honors." He scratched his beard, studying Bruce and Enid with a knowing grin. "Maybe we better go out and talk it over, while these two reunite."

Bruce had been watching Enid, whose eyes had never left Garrit. "Perhaps it is I who had better go out with you, Farrier," he said.

Enid turned sharply to him. "Bruce, I — "

"Never mind, Enid." His voice had a dead sound. "I guess I should have known how you felt, ever since you saw Garrit here last April."

He turned, shoulders dragging, and went out with a perplexed Farrier. Garrit felt sorry for the man. He knew he should have felt elation for himself, however, as he turned back to Enid, but it did not come.

"I have always wondered, Vic, why you let her make such a fool of you, that first time, on the Platte," Enid said.

He stopped, frowning deeply. "I've wondered that myself."

"Perhaps, Vic, it was because she is really

the woman, and I never was," she said.

He turned to her, tried to say something. She shook her head.

"You'll never be happy with the old life. I can see that now. If you want to go to her, Vic, you're free."

He stared at her a long time, realizing she had touched the truth. And he knew now why Anne Corday's face had been with him in so many dreams. It hadn't been there as a symbol of his revenge, or vindication.

"Thank you, Enid," he said, softly.

He left the fort with but one pack horse and enough supplies to take him as far as Flathead Lake. He rode across the flats and into the timber where a magpie's scolding drew a fleeting grin to his lips. He stopped, to take one look backward, and then he turned his face toward the mountains, and rode.

Silver and Shells for General Kearny

DEATH'S MESSENGER IN BUCKSKIN

The echoes of the shots were dead now, and the peons were crowding back into Sante Fe's moonlit San Francisco Street, looking after the four horsemen who galloped on down toward the plaza, driving Danny Macduff's mules in front of them. His left arm hanging useless, his right fist gripping his Remington .44, Macduff crouched, hidden in the shadowed hacienda doorway. Those four riders had galloped from beneath two of the hovels across the way with guns flaming at Macduff. He wondered bitterly, who wanted him dead that badly, and what they expected to find in the pack-saddles of his mangy mules.

Iron hasps creaked behind Macduff. He whirled to the opening door, Remington jerking up. He stopped his tightening finger just in time.

"Señor Riley?" said a woman's voice. "We didn't know if it was you they were shooting at. The peons are so stirred up. They have been firing their guns all night anyway. Come in quickly, please."

Patently, she took him for someone else. But right now he would feel safer behind that solid oak door, and he had to get his wound tended. He stepped inside, and iron hasps creaked as the door closed.

"This way, Señor Riley," said the woman.

Macduff followed her toward a faint line of light that came from beneath another door at the end of the hall. She opened that door and stood by it, apparently wanting him to enter first. He stopped too, momentarily, to look at her.

Light spilled over blue-black hair piled up under a white mantilla, deep brown eyes that held his for a moment, scarlet lips, startling against the pallor of her face. She wore a camisa — the pleated white blouse of these señoritas — and a full silk skirt that trailed on the floor, revealing only the toes of her red slippers.

He looked past her to the inner sala, a large room, walls white-washed with yeso, barred windows set with semitransparent mica. A banco ran all the way round, forming an adobe bench, covered with red blankets from Chimayo and fringed satins from Mexico City. There were four men.

The candles of the big center table lighted only the front part of the room, and in the deep rear shadows stood two of the men, their faces mere blots in the darkness. The other two stood within the circle of light.

Macduff shot them a hard glance, then limped ahead into the sala. He stopped before the table, putting his gun away, cuffing his black felt hat from his dark hair that curled long down the back of his neck. The sun had burned his stubborn-jawed face an Indian-brown, but hadn't quite obliterated his Irish freckles.

"Did they hit your leg?" asked the woman, coming from behind.

Automatically, Macduff glanced down at his leg. "No, that's an old one," he said wryly, then held out his left hand, sticky with the blood leaking down from his wound. "This is where they hit me; here."

"Sit down, please," she said, "and I'll have a criada bring some hot water and bandages."

She turned to call the servant, and before he had taken the chair by the table, a Navajo woman came through another doorway, the heavy silver-embroidered curtain rustling as she dropped it behind her. The señorita spoke softly in Spanish, and the criada, her face darkly impassive, bowed herself back through the curtain.

"Now, Señor Riley," said the woman, turning back, "I am Señorita Lajara Costillo." She indicated a hawk-faced young man, the silver-chased scabbard of his rapier showing beneath a blue, silk-lined riding cloak. "This," she said, "is Don Caspar Jamarillo."

He nodded curtly to Macduff, eyes narrowed.

"Look here," said Macduff, half-rising. "We'd better get this straight. I'm not — "

"Now, now," said the other man, stepping around the table and gently shoving Macduff back down. "We'll fix that wound before we do the business. Incidentally, I'm Doctor Leo Britt. Did you recognize who shot you?"

He was a pot-bellied, dowdy man in soiled fustian and rumpled waistcoat, black string tie hanging from a frayed choke-collar. Yet, for all his sloppiness, there was something about his eyes. . . . He began taking Macduff's shaggy old buffalo coat off.

"I only got a good look at one of them before they high-tailed it with my mules," said Macduff. "He was a big tall hombre with long mustaches and Apache botas — "

"Anton Chico," said Lajara Costillo heatedly. "That *maldito!*"

"Anton Chico?" asked Macduff.

85

"A bandit," explained the doctor, fishing out a Barlow knife and slitting Macduff's flannel shirt sleeve. "Though how he found out you'd be here tonight only the devil knows. That's an ugly wound, Riley. What you need is a drink. As the immortal bard says, 'Be large in mirth. . . .' "

" 'Anon, we'll drink the table round,' " Macduff finished the quotation almost automatically.

The doctor had reached for a silver jug of pulque on the table; he turned, jug and tumbler still held in his hands. "By Harry — an Irishman who quotes Shakespeare! It's rare one finds a gentleman of the old school in these God-forsaken mountains."

Macduff shrugged, almost sorry it had slipped out. Then he turned, his eyes riveted to the man who had moved out of the shadows by the rear wall. Candlelight fell on broad shoulders and deep chest, an expensive tailed coat, pin-striped trousers, razor-creased, and polished Anson boots. Beneath a sweep of fair hair, clear blue eyes regarded Macduff candidly, but they held no hint of recognition.

"Mr. Riley," said the man. "I trust you weren't indiscreet enough to carry the money on those mules."

For just that moment, Danny Macduff was caught off guard, and his mouth opened in stunned surprise. Then his dark face became carefully blank, and his mouth snapped shut. He looked at his tall, fair brother with veiled eyes, thinking, All right, Terrance Macduff, if that's the way you want it, all right!

But the others had caught that unguarded moment, and the woman was watching Danny closely, a new speculation in her glance. The little lights that came and went in Don Jamarillo's eyes might have been a trick of the flickering candle, or a new, growing suspicion. Doctor Leo Britt took a step forward and leaned toward Danny, his voice ironic.

"The man who asked you the question is Mr. Coe, the agent for Klierman Shippers, here in Santa Fe. He is, let me assure you, one of us."

"Oh," said Danny, "Mr. Coe. Well, Mr. Coe, I didn't carry any money on my mules, if that makes you feel better."

The last time Danny had seen his brother, Terrance had been stationed at Leavenworth, the blue coat and brass buttons of the United States Cavalry over his big chest instead of these expensively tailored civilian clothes. It struck Danny Macduff that he had stepped into something deep here, and that he might very well be in over his head right now. . . .

The Navajo criada had come back with a big jar of hot water and strips of clean white cotton. The doctor peeled Danny's split sleeve away from the wound and swabbed it clean.

"Perhaps," he said, "perhaps you would like to tell us where the money is, then, Mr. Riley. We haven't much time."

Jamarillo shoved his cloak back and let one hand slide to the hilt of his sword, leaning forward a little, eyes glittering. The woman shifted impatiently, pulling her mantilla tighter. The doctor finished bandaging Danny's arm, stood up.

"Well, Mr. Riley . . . ?"

Whatever Danny would have answered was stopped by the muted thud of hoofs from the street outside, the creak of men swinging down from saddles. Doctor Britt turned.

"That might be our good Captain Antonito Valdez coming after the money, and then again, it might not."

Lajara Costillo snatched up Macduff's buffalo coat, helping him out of the chair. "You'd better get in the other room till we make sure. And you too, Señor Coe. Conchita, get rid of this stuff, pronto."

The criada collected the jar and soiled cotton, padding from the sala. Britt disappeared into the shadowed hall, going to the front door as Señorita Costillo herded Danny and his tall brother into a darkened room. Danny slipped his buffalo coat on, turning to his brother.

"That was a fine greeting you gave me out there, after four years," he said.

"I didn't think you wanted to be given way — Mr. Riley," said Terrance.

"I thought it was *you* who didn't want to be given away — Mr. Coe," said Danny. "What is this, Terrance? Who's Riley? And why did that bandido expect me to carry money on my mules?"

Terrance spoke very carefully. "Wait a minute — you mean to tell me you're *not* going under the name of Riley?"

"No, dammit, no! I'm Danny Macduff and I'll always be Danny Macduff. I've been up north, hunter for Bent's Fort. Bent paid me a year's wages in beaver plews and I was coming down here to cash them in. If that Anton Chico expected to find any money on my mules, he'll get a mighty big surprise."

Terrance laughed wryly. "You can bet he will. They expected to find thirty thousand dollars in silver on your mules."

Danny grabbed his arm. "Tell me what it's about, Terrance."

"Ease up on my arm and I will," said the other. "If you've been north, you wouldn't know the United States declared war on

Mexico in May, 1846. New Mexico's a northern province of Mexico and it rates a first class attack. General Stephen Kearny is approaching Las Vegas right now with the Army of the West. As soon as he takes Las Vegas, he'll move on Santa Fe."

Danny let a low whistle through his teeth. "War — no wonder the peons were raising such a ruckus outside. But how come you're here in civvies, instead of out there with Kearny, where you belong?"

"The War Department had been preparing for this ever since the Texas trouble," said Terrance. "I'd been riding escort on the wagon trains over the Santa Fe Trail, knew this country, spoke the language. We always stopped at Chouteau's Island and let the wagons come on to Santa Fe, then picked them up on the return trip, so I wasn't known here in the town.

"Last January I was transferred from the Cavalry to Intelligence and planted in Santa Fe as Mr. Coe, agent for Klierman Shippers, a Yankee outfit with a branch at this end. My job is to do all I can to aid our troop movements, and to try and stop any conspiracies that will work against us. And this thing you've stepped into, my boy, is a conspiracy to end all conspiracies."

He stopped a moment, listening to the

muted hubbub of talk at the outer door. Doctor Britt seemed to be arguing with someone. Then Terrance turned back to Danny.

"Marching into Santa Fe, Kearny will have to take Glorieta Pass and Apache Pass through the Sangre de Cristos. Either of those canyons holds a dozen spots perfect for ambush. Manuel Armijo, the governor here, and also general of the Mexican army, is an unscrupulous, conniving despot who'd sell out his own mother for a few pesos. His tyranny has created a host of enemies for him in Santa Fe. They'd do anything to get Armijo out. I put it into their hands to offer him money to withdraw his troops, and to abdicate."

"That's the money that was to be brought by Riley?"

Terrance nodded. "Armijo must have realized what a powder keg he was sitting on. He agreed to sell out for thirty thousand dollars. This James Riley isn't known here in Santa Fe; none of us has ever seen him. But we were given his description by partisans who chose him for the job. He was in Las Vegas collecting the last of the money, was due here tonight at seven, with the whole sum."

"And if Armijo doesn't get that money?"

"General Kearny and his whole command," finished Terrance, "will ride into an ambush somewhere between here and Las Vegas, and will stand a good chance of being wiped out!"

He turned toward the door suddenly. Boots thudded down the front hallway and into the main sala. There was the muted clank of accouterments, and a young, arrogant voice said in Spanish:

"*Buenas noches,* Señorita Costillo; Don Jamarillo. Governor Armijo grows impatient. It is past the time when the money was due at the palacio. He sent me after it."

"Captain Valdez," Terrance whispered to Danny. "Mexican dragoons. Tough hombre to meet in a scrap."

Valdez's voice sounded again, sharp with rising anger. "*Por supuesto,* Doctor Britt, you told me Señor Riley had not yet arrived. But you forgot to wipe the blood off his chair. Are you trying to hide him from me? Cabo, take that door — I'll take this one!"

Before he had finished the order to his corporal, his steps sounded swiftly toward the curtained doorway to the room in which the two brothers stood. Already, Danny was forcing Terrance to the big chest that stood on the far side.

"Let go," said Terrance. "This is my business!"

"Don't be a damn' fool!" snapped Danny,

92

shoving him down between the wall and the chest. "You know what they do to spies as well as I do. If they got suspicious about you being here with me, it'd be the firing squad."

Then he was taking a swift step toward the door, digging back his buffalo coat to get at his Remington. The curtain was yanked aside with a tinkling clash of silver, and Macduff stopped with his gun half-drawn.

Captain Antonito Valdez stood there with one hand holding the curtain back, the other gripping a big Walker Colt.

"Ah," he said. "Señor Riley. Won't you please come out."

Danny Macduff stepped through the door and the captain moved aside to let him pass. He was a rakish young dragoon, Captain Valdez, a tight cuirass of double-folded deerskin worn beneath his blue jacket with its red cuffs and collar; his eyes had a flash and an arrogance that matched his voice.

"Why did you hide him, Doctor?" he asked. "I thought we were all compadres in this."

"I wasn't sure it was you," said Doctor Britt, blandly. "Anton Chico has already made his appearance tonight. If he knows, aren't the others just as likely to know?"

"You brought the money?" Valdez asked Macduff.

"Apparently," said the doctor, "he didn't. Chico jumped him outside and ran off with Mr. Riley's mules. But Mr. Riley said he didn't have the money on them. And Mr. Riley hasn't yet told us where he did have it."

Valdez looked at Macduff, face hardening. "You will tell me, señor, where it is."

Terrance was out of it now, and Danny knew he should have told them long ago who he really was.

"I think you ought to know," he said, "that I'm not James Riley. I'm a hunter for Bent's Fort. The name's Macduff — Danny Macduff."

Valdez's eyes widened. He looked from the doctor to the girl, then back to Macduff, his surprise clouded by anger. Lajara Costillo made a small, unbelieving gesture.

"Señor, this is no time for joking, I assure you."

"I don't think so either," Danny told her. "That's why I'm not joking."

Doctor Britt leaned forward, and his eyes suddenly held a dangerous flame.

"I always thought thirty thousand dollars was a lot to trust with a man we'd never seen," he said. "And he chooses Macduff, of all names!"

94

"Perhaps we'd better take him to the palacio," said Valdez. "Governor Armijo has a way of dealing with such as Señor Riley."

"Macduff is the name," said Danny. "Macduff. And I'm not going to any palacio. This isn't any of my business."

The two dragoons who had come in with the captain moved toward Danny from the side. Don Jamarillo stepped around the table.

Danny took a jerky step toward Valdez, bending forward almost unconsciously, hand taut above his gun. Valdez curled a thumb around the hammer of his Walker, cocking it. Danny hung there for a moment, almost mad enough to go for his gun anyway. . . .

There had been two men standing in the gloom at the rear of the room when Macduff had first come into the house. One had been his brother, Terrance. The other was still there. Now that man moved forward. The light suddenly caught his face, beetling brows over jet black eyes that flicked from Valdez to Britt to Macduff, and finally to the señorita. Still with his hand clawed out over his Remington, Macduff caught the almost imperceptible movement that might have been the man's hand dipping for his gun.

Then the señorita gave the man a quick,

hard look, and he subsided back into the shadows. Almost at the same time, she stepped forward and caught Macduff's good arm.

"Don't be a fool," she said hotly. "Don't be a fool!"

Valdez smiled thinly. "I almost believe you'd do it, Señor Riley!"

Eyes on the black bore of that Walker Colt, Macduff finally let the whole knotty tension slip from his body. Valdez indicated the Irishman was to precede him into the hall. Macduff limped forward, and the shadows in the hallway reached out for him, falling darkly across his square, broad shoulders.

INTO THE TRAP!

New Mexico, as a northern province of Mexico, had bowed for ten years under the heavy, despotic hand of the fabulous Governor Manuel Armijo. Standing before him now, in the executive office at the governor's palace, Macduff could well believe all the bizarre tales he'd heard of the man.

Armijo was mountainous behind his great, ornate desk, his tight charro jacket strained to the bursting point by its tremendous torso, hands thick-fingered and fat beneath the flowing sleeves of his white silk shirt.

But it was the eyes that marked the man. The heavy, narrowed lids couldn't veil the craft and ruthless intelligence it must have taken to build such an intricate, despotic empire out of this barren province. Macduff sensed that the great, fat Armijo could play a dozen different parts, as the occasion demanded, and that right now he was playing the suave, magnanimous governor up to the hilt.

"My palacio is yours, Señor Riley," smiled Armijo. "Sit down, please. Have a puro?"

Macduff declined the cigars, and took a carved oak chair in front of the desk. Living among the Indians up at Bent's Fort, he had learned to see things without actually seeming to. And though his eyes never left Armijo, he had taken in the whole room.

Hung on the walls were festoons of Apaches' ears, collected by Armijo in reprisal for the Indians' scalping of Mexicans. Beneath the strings of ears were ancient spears and rusty cuirasses that must have dated back to De Vargas. Black Bayeta blankets and red Chimayos were draped over the usual banco running all the way around the room, and upon one sat the dowdy, smiling Doctor Britt.

Valdez stood very close to Riley. He had taken the Irishman's Remington; it lay on the desk before Armijo. There were two guards by the open door, one inside, one outside in the hall, both armed with the huge, smooth-bore escopetas of the Mexican dragoon.

Armijo took one of his own puros, bit off the end, took his own time lighting it. His chair squeaked as he eased his prodigious bulk back in it.

"I'm disappointed in you, Señor Riley," he said heavily. "I made a bargain with your go-betweens, was very specific about how it was to be carried out. In the first place, my name wasn't to be mentioned — I wasn't to appear in it till the money finally reached me. You must realize what would happen if the people of Santa Fe realized I was. . . ."

"Selling them out?" Macduff supplied.

Armijo flushed. "Señor . . . please!"

"That's what it amounts to," Macduff shrugged. "You get paid for withdrawing your troops and throwing over your office. Why not put it plainly?"

"This is intrigue, señor — one never puts things plainly in intrigue," growled the governor. "However, you don't seem to realize that every minute you spend in Santa Fe is another minute in which a dozen different factions will try their best to kill you.

"You saw how Anton Chico was willing to murder you for that money. He and his bandidos form only one party. There are the common soldiers; they would tear you to pieces if they knew you brought the money that would mean the Americanos march into Santa Fe without a shot. And the peons. . . ."

"And the Farrerra party," said Britt.

Armijo's face darkened. "Sí. They are the strongest of all — minor politicians who have become fat under my rule. They would stand to lose everything if I — ah — abdicated. They would stop at nothing to keep the money from reaching me. Their nominal leader is the emigration officer appointed from Mexico, Carlos Farrerra. But behind him stands another, an unknown, whose backing makes them more powerful and more dangerous than any of the other factions. Now, Señor Riley, you must see how stupid it would be to continue this farce. Surely your life is worth more than a paltry thirty thousand dollars — "

Anger again flared inside Macduff. He gripped the carved arms of the chair till his knuckles showed white.

"I'm *not* Riley. Why won't you believe that?"

Armijo sighed heavily. "We were given Riley's description. Irish, obviously — short and broad-shouldered with brown hair and brown eyes, in this country long enough to be darkened by the sun — "

"All of which might fit five out of ten Irishmen," snapped Macduff.

"And of course," said Armijo, "it was just by chance that you came down the entrada at the time Señor Riley was due; and just by chance you chose the señorita's doorway."

"They were waiting for Riley just opposite," said Macduff. "There wasn't another place to hide within a hundred yards."

Armijo leaned forward, his voice catching with impatience. "Señor, were you fool enough to think you could begin conspiring also, to think you could play one side off against the other and maybe be left with the money, yourself?"

" 'Now, whether he kill Cassio,' " quoted the doctor with a chuckle, " 'or Cassio kill him, or each do kill the other, every way makes my gain.' "

Armijo cast a glance at Britt. "Sí, doctor, that is it. *Pues*, it seems our Señor Riley wasn't cut out for intrigue. There are right times to play that kind of a game. And wrong times."

Macduff stood suddenly. Valdez made a swift, instinctive move toward his gun, then stopped like that, waiting.

"Let's quit fencing," flamed the Irishman. "I'm fed up. I'm not Riley and I don't know where the hell your filthy bribe is. That's all I've got to say, whether you believe it or not!"

Armijo's eyes took on a cruel glitter. "*Pues,* there is always La Garita."

"La Garita?"

"Yes," explained Doctor Britt softly. "It's the old Spanish prison behind the palacio. Whenever a man disappears suddenly, here in Santa Fe, it's rumored that a questioning party might find him in La Garita — if the party was fool enough to question."

Macduff saw it was the end of the rope. He took a slow breath, setting himself. The doctor had no obvious weapon, though he might carry a gun beneath his coat. Armijo could reach the Remington lying on the desk, but Macduff felt sure he could move a little faster. Valdez, then, was the man, his big bone-butted Walker riding high out of his hand-tooled holster.

Armijo's voice was sly. "There are some marvelous implements in La Garita — left there from the Inquisition. My hombres have become artists in their use. Persuasion, you know, Señor Riley. . . ."

The desk was slantwise across one corner of the room, and the way Macduff stood, the doorway was within his line of vision. An awareness of the dragoon standing outside the door had been growing on Macduff ever since he had risen from the chair. Macduff turned imperceptibly, and caught the man's face, the beetling brows over beady eyes.

The last time Danny Macduff had seen that man, he had stood in the shadows at the rear of the main sala in Señorita Costillo's hacienda, and he hadn't worn any dragoon's uniform then.

The hope of it almost hurt Macduff. He knew whatever he did here by the desk would be useless because of those two guards. But if one of them was the señorita's man, if she had sent him. . . .

It was the chance Macduff would have to take, and he gathered himself for it. Then the doctor came forward, leaning his hands on the desk. The twinkle had gone from his little blue eyes, and his soft voice held a strange menace. Macduff suddenly realized that the doctor might be more than just a chuckling pot-gut who spouted Shakespeare.

"Now, Riley," said the doctor. "We've given you your choice. Tell us where the money is, or — La Garita."

Perhaps they didn't expect a lame man to move quite so fast. Macduff's eyes were still on the doctor when he threw himself aside in a sudden, lurching movement toward Valdez.

With the Irishman's shoulder in his middle, Valdez let out an explosive wheeze, reeled back, hand grabbing for his Walker. But Macduff already had both his hands on the gun. They slammed against the banco, rolled off, pulling a Chimayo blanket with them. Macduff hit the floor with Valdez on top of him, and had the Walker out, jerking it to bear on the doctor and Armijo from beneath the captain's body.

The huge governor had risen, one fat hand outflung for Macduff's .44 where it lay on the desk. He stopped that hand just above the gun, heavy-lidded eyes still wide with surprise.

The doctor had taken his hands off the desk. One of them was sliding back out of his coat where he had reached for something a little too late.

"I thought maybe you were heeled, Doc," said Macduff.

" 'Why should I play the Roman fool and die on my own sword?' " quoted Britt, forcing a chuckle.

"Get off, Valdez," said the Irishman. "And

103

do it right, unless you want one of your own slugs through your brisket."

The young captain rose carefully, face dark with rage and shame. The guard who had stood inside the door was sprawled on the floor where Señorita Costillo's man had knocked him with the butt of his escopeta.

Macduff began backing toward the door, glad he had taken that chance.

"You're a fool," Doctor Britt said. "There are a hundred soldiers between you and the outside. And if you do escape, there are a dozen different factions that'll be hunting your hide. . . ."

Macduff slammed the door on his words. The big hulking man outside grabbed his shoulder, turned him toward the rear of the palace.

"I'm Ancho," he said. "The señorita is waiting in the Arroyo Mascaros with horses."

He was peeling off the blue dragoon's coat. Beneath it were his two sixguns, belt buckled up tight around his thick waist so the holsters wouldn't show beneath the bottom of the coat. As they reached the turn in the corridor, Armijo's voice rang down the hall after them like angry thunder.

"Capitan del Guardia, call out the guard! The Yankee has escaped. *Capitan del Guardia!*"

104

Macduff and Ancho were already pounding around the turn when from ahead came the sound of the dragoons running. From a barrack room, dark figures lurched into the hall. A gun blared. Lead ricocheted off the wall chipping adobe into Macduff's face.

Ancho dug high heels into the earthen floor, trying to stop. His twin sixes were already out. One of the dragoons charging down the hall suddenly pitched forward with a scream. Another tipped over sideways, still running, hit the wall and slid down, finally rolling to a stop. The Captain of the Guard tripped over his body and fell, bullets from his gun plowing the floor.

Macduff yanked Ancho back around the turn. But already from behind them came the pound of other feet — Britt and Armijo and Valdez.

The Irishman spotted a square blot across the hall, and both he and Ancho jumped toward it, shoving open the door and lurching into the dark room just as the remaining dragoons came around the turn. A soldier tried to follow them in through the door. Valdez's Walker felt heavy and unfamiliar in Macduff's hand, but his first shot caught that man in the door, spilling him over backward into the hall.

Outside they could hear the Captain of

the Guard calling: "We have them trapped in that sala, Governor."

"Well, go in and get them!" roared Armijo.

Backing farther into the room, Macduff brought the smoking Walker up again. He didn't know how many there were. It didn't matter much. They had made a good try, anyway.

But the body of the dragoon Macduff had shot was lying half in, half out the door, and it must have discouraged those outside. Now that the action was over, he could feel the insistently throbbing pain in his wounded left arm. Ancho was fumbling with something behind Macduff.

"Dios!" he muttered. "There's a door here, but it's locked!"

Macduff stumbled around a big table, lurched up against the solid sweating body of the man. He felt for the door handle, found it, an ancient relic of hammered silver.

"Get away," he said. "I'll try to shoot the lock apart."

His shots were deafening, echoing out into the hall. With acrid powdersmoke choking him, he heaved against the iron-bound door. It gave, hurling him into another dark room. Ancho followed behind, and over his lumbering footsteps, Macduff heard Armijo's raging voice.

"Go in after them, you *barrachónes*. What kind of coyote soldiers do you call yourselves?"

There was a sudden rush. The thunder of gunfire rolled inside. Then there was a moment of silence as the dragoons must have realized they had rushed an empty room. Macduff found another door in the dark, unlocked. It led into the corridor beyond the turn. Their feet made a muted thud on the earth, past the deserted barrack room, to the end of the hall.

The apartments behind the Palace of the Governors had been built in an earlier century, to house the dignitaries of the Spanish government. Now they were officers' quarters, adobe houses grouped around flag-stoned courtyards with green willows sighing above bright-roofed wells. Hugging the shadowed gloom of an adobe wall, Ancho led through the first placita to an iron-grilled gateway. The sound of pursuit was becoming audible behind them as they reached the main gate.

Macduff saw where Ancho had gotten the uniform, then. In the shadows of the wall lay the guard, stripped to the white pantaloons dragoons wore beneath their blue trousers. The iron grille complained rustily as Ancho shoved it open, poking his black head out carefully, looking up and down the street.

Across the way was a row of mud-walled hovels. Between two of these Ancho led Macduff, rounding a crude piñon hayrack. Somewhere a baby cried plaintively. A burro grumbled on its tether behind the houses. A narrow winding alleyway led finally to the Arroyo Mascaros.

They half slid, half ran, down its steep bank, feet plunging into the shallow water at the bottom. A fringe of cottonwoods bulked across the stream, and Ancho pushed through the underbrush. Macduff followed, thorns catching at his shaggy buffalo coat, scraping across his elkhide leggins. In a clearing stood four horses, held by a criado in white trousers and shirt. The girl had changed to a split Crow riding skirt, and was muffled to the chin in a dark cloak, black felt soft brim taking the place of her mantilla.

She turned nervously as the two men broke through the agrito. "Ancho?"

"Sí, señorita," said Ancho. "It was easy."

She was only half listening. Her eyes, shadowed beneath the hat brim, were on Macduff.

"Why send Ancho after me?" he asked. "I thought you were with the doctor."

"Doctor Britt still thinks you are Señor Riley," she said. "But after you left, Ancho told me about you — El Cojo!"

A fleeting grin caught at Macduff's mouth in the gloom. El Cojo — The Lame One. The Apaches had tacked that on him up around Bent's Fort.

"How did Ancho know? I never got this far south."

"Ancho is part Apache," she said. "They have sort of a grapevine, the Indians. I imagine you're known to every Apache from the Territories to Mexico. It's a real compliment to have them admit a white man can outtrack them."

He shrugged. "I was a hunter. Tracking was just part of my business."

"You may not be Riley," she said. "But if you're as good as Ancho said, you're about the only man in Santa Fe who can save Kearny from that ambush."

He turned sharply to her, but Ancho's voice stopped him. "Señorita, the dragoons!"

DESPERATE BROTHERHOOD

For a long time they stayed there in the thicket, holding the horses, waiting. Valdez appeared at the top of the arroyo periodically, rode parallel to it for a block, then turned

109

up another street. The girl moved closer to Macduff, and the scent of her hair made him shift uneasily.

"How do you fit in with this thing?" he asked.

"From the very first, the ricos — the landowners — have opposed Governor Armijo," she said. "My father led their party, and it became known as the Costillo faction. We tried every way to force Armijo out, but he was too strong. Two years ago my father disappeared. . . ."

"La Garita?"

Her face paled. "Probably. That's where Armijo puts most of his political enemies. Since then I have led the Costillos."

"If you're so bitterly against Armijo, why try so hard to see that he gets this money?" asked Macduff.

"Only to get rid of him, don't you see," she said hotly. "Anything to get him out — *anything!* He is such a despot, so cruel, so greedy. He's taxed us heavily; yet almost every landowner north of Socorro put money into that fund of thirty thousand. With all the Ferrerras and their spies in Santa Fe, and Anton Chico, and all the other parties who would stand to lose if Armijo abdicated, we couldn't collect the money here. We chose Las Vegas. And when the thirty thousand was gathered, our partisans there were to choose a man who could get through with the silver.

"The Costillos know how little chance they stand of removing Armijo by force — we tried it a couple of times before. But if that money doesn't reach him, we're desperate enough to try it again, to storm the palacio and take him ourselves!"

"Doctor Britt — is he with you, or Armijo?"

"He was the go-between for Armijo," she said. "On the surface, he's just a harmless little man Armijo keeps around to doctor his gout and to amuse him. But I've heard it whispered that Britt is master of Armijo when it comes to intrigue, that he has just as many irons in the fire as the governor."

"Valdez?"

She shrugged, smiling faintly. "About the only honest man in Santa Fe. A blind, hot-headed young fool who would die for Armijo. He and a few other trusted dragoons are the only soldiers who know of this thing. Naturally, if the rest of the army found they were being sold out, they'd revolt. The same with the peons. No telling what would happen to Armijo then."

"Now," he said, "that we have all the other characters in their proper places, we come to me. You said I was the only man who could save Kearny. . . ."

"Something has happened to Riley, obviously," she said. "He was due at my hacienda five or six hours ago. Apparently he has been intercepted somewhere between Santa Fe and Las Vegas. The fact that Anton Chico was waiting for him opposite my doorway proves the secret leaked out. . . . A good tracker, working backward on the trail from here to Las Vegas, would stand a chance of finding Riley's sign, and trailing from there. . . ."

"But why me? You must know a hundred Indians who could do it."

"The only Indians I would trust are my servants, and they can't track like you. Ancho himself told me that."

"Everybody thinks I'm Riley," he said. "Here's a bandido and his killers after my hair because they want the money. Armijo's after my ears because he thinks I'm playing both ends against the middle, and because he wants the money. A man nobody knows leading a bunch of small-time politicians who don't want the money to reach Armijo, and who, incidentally, want the money themselves. Every peon in Santa Fe is set to murder me if they find out about the plot. The whole Mexican army in between here and Las Vegas. I'd be a fine fool, wouldn't I, to go wandering down the Pecos Trail to Las Vegas — like a foolhen sitting on a branch, waiting for every chicken hawk in the Sangre de Cristos to jump it."

"Sí señor," she said. "But sometimes it takes just that kind of a fine fool to save an army, or a nation, or a people. I thought perhaps you were he."

He looked down at her, a grin catching at his mouth. There were other issues involved, of course. There was Kearny's Army of the West that would stand a chance of being wiped out. There was Terrance, whose mission would fail, and who would probably be discovered and stood up against the wall. There was even James Riley, who, by all the Irish in him, Danny would have helped. Any of those things were enough for Macduff. Yet, somehow, they didn't mean as much as the woman, standing there with the scent of her blue black hair disturbing him, her eyes shining up at him, asking him to do it.

"You thought right," he said. "I'm just exactly that kind of fool!"

It was long past midnight, and only a few peons lurched drunkenly homeward down the entrance of the Santa Fe Trail into San

113

Francisco Street. Bordering the road on one side was a line of hovels, and on the other, two walled haciendas, one of them Señorita Costillo's. Macduff and the others had waited there in the arroyo until Valdez had ceased searching the city for them, then had wound through narrow back alleys and streets in the poorer section of town, finally nearing the woman's house. Halting in the shadow of a vine-covered wall while Ancho scouted ahead, Macduff leaned forward to tighten the nose band on his gelding.

"Isn't it dangerous going back to the hacienda this way?" he asked. "If anyone in Armijo's office recognized Ancho, they'd know where I would go."

"Ancho was careful not to be recognized," said Lajara Costillo. "And the servants wouldn't allow anyone in but those who have been working with us."

Still, Macduff felt the skin crawl along the back of his neck as they rode along the wall and through the entrance that led into the placita. The girl swung gracefully from her skittish little palmetto, calling for a servant.

"Where is that Pepe?" she said impatiently. "Ancho, is he drunk again?"

Ancho shrugged. "Probably, señorita. I will have another criado attend to the horses as soon as we are inside."

The girl dropped her reins and followed Ancho toward the house, and Macduff took up the rear. He didn't know exactly why, but as he moved into the gloom beneath the arcade down one side of the placita, his hand slipped down to the bone butt of Captain Valdez's Walker Colt. The woman's skirts rustled through the door into the main sala ahead of Macduff, and her voice sounded strained.

"Caracoles, have they all gone to bed? Conchita, you lazy Indio, will you bring some light. . . ."

"That's quite all right," said a sardonic voice. "I don't mind the dark at all."

Before the voice had finished, Ancho gave a sick grunt. Macduff threw himself forward with some wild thought of protecting the woman, his gun coming out even as Ancho's heavy body hit the floor. The Irishman's finger was tightening on his trigger, his arm raising to throw down on the blot of scuffling figures ahead of him. Then he realized he might hit Señorita Costillo. She gave a terrified scream that was cut off sharply.

A man lurched in between Macduff and the sound of her voice. Sensing a blow, Macduff ducked in, hard and fast. Instead of the man's gun hitting Macduff's head, the man's elbow hit his shoulder.

Macduff lunged up, pistol-whipping the unseen face above him. He heard a sharp cry. Then the man was gone from in front of him, and he was stumbling over a body that must have been Ancho. He would have gone flat, but his hand found the big center table, pain burning through him as he put his weight suddenly on his wounded left arm.

The front door slammed open. On his knees by the table, Macduff saw three figures silhouetted in the door. Two men went through first, a struggling shape between them that was the girl, head covered by the blanket. Then the last man followed them out, running.

Macduff lurched after them. Before he reached the outer door, he heard the creak of saddles, the clatter of horses breaking into a gallop. Then he was out in the street, still not daring to shoot after them, because one rider carried the woman across the withers of his mount, head on one side, kicking feet on the other.

Hopelessly, he watched the swiftly receding figures disappear down the entrada and onto the Santa Fe Trail. One of the men turned, and a strange wild laugh pealed back to Macduff, mocking him. . . .

He turned finally, realizing that many peons were in the street, brought by the

116

noise. They were moving toward him in little knots. None of them had slept off their Taos lightning and their Pass brandy. Their faces were sullen and ugly. Macduff began backing toward the door of the hacienda.

"Holá," shouted a big Mexican with mustaches a foot long. "An Americano, compadres — a gringo!"

Another dressed in flapping white trousers laughed nastily. "Maybe he doesn't know there's a war on, Pedro. Maybe we better let him know."

"Sí," laughed Pedro, yanking a gleaming machete from his red sash. "Cut off his ears to hang on the Governor's walls."

The butt of Macduff's gun was sticky with perspiration. They were closing in, and others were drawing dirks, and one or two carried escopetas. Macduff's foot hit a rock and he stumbled a little.

Pedro laughed, drawing back his machete. Macduff had seen that kind of throw before, but he took another step, waiting, knowing what his shot would start.

Pedro's machete was behind his head. A man brought up his escopeta. Someone shouted.

With that shining machete for a target, Macduff fired, throwing himself backward. Lead ricocheted from steel with a scream, and the Mexican's howl was drowned by the swift pound of feet as the others broke forward. The man with the escopeta fired, but Macduff was already rolling through the door, and the lead plunked into adobe a foot above his head. Running forward, another peon brought his escopeta flat against his belly for a spot shot.

Macduff's second slug caught him in the chest. He dropped his escopeta and slammed into the wall before he could stop himself, then slid to the ground, clutching at his chest. Macduff was inside the door then, scrambling to his feet, slamming it shut and shooting the bolt.

He could hear them milling around outside, cursing and talking in swift, angry Spanish. But even the excitement of war wasn't as strong as the century-old traditions that held them from breaking into the hacienda.

Macduff turned, feeling his way along the pitch-black hall and into the main sala. There were still some coals gleaming faintly from the stove that stood in one corner of the room. He hunted for the silver tongs, and fished out one of the live coals. Holding it with the tongs, he stepped over Ancho's body to the table, lighting a candle.

Ancho lay sprawled by the table, stabbed, dead.

Then, the flaring light revealed the other man, over against the banco. One big hand was at his chest, dark blue fustian coat drawn up into little folds by his clutching fingers. Macduff's face went dead white beneath its tan.

"Terrance!"

Terrance opened his eyes, looking at Danny a long time before he seemed to see him. Blood frothed from his lips when he spoke.

"Waited — waited in the other room till you left with the captain, Danny. Was going to help the señorita get you from the palace. She said to stay here and wait for Riley. I had to, Danny. . . ."

"I know," said Danny huskily, trying to help him up.

"No," choked Terrance Macduff. "No, Danny. I'm done. Don Jamarillo must have been a Farrerra all along. Planted in the Costillo party."

"Jamarillo?"

"Remember the hawk-faced gent. . . . Blue riding cloak and sword, here with the doc when you first came? He put his blade through me from behind, after the señorita left with Ancho. Then he took care of the servants, let those other hombres in when they came. Farrerra came too. He's not the real leader, though; just a stooge. . . ."

He coughed weakly. Danny tried to say something, but Terrance waved it aside.

"It's your job, now, Danny," he gasped. "They must've thought I was dead. Left me lying here. I learned who's really behind the Farrerras. He's the one you have to get, Danny. Armijo doesn't compare with him, or Anton Chico. He's the most dangerous . . . Your job, Danny. . . . It's up to you now."

Danny grasped his shoulders as he trailed off, almost shouting: "Terrance, who is he? Terrance. . . ."

Then he stopped shouting, because Terrance Macduff was dead.

He knelt a long time beside his brother, looking at the wall without actually seeing it, his dark face hard and bleak.

EL COJO TAKES THE TRAIL

Centuries before, when the first Spaniards had come north from Mexico and had seen the mountains east of Santa Fe, lifting their crimson spires above the valley, they had called them Montes del Sangre de Cristo — Mountains of the Blood of Christ.

Two passes, Apache and Glorieta, formed

the gateway through the Sangre de Cristos to Santa Fe, and riding along the trail of the horsemen who had carried off Lajara Costillo, Macduff reached Apache Pass an hour after the sun had risen.

Behind the stables, Macduff had found the man who might have been Pepe, only he wasn't drunk, he was dead. Jamarillo had finished off the other male servants, too, and had tied the woman criadas in their quarters.

After Macduff had released them and waited for their hysterical sobbing to cease, they had helped him stuff tortillas and maize in the beaded saddle-bags on the gelding. Slipping out the rear way, he had been on the trail less than an hour after the horsemen had ridden away down the entrada, with Lajara.

That's how it was in his mind now. No longer the formality of Señorita Costillo, but just Lajara. The way a man thought of a woman when he'd known her for a long time, or when he suddenly realized how much she meant to him.

The trail, for Macduff, was like the pages of a book, every mark was a word that told him of the men he was following. He knew that one of the riders must be an Indian because one of the horses was unshod; and that the woman was still being carried across a horse's withers, because the front hoofs of one animal were sinking in deeper than its hind hoofs.

At mid-morning he had gone through Apache, and was entering Glorieta. He saw that the riders had passed through there ahead of him shortly before dawn, for the dew had dried in their tracks.

Live grass began to rise immediately after being trodden on, and rose for three days afterward until it was straight again. When Macduff crossed a glade of short green grama, he dismounted and studied it, able to tell just how many hours ago the hoofs of horses had crushed it.

Finally the trail cut up the side of the pass into dark stands of piñon and cedar. Up on the slope that way, Macduff got a view down the pass. A quarter mile ahead was a vedette of Mexican dragoons, red cuffs and collars gay in the sun, accouterments glittering, horses ground-hitched.

Farther on, dust hung over the canyon in a dim yellow plume. That was Armijo's main army then, and Glorieta was where he planned to ambush Kearny. It was a good position, not a very long line to hold with the slopes rising steeply on either side. It wouldn't be hard to hide in the thick timber on each slope, letting Kearny's skirmishers and scouts filter through, then come down on the main force of Americans.

Kearny didn't know the country, and his Army of the West would be weary and sick from the hellish march across the Jornada del Muerto. Armijo would have everything just about all his own way.

The pines formed a heavy forest that let the sun through now and then in dappled patterns, and Macduff rode for the most part in deep gloom. Then, ahead, showed the broad sunlit space of a clearing, jade green grama grass spread over it like a soft carpet. At the fringe of timber, Macduff dismounted and searched the forest around him. But the only men seemed to be the dead ones, lying there in the sun of the clearing, flies making a lazy, funereal buzz around their bodies.

It must have been a big fight.

The man nearest Macduff was an Apache, and he remembered there had been the un-shod prints of an Indian's pony among those he had been following. Farther on were two hardfaced young peons, both wearing Colts buckled around their dirty white cotton trousers. Sprawled across one of them was a man in more expensive clothes, silk-lined riding cloak hitched up over his head and hiding his face, blood spreading blackly over the back of his embroidered Spanish vest. And on across the meadow were two more, in the same cloak and vest.

The tracks Macduff had been following led right into the clearing. He stood there for ten minutes, searching the forest around the glade carefully, and it seemed silent, empty. Even so, the safer thing would have been to skirt the clearing and see if he couldn't pick up the trail on the other side. He was about to do that when he caught sight of another body, half hidden in the grass.

Cautiously, Macduff stepped into the open, leading his gelding. He passed the Apache, and the richly dressed man sprawled over the two peons, and the pair of bodies beyond them. Then he stood looking down at that last one.

He was short and thick-set, dressed in Yankee jeans and a dark fustian, gold watch chain gleaming across his white waistcoat. His brown hair curled long down the back of his neck, and though the sun had burned his face to an Indian darkness, it hadn't quite obliterated the Irish freckles on his snub nose.

Armijo and the others had never seen the man they expected to bring the money, but they had been given his description. And now Macduff could well see why they had taken him for James Riley. . . .

In Macduff's four years at Bent's, he had seen enough men die when they became careless. He knew, suddenly, how careless he had been. But now it was too late.

"I'm disappointed in you, señor — I always thought El Cojo would be a harder man to snare," said a voice behind Macduff; it was the same sardonic tone Danny had heard in the Costillo hacienda the night before.

Macduff turned, keeping his hand carefully away from his gun. The man who had spoken sat a big black just outside the fringe of timber behind Macduff. Over the man's grease-slick leggins were a pair of gaudy Apache boot moccasins of deerskin, long enough to reach the hip, folded over until they were knee-high, forming a double thickness of hide as protection against the clawing brush.

"Well," said Macduff, "Anton Chico! And what did you do with the girl?"

The bandido held a big Dragoon pistol in his right hand, single action hammer at full cock under his thumb. He waved the gun at the richly dressed man sprawled across the body of the white-trousered peon.

"That is Señor Carlos Farrerra. And those other cabrónes in the cloaks are men of the Farrerra party. They said they'd give me half the money they got from Riley if I met them here this morning with the girl. As soon as I handed her over, they jumped me. I should have known a bunch of small time politicos like them wouldn't part with any fifteen thousand silver dollars. They could have finished my tortillas right then. But the fools started shooting while I and some of my men were still on our horses."

"But why should they want the girl?" asked Macduff.

Anton Chico's sardonic mouth tightened impatiently. "The Costillo party plans to storm the palacio and take Armijo themselves if the money doesn't reach him by tonight. Naturally, the Farrerras don't want that any more than they want Armijo to get the money. Either way he's out of the office, and they fall with him. When the Costillos find the Farrerras have the girl, their leader, they won't dare make a move, knowing it would mean her life."

There were four wild ladrones behind Anton Chico, sitting jaded horses just under the fringe of pine, their eyes filled with the fierce wildness of the lobo wolf that has run alone for so long he doesn't know what it is to feel safe. One of them had a ragged serape over his left shoulder and a big Green River knife through a broad belt of Cheyenne wampum. Down one side of his face, from temple to jawbone, the flesh had been laid open. He gave Macduff a murderous glance, and Macduff realized it must be the hombre he had pistol-whipped the night before.

"Let's not palaver here like a bunch of duennas, jefe," he said to Anton Chico. "The dragoons will be coming sooner or later. They must have heard our guns."

Anton Chico leaned forward in his silver-mounted California saddle, flapping his legs out wide for support. Only then did Macduff see how he held his left hand tightly over his side.

"Sí, compadre, you are right," he growled, then he nodded indifferently toward the dead Apache in the grass. "They got my Indian. I managed to escape with these four hombres. We waited up on the slope till the Farrerras left with the woman, then tried to follow their trail. But the Apache was my tracker, and we lost it down by Rio Espiritu Santo.

"I remembered how you ran out of the house last night, and figured you would be following us. I came back here to wait for you. And now, El Cojo, you're going to follow the trail of those Farrerras, if necessary, all the way to hell!"

"If you know I'm El Cojo, why did you take my mules last night?" asked Macduff bitterly.

"I thought you were Riley then. My Apache recognized you when you chased us into the street last night — " Suddenly the sharp intelligence in Anton Chico's black eyes was turned into a vicious, impatient anger. "You ask too many questions, señor. I took a hunk of lead in that fight, and I've lost a lot of blood, and I want to catch those Farrerras before I fall off my caballo like a drunk — a *barrachón*. Now get on your horse and start tracking or I'll shoot you in the legs and make you follow the trail on your hands and knees!"

The tracks were easy to follow to the Rio Espiritu Santo — Holy Ghost Creek. Macduff followed the hoofprints of some ten horses down into the water. They didn't come out on the other bank.

"They've either gone upstream or down," said Macduff. "Using the water to hide their tracks."

"Obviously," said Anton Chico. "And now, señor, you had better live up to the things the Apaches tell of you — if you understand me."

He waved his Dragoon, and Macduff saw what he meant. Either way he stood to lose. If he couldn't find the trail now, the bandido would kill him. And if he did find it, when they reached the end, Anton Chico would kill him anyway.

Yet he had to finish the thing now. The Farrerras had killed his brother; he owed them for that. Also, they held the lives of countless American troops in their hands, and they had the woman.

With infinite patience, he coursed up and down the stream, hunting for sign. He spent much time where the thickets of choke-cherry and wild rose reached out over the water. Anton Chico had carried Lajara across the withers of his mount. With her head hanging over on one side, if the horse passed near the bank. . . .

Finally, he found a strand of blue-black hair caught in a thorny bramble that stretched out over the cut bank. It was about a mile up-stream from where the tracks had entered the water. He straightened, standing knee-deep in the icy stream, holding the hair up for Anton Chico to see.

The bandido sat on the bank, the four ladrones nervous behind him. He grinned sardonically.

"Señor, if the Apaches said you could trail a bald eagle, I wouldn't doubt them. It is unfortunate you were born an honest man. Your talent could be put to so many better uses than hunting for Bent's Fort."

Macduff mounted his gelding, slapped his wet legs against its flanks to stir his circulation. "And when we find the Farrerras, how do you know they'll have the money?"

The bandit spurred his black into the shallows after Macduff, turning upstream. "You saw Señor Riley there in the clearing. The Farrerras wanted him stopped last night. All they had to do was let me know he was due at Señorita Costillo's hacienda with the money. Then, you came, instead. When I found beaver pelts instead of silver, I got in touch with the Farrerras. They still thought you were Riley, thought you'd come ahead as decoy, leaving someone else to bring the money.

"They headed back toward Las Vegas to intercept whoever that was, telling me they'd give me half the money anyway if I'd get the girl and bring her to that clearing. Riley must have been late, and they caught him somewhere in Apache Pass, because they'd already killed him when I arrived with the girl."

Macduff started as a long-legged paisano flushed from some wild plum bushes on the bank. He hadn't realized how keyed up he was.

"What's the matter, El Cojo?" grinned the bandido. "Are you getting nervous?"

Macduff didn't answer, because he had caught sight of prints leaving the Rio. The horses were glad to get out of the cold water. Blowing and snorting, they passed through the aspens fringing the stream, yellowing with summer color, then through the pines that covered the lower slopes, the thick blanket of needles muffling the hoofbeats.

It was harder to follow the trail through those needles, and Macduff had to dismount. They were rising steadily, and though it was growing colder, Macduff could feel the sweat moistening his palms. The growing excitement made him breathe hard, leaving his senses abnormally acute. He had faced many kinds of death before, but not this certain, waiting kind, his life hanging on the shortening time, and on the cocked hammer under Anton Chico's thumb.

They had left the carpet of needles behind and Macduff could read sign from the saddle again. He swung aboard the gelding, glad for that, at least. He wanted to be mounted when it came. There was little enough chance that way.

"All right, señor, we have come far enough," called Anton Chico softly.

Macduff could see it now, the black hole in the side of the cliff, partly hidden by brambles and scrub-oak. A big bunch of jaded horses stood before the cave with a knot of men dressed in riding cloaks, high black boots and heavily glazed sombreros.

"Farrerras," muttered Anton Chico. "Small time politicos that grew fat under Armijo's rule and stand to lose everything if he runs out on them."

Macduff wasn't looking at the cave any longer. He knew that if Anton Chico wanted to take Farrerras by surprise, he wouldn't risk a shot down here. It would come from behind them, from one of Chico's men, and the bandido was just talking to cover whatever they were going to do.

"I've heard of this cave in Cañon Espiritu Santo," said Chico. "Some say it leads to subterranean passages that open out in the mountains above the Nambe Pueblo. . . ."

Beneath Chico's voice, Macduff heard the swift swishing sound he'd been waiting for, the sound of a man's cotton-sleeved arm raising for a blow.

With a sudden jerk to the side, Macduff kicked his gelding's right flank, and yanked cruelly on the big Spanish bit. The horse danced hard into Chico's back. Throwing himself at the bandido, Macduff heard the man behind him grunt with having missed the blow, heard the slide of his leggins over leather as he tried to stop himself from going out of the saddle.

The Irishman was already crashing into Chico, putting all his chips on the bet that the bandido wouldn't use his gun. He felt the muzzle of that Dragoon dig into his belly, then both of them were slamming down off the black and onto the ground.

THE FIGHT IN KILLER'S CAVE

They hit hard. Macduff was on top with that gun still sinking into his belly. All the air went out of Anton Chico in a big burst. Macduff tried to grab the gun. Chico wrenched it from between their bodies, holding his thumb desperately across that cocked hammer, striking at Macduff.

Head rocking to the blow, Macduff sprawled flat on the man, clawing at the gun. Then the steel of a blade, burning like fire, slipped through his ribs from the back. The man he had pistol-whipped the night before straightened, the bloody knife in his hand, and Macduff collapsed across Anton Chico. The bandit heaved off Macduff and stood up, face twisted with pain, left hand going again to the wound in his side.

"I knew he wouldn't give up without a

fight," he panted. "Por Dios, I didn't expect a lame man to move so fast!"

The first pain held Macduff in a strange lethargy. Dimly he could hear Chico's voice, the shuffle of feet. He knew he would be helpless against that second thrust. He wished, somehow, that he could have seen the girl again. It would have been easier to die. . . .

He saw the blurred figure of the ladrone with the knife move to stab him again, then Anton Chico grabbed the man's arm, growling angrily:

"Caracoles, you're wasting time. I can't last much longer with this bullet hole through me and you want to stand around putting that knife in a man you've already killed. Look at all the blood on him, you cabrón! He was dead before you pulled the blade out."

They moved away up the hill, and only the horses stood there, cropping halfheartedly at some bark. Tentatively, Macduff raised to an elbow. Pain stabbed at him, subsided. The bandit leader and two of his men were working up through thinning timber toward the cave. The other two ladrones had worked around above the Farrerras, were sliding down through the knee-high clumps of wild hops that grew on the slope over the cave mouth.

Macduff crawled on his hands and knees to Chico's black, the nearest horse. He reached up and grasped the stirrup, hauled himself to his knees, then to his feet. He leaned weakly against the horse, breathing the stink of sweaty leather.

Then the guns opened up. Anton Chico and two of his men broke from the edge of the timber, firing. And the pair above the cave rose up, six-shooters clattering. The Farrerras were taken completely by surprise. One of them folded without a sound. Another took a half step forward, clawing spasmodically at his gun, then fell over on his face. The other two whirled wildly toward the cave. One of them made it.

The two ladrones above slid down the shale over the cave's mouth and dropped to the ground. Anton Chico and his pair joined them, and they all disappeared into the black maw.

Macduff let go the black and staggered from the junipers toward the cave, every step a separate agony. Chico had taken his gun, and he stopped a moment beside one of the dead Farrerras, stooping for the man's weapon. Black nausea swept him and he felt himself falling. It was a terrific effort of will that jerked him erect, the dead man's six-shooter clutched in his fist. Then he swayed toward the cave, footsteps fumbling into the cool darkness, the smell of rich black loam softly enveloping him.

A blast of gunfire sounded from farther back, rolling down to Macduff in warped, hollow echoes. And then came Anton Chico's wild laughter. And silence again.

When the Irishman came across the first bodies, it was still quite light in the cave. The Farrerras must have made a stand here, because Anton Chico's four men were sprawled on the black earth, one after another, and beyond them a little huddle of Farrerras in their cloaks and boots and rich vests. Macduff had just moved past when a sudden movement on his right whirled him.

Two dim shapes hurtled from a recess in the caves. Macduff caught a flapping cloak, light glinting along a sword blade. He jerked backward, trying to dodge the sword, gun bucking up in his hand with the first shot.

One of the men went down. Macduff's thumb was snapping his hammer back for the second shot when the other man smashed up against him, carrying him back against the opposite wall of the cave.

With his gun against the man's body, Macduff fired. The sound of the explosion was muffled.

For a moment he thought he had missed,

and with the sword quivering in him like that, he wondered why he felt no pain. Then the body against him relaxed, and slid down to the ground, limp and falling from the rapier hilt, leaving the sword sticking there.

For a long moment, Macduff sagged against the wall, looking down at the man. The sightless eyes that stared up so gruesomely were those of Don Gaspar Jamarillo, the man who had put that same blade through Terrance, back at the hacienda. Macduff knew a moment of grim satisfaction — that score, at least, was settled. Then he saw why he felt no pain. He had managed to dodge the rapier, after all, and the blade had only gone through the sleeve of his buffalo coat, pinning him to the cave's wall. He pulled free, dropped it, stepped across Jamarillo.

If the don had let Anton Chico go on by, then there might well be other Farrerras who had done the same thing, not wanting to meet the bandido's skill with the Dragoon pistol.

That last effort seemed to have taken all the will to move from Macduff. Fighting an enveloping lethargy, he stumbled into the darkening recesses of the tunnel, and the thought of the woman back there somewhere was the only thing that kept him going. Lajara. . . .

There was another clatter of gunfire, and flame stabbed the gloom ahead of Macduff. Anton Chico's voice followed, calling to someone:

"It's only you and me left now, isn't it? You've played your pretty game for a long time! Nobody would have guessed you were the real leader of the Farrerras. But you can't double-cross everybody all of the time, and you made a mistake when you tried it on me. This is Anton Chico, you fat cabrón, and I'm going to kill you. . . . I'm coming to get the money and kill you!"

The answering voice was so muffled and warped that Macduff couldn't recognize it: "Don't come around that turn, Chico, you won't stand a chance."

There was the sound of a moving body, pounding feet, a crazy yell. Then guns drowned everything else.

Macduff heard the bandido scream once in mortal pain. The echoes of the gunfire and of the scream, slapped mournfully back and forth down the tunnel until they died.

There was a turn ahead, then, and the mysterious leader of the Farrerras was beyond it. Whoever tried to get him would be going from a lighter part of the cave to a darker part, and would be a perfect skylighted target. . . . would die, as Anton Chico died.

Forcing himself ahead, against that pain and lethargy, Macduff stumbled over another body. He went down, dropping his gun. The man he had tripped over was another Farrerra. His hand still clutched the ornate butt of a sixgun that had been so useless against Anton Chico's deadly Dragoon. Yet, not even Anton Chico's gun-skill had been able to meet the unknown leader of the *nuevo ricos* around that turn.

Terrance had said that the unknown Farrerra leader was the most dangerous of all. Danny could believe it now, because Terrance was dead, like Farrerra himself, and Anton Chico with all his ladrones was dead. And, too, all the Farrerra *nuevos ricos*. . . . And now only that man beyond the turn remained, with everything his own way, playing the game out with all the top cards in his hand.

What could Macduff hope for? Nothing but what Chico had gotten, what all the others had gotten.

The Irishman must have made considerable noise in falling, for that muffled voice around the turn called out: "That you, Jamarillo?"

Macduff was concentrating too hard on finding his gun to pay much attention. He hardly heard. Then he found the weapon, the bond handle covered with cool black loam.

"Jamarillo?" came the voice again, still muffled and unrecognizable.

Macduff shook his head to clear it, tried to place the voice. It had a familiar ring, a tantalizing familiarity. Then the man chuckled.

"All right, so it isn't Jamarillo. Come on around the corner and you'll get the same thing Chico got. Macbeth had the right idea — 'I bear a charmed life, which must not yield to one of woman born.' "

Suddenly Macduff knew who was waiting there for him, knew who had led the Farrerra party all along. His voice boomed down the cavern in hollow, ghostly answer.

"Don't you remember the rest of it, Doctor? 'Despair thy charm, and tell the angel thou hast served. Macduff was from his mother's womb untimely ripped.' "

There was a moment of stunned silence. Macduff took it to fight erect. He was so weak he had to lean against the wall for support. He couldn't seem to think straight, and finally, to focus his thoughts, he began saying a name. It gave him strength, somehow; Lajara, Lajara. . . . .

Doctor Leo Britt's chuckle came finally, and it sounded forced. "If it isn't our lame Irishman, by Harry! And I thought that Macduff business was just some of your blarney. Sorry I got you into this, really. You caused me no end of trouble. I didn't realize who you really were until my Farrerras picked up the real Riley in Apache Pass. But you won't cause any more trouble, will you, not if you try to come around that corner?"

The woman's voice was high with fear. "Macduff, don't do it. You'll make a perfect target. Chico couldn't do it. You won't stand a chance!"

Lajara's voice sent a new power coursing through him, and he jerked away from the support of the wall, wiping his sweaty hand against his leggins, then slipping the gun into it. He began moving forward in a half-blind stumble.

Yet he'd be a fool to march around and take it like Chico had.

That was the normal way, though, to go around the turn standing up. Britt would expect him to come that way. It would take his eyes a moment to accustom themselves to the darker portion of the tunnel. And that moment would be all Doctor Leo Britt's. He couldn't miss.

A black curtain kept sliding over Macduff's eyes. The cave reeled around him. He wanted to lie down and give way to the pain and cry like a baby.

"Macduff, don't be a fool. . . ."

It was Lajara's voice, and it was the spur. Teeth clamped shut, he gathered himself for that last rush. Then he began to run, his gun coming up, his square, broad-shouldered body moving into a pounding, lop-sided charge, moving so much faster than anyone would expect of a lame man. And in his mind was that single driving thought: Lajara. . . .

On the last step that took him banging around the curve, he launched himself into a low dive, body hurtling forward from the vertical to the horizontal just an instant before Doctor Britt's gun flamed from the gloom.

The lead whined over Macduff and plopped into earth behind him.

It wasn't as dark as Macduff had thought, and in that instant before he hit on his belly, his eyes became accustomed to the gloom, and he could see the doctor back against the cave's wall. Spasmodic anger at having missed that first time twisted the doctor's pudgy face, and his thumb was twitching the hammer back for a second shot, gun jerking down toward Macduff's hurtling body.

Then the Irishman hit, sliding along on his belly, rocks ripping his coat and flannel

142

shirt from collar to belt, head rocking as his chin slammed into the ground. But somehow he had managed to keep his gun out in front, holding it desperately in both hands. And even as he began to slide forward, he shot.

Britt stood there for one moment, face blank with surprise and pain — as if he really believed he bore a charmed life and couldn't understand how Macduff had hit him. Then he took a faltering step backward, trying stubbornly to catch at his gun's hammer again.

It took all Macduff had left to lift his six-shooter and fire again. The doctor dropped his gun and went over backward.

For a long time Macduff tried to gather the strength to crawl to the woman, where she lay beside Riley's Mexican packsaddles, bulging with silver. He managed to get his Green River out, finally, and cut her loose from the rawhide lashings. She helped him up, then was suddenly in his arms, sobbing with reaction.

"It was the doctor all along," she cried. "With the backing of the Farrerra party, he was going to overthrow Armijo after the governor had ambushed the Americanos; was going to take over the government himself. He was the master conspirator of all, and none of us suspected. Not even Armijo."

Her voice had drowned whatever sound Valdez must have made coming in.

"What have you been doing, señor?" he asked. "It looks like the Taos Massacre."

Macduff tried to keep himself from falling with the girl's weight against him. "I thought you were in Santa Fe, Captain."

"When the money didn't come, Armijo sent me out with final orders for the preparation of the ambush," said Valdez. "A few hours ago, we heard the first firing. I thought the Americanos had flanked us, and took five squadrons up the slope. We finally found that clearing. And then we heard more firing from up Cañon Espiritu Santo."

"There's your money," said Macduff, motioning to the aparejos. "You're about the only man I'd trust it with. You can take your five squadrons and get it back to Armijo today."

"Sí," said Valdez. "Just in time, too. We have already received word that Kearny has taken Las Vegas and is advancing on Santa Fe. . . ."

He stopped talking, because the girl had taken one of her arms from around Macduff and was staring at the blood on her hand, eyes widening.

"It's all right," said Macduff, weakly. "I

144

was jerking around a lot when they stabbed me. Makes me sort of dizzy — just lost a lot of blood."

She put her arm around him, supporting his weight. "I don't think the blade is made that could kill you, not after coming all the way from Santa Fe with every hombre in the city looking for you, getting through all the peons and Armijo's dragoons and Anton Chico and his bandidos, and the Farrerras, and the doctor. I didn't believe any man could be that good. But I do now. . . ."

He found it hard to choose the right words, because his head was swimming, and because he always felt awkward with a woman, anyway. "Some men come west to run away from something, others hunting something. I guess I was hunting something. Only last night, when Anton Chico took you, did I realize what it was — what every man hunts for, whether he knows it or not. . . ."

She seemed to understand, for her arms were soft around him and her eyes were shining. "You'll like it in Santa Fe now that everything is settled, Danny Macduff," she said softly.

And he knew she spoke the truth.

Dangerous Orders

Lieutenant John Hunter, First Dragoons, stood beside his two big cavalry mounts on Tucson's *Calle Real*, watching the last Federal troops march eastward down the ancient street. It was June seventeenth, 1861. The withdrawal of Union troops for service in the East had loosed the long-restrained vengeance of the Apache. Southern Arizona was being laid waste, and refugees were streaming into Tucson, the only white outpost left for hundreds of miles.

The creaking wheels and tramping feet of the incoming mob beat up the dust till it filled the air with a mealy haze and settled in whispering white layers on the young lieutenant's uniform and face. It was a long and thoughtful face, already turned gaunt by the rigors of this land, with crevices of perpetual watchfulness at the corners of the eyes.

He straightened a little as he saw Sheridan Wade elbowing through the press. They had told Hunter it might start anytime. But somehow he had not considered Wade.

The tanned, youthful smoothness of Wade's face was a painful cultivation against the insidious signs of whitening hair and thickening belly which even the impeccable cut of his bottle-green frock coat failed to hide. He saw Hunter as he struggled free of the mob, and a genial smile curled his mouth.

"Aren't you going with your company, John?"

Hunter kept his face blank. "I'm on orders to Sante Fe."

Surprise seemed to widen Wade's tawny eyes a little too much. "What a wonderful coincidence, John. I'm bound there myself. The last stage left yesterday and the bank closed before I could get my money out. I haven't been able to get hold of a horse."

His gaze turned covetous as it settled on Hunter's extra animal, and the lieutenant spoke sharply.

"That's my spare, Wade. I can't let anybody have it."

"What a way to treat an old friend," Wade said chidingly. He grasped Hunter's arm.

"You have no idea how happy I was to find you stationed so close to Tucson when I came here last March, John. I swear I'd have seen more of you if I hadn't been so infernally busy. But now we've got to make up for it. You can't turn down a man from your own hometown, boy — "

"I'm sorry, Wade," Hunter said.

Wade's hand slid off; it seemed an effort to keep the paternal indulgence in his chuckle. "You must be doing something infernally important to be so damn stiff."

Something slyly knowing licked through Wade's eyes. "Is it this last order issued by department headquarters at Santa Fe, John? All commanders in the Territory were to destroy what supplies they couldn't transport when they evacuated, weren't they? It's common knowledge that Apache raids have kept Fort Warren cut off from Santa Fe for months. Warren probably got the first order — to evacuate — on the twentieth of June. It was sent out some time ago. But they couldn't possibly have gotten this new order to destroy, could they?"

Hunter could hardly keep the shock from his face. How could the man know so much? If Fort Warren didn't get the order to destroy what supplies they couldn't carry, they'd move out in three days, leaving behind them enough stores for a regiment. It was as if Wade had read Hunter's mind.

"The only way Fort Warren could get the order to destroy is for one of the commanders down here to relay it by messenger," the older man said. "Are you the messenger, John?"

Hunter shook his head stiffly. "You've got it wrong, Wade."

"In a way, I hope I have," Wade said. "You must know the Confederates will have an agent out to stop those orders from reaching Fort Warren. You must know what that agent is capable of doing to attain his ends."

"You — Wade?" There was a soft disbelief in Hunter's voice.

The man chuckled heartily. "Lord Harry no, John. I'm just a banker. You know that. I only come to you as a friend."

He grasped Hunter's arm again. "Baylor and his Confederates are within a day's march of Tucson right now. They need supplies desperately. Those stores at Fort Warren would mean the difference between taking Arizona or not. All you'd have to do is see that the order to destroy doesn't reach Fort Warren, John. As simple as that. You can't let your own people down."

"You talkin' about white trash, Wade?" John asked softly.

Anger mottled the man's cheeks, but he checked it with palpable effort. "Don't be like that. It's in the past. We're both in this together now, John. We're both fighting for the South."

Hunter's eyes were narrowed to slits. "What South, Wade? Yours or mine? Do you think mine's worth fighting for? Do you think I'd have left if I'd wanted to fight for it? A one-room shanty on a stinking backwater and a rag for a shirt and a handful of hominy — "

Wade held up a protesting hand. "John — "

"Or your South, Wade? You wouldn't give me a crumb of it before. Mint juleps and white houses and dimity women. Would Lucy speak to me on the street now? Would you keep me standing all evenin' at the back door with my hat in my hand now — "

"Damn you, shut up!" Wade had leaned so close their faces almost touched. Though his voice was barely a whisper, it was as venomous as a snake's hiss. "I made the mistake of treating you like a gentleman. Now I'm goin' to treat you like the white trash you are. No wonder my daughter laughed at you when you asked to court her. Lucy knew what you were, even better'n I. And it didn't change you none to run away. I'm through askin', John. I'm tellin'.

I'm ridin' with you, and if you don't take me you know what will happen. There are a hundred Confederate sympathizers in this town that would jes' love to know you're carryin' those orders to Fort Warren."

Hunter felt his belly knot up with violent reaction. But somehow he checked himself, the blood pounding hotly through his head. Dimly, he realized Wade was right. A hundred sympathizers. They'd be on his tail the moment Wade told them. And it wasn't the sympathizers Hunter wanted. He stared at Wade, realizing what he would have to do. He felt his shoulders sag in defeat.

"All right, Wade," he said in a low voice. "Let's go."

He saw triumphant justification lick through Wade's tawny eyes. A justification of Wade's whole class, his whole way of life. The man settled back with a smug smile, squaring his coat with a pull at the lapels.

"Yes," he said, with a return of that lubricious geniality. "By all means, let's go."

The road unfurled like a saffron banner before the two men as they trotted northward from Tucson. The sun cast grotesque shadows at the foot of mesas flung like giant blockhouses across the desert. A field of sacaton grass slipped over the horizon, turned to a glittering sea by the brazen sun.

Hunter rode hunched forward in the saddle, eyes tirelessly moving across the endless expanse of earth which swept at last into the Superstitions lying in a jagged silhouette against the sky.

The lieutenant's mind was on Wade, at his side. He could not see the man's face, but he knew the expression it held: It seemed to symbolize the insidious pressures which had driven Hunter from his home in the first place. He had tried since early boyhood to rise above the degraded level at which his birth as the son of a river rat had placed him. He had battered his head for years against the cottony wall of patronization and tacit exclusion by Wade's decaying society. Perhaps the final blow had been Wade's daughter.

Hunter had worshipped Lucy Wade from childhood. As long as he had kept it impersonal, she had tolerated him. He had even taken a job as a stable boy on the Wade plantation — when few white men would be seen at such a task — to be near her. He could ride behind her on the hunt and drive her gig to town when she shopped. There had been a certain comradeship between them even under those circumstances. He had been blind to the patronization. But finally he had been unable to contain himself.

He had told her how he felt.

Hunter could still hear her laughter, rich with derision and contempt. The whole town had known the next day. The whole town had laughed.

He had run from her laughter. Also he had run from something deeper. More than anything else, it had made him realize the futility of trying to change his station in such a society.

Wade's voice broke him in on Hunter's thoughts. "Can't I have another drink, John? My throat's closing up."

Their canteens made a hollow clanking against the flanks of Hunter's horse, as he turned to look at Wade. The desert was beginning to take its toll. Wade lagged behind Hunter, his soft weight settled deeply into the saddle. But that smug haughtiness still lay in his eyes.

Hunter knew what was going through the man's mind. Wade thought the lieutenant would comply with this as he would have back in Virginia, bowing automatically to hereditary authority, reverting without a struggle to the old servility. That was the worst for Hunter. Knowing he could not strike back. Knowing he could not show the man how different the standards were out here; how a man's worth didn't depend upon his birth or his wealth; how he, himself, had changed.

"We drink at four, Wade," he said. "We don't reach water till night. I don't see how you ever thought you'd get through alone."

"I'd have managed," Wade said condescendingly. "My home office in Richmond needed a man to get what Confederate funds he could out of Santa Fe, before the Union confiscated them."

He broke off to cough as a hot wind swept parched dust into their faces. Then he brought his horse against Hunter, reaching for the canteen. "Damn it, John, give me a drink."

Hunter reined his horse sharply away.

"Don't crowd me, Wade," he said. "We drink at four."

Wade's eyes widened in surprise. Then the expression changed within them, and his mouth furled with contempt.

"White trash is gettin' high and mighty ideas again," he said.

Hunter's voice came out thinly. "You haven't got your hundred Confederate sympathizers out here, Wade."

The man settled back into his saddle, studying Hunter with a new calculation in his eyes. But he spoke derisively. "Think I'd really need them, John?"

Hunter glanced at him, trying to read all the implications in his face. Then he gigged his horse on ahead.

The heat seemed to grow greater through the afternoon. Hunter was seeing mirages now, lakes in the middle of a dry salt flat, cities where only the gnarled saguaro grew. They came to eroded bluffs and dismounted for a rest in the meager shade. Hunter was barely on his feet before he saw the prints in the sand.

"Get aboard, Wade."

The man had just lowered himself against the sandy *barranca,* and looked up in surprise. "What for? We've got to rest."

"Not here. Can't you see those hoofprints? It's an Indian war party and it passed here within the hour."

To the east were badlands, gullies, and fissures cut by centuries of wind and water into a weird labyrinth without end. They sought cover here and sweated without shade for the rest of the afternoon.

Hunter lay on his belly against a bank, scanning the sky in all directions with his four-power cavalry binoculars. At last he saw the stain against the ruddy banners of evening clouds. He let Wade see it.

"Smoke," he said. "It would come up in puffs if they were signaling. They've burned out somebody. We'll head toward it."

An edge of tension ripped at the cultivated geniality of Wade's voice. "Why go directly toward them?"

"Because they're about finished when they start a fire. They won't backtrack. They're out looking for something else to raid now and they didn't find anything on their way through here."

Night darkened the sky till the smoke was no longer visible as a separate hue. They halted a few minutes for a cold supper from the lieutenant's saddlebags. The moon had risen by the time they reached the gutted buildings. Smoke still curled dismally into the night, and somewhere off a wolf was howling.

"This is our first water hole," Hunter said. "It's the Chicataw way station."

Seeing no sign of bodies within, Hunter led around the buildings to the rock sink. He dropped his reins to the ground and hunkered down, scooping up a handful of water. He tasted it and spat it out.

"They've dumped alkali into the water," he said. "We can't use it."

Wade's rigging squawked as he swung off, his mouth starting to open in horrified protest. Before he could speak, there was a sharp rattle from the brush across the sink.

Wade's hand darted instinctively inside his frock coat.

Moonlight spilled across the figure of the man who crawled feebly from the sagebrush across the water.

"I thought you was them warwhoops at first," he said feebly.

Hunter rose from his squatting position, hand still on the butt of his holstered Dragoon Colt, giving a glance to the snub-nosed derringer Wade had pulled from under his coat.

"I didn't know you carried a gun, Wade," he said.

There was a flutter of guilt in Wade's eyes. He shoved the derringer back into its harness under his lapel. His chuckle held a forced urbanity.

"Ace in the hole, John, ace in the hole."

Hunter was already hooking a canteen from his horse and moving around the tip of the sink. The third man sat heavily back into the sand, reaching eager hands up to hold the canteen as Hunter tipped it to his lips. He was a big rawboned figure with long-sleeved red woolens for his shirt and a pair of grease-blackened rawhide leggins stuffed into cast-off cavalry boots.

"You're Hock Ellis, aren't you?" Hunter asked.

"That's right, Lieutenant. Station-keeper

here. I was the only one left when them warwhoops jumped the station. I got out the back way and hid in the bushes. Been there without water all day. Damn sun clabbered my brains."

Hunter frowned suspiciously at him. "I thought that last stage out of Tucson was going to pick up all personnel as far as Salt River."

Ellis got unsteadily to his feet, handing the canteen back. "That's what saved me, I guess. Them Apaches thought the crew here had left and didn't bother hunting for me."

"We can't take you," Wade said. "We'll be lucky if we make it ourselves to the next water hole."

A wild look widened Ellis's eyes, then he caught at the pommel of Wade's horse. "You got to take me along with you, them Apaches are everywhere — "

Wade caught Ellis by one arm and jerked him loose, spinning him back so hard the man tripped and fell. Ellis rolled over onto his belly, staring dazedly at Wade.

"I wouldn't have thought you were that strong," Hunter told Wade.

The man turned sharply, almost angrily. Then he collected his gentility with effort, and that oily chuckle slipped from him.

"You don't want to underestimate us bankers, John."

Hunter's eyes traveled back to the station-keeper, seeking some capacity for guile, for intrigue, in the man's equine face. He could read nothing but grim weariness. Then the irony of this struck him and he could not help a grim smile.

"Ellis will ride with you," Hunter told Wade.

Wade stared blankly, "We'll never make it. Three men on two horses. No water. All those Apaches between us and the Salt River. You're crazy, John — "

"But still a white man, Wade. Let Ellis go on first."

A raw wind mourned down off the Superstitions. It rattled through miles of creosote brush like the beat of an Indian tomtom. It made Hunter shiver and huddle in his tunic.

The stage station was hours behind. Sheridan Wade's horse was beginning to falter beneath the double load. They had given the last of their water to the animals. Hunter knew if they didn't come up with the next sink before dawn they would have to spend all day without water. It was too risky to travel during the day with Apaches all around.

He began to keep his eyes open for a safe campsite. He was so intent on this that he did not notice how Wade's horse was lagging behind. Suddenly he realized it was no longer visible from the tail of his eye, and he jerked sharply around in the saddle. The two men were a full length back of him, Wade sitting behind Ellis.

"What's the matter, Lieutenant?" Ellis said. "You look like the cat caught stealing the cream."

"Get ahead of me where I can see you," Hunter said.

The station-keeper gigged the horse up. "What makes you so suspicious? You ain't got any more water left to steal."

"Perhaps he's wondering what your policies are," Wade said.

"I'm the best Unionist of 'em all," Ellis said. Then he spat disgustedly. "How do you get off wondering about my politics, Lieutenant, you traveling with a damn Secesh banker from Virginia?"

"Don't rile the lieutenant," Wade said smugly. "He'd like to forget his origins."

Ellis glanced at Hunter's hands. The calluses were beginning to wear off, but the gaunt knobbiness that came from a lifetime of common labor would never leave. The station-keeper read the story.

"You didn't git to live up in the big house, I guess, sipping them juleps and watching them pretty horses." His voice grew sly. "Is that what they call white trash down there, Lieutenant?"

Hunter felt his ears begin to glow. Wade chuckled, and it was filled with husky mockery. Hunter's hands closed tight on the pommel, and he would not look at them.

"How did a man like you git to be an officer?" Ellis said. "You sure ain't West Point."

"He was always a good bootlicker," Wade murmured.

Hunter looked straight ahead. He could feel the blood beating at his temples. But he realized there was even more reason to contain himself now. He had seen it as ironic, at first, that they were forced to take Ellis with them. Now he realized it might contain more irony than he had bargained for.

"You never did tell us how you happened to get left at the station," he told Ellis thinly.

"No room on the coach. They left me a horse. But he got away."

"*Did* he now?" Hunter said.

He saw surprise turn the man's seamed face blank. He jerked his head for them to go on. Ellis dug heels into his horse. Wade said something softly into the station-keeper's ear. Ellis laughed gutturally.

They found the rotting building in the

darkest hours before dawn. It was up in the wind-swept mesa land, crouched in the lee of a lonely bluff. Hunter checked his weary horse, peering through the thick texture of darkness at the ancient logs stacked into a beehive shape.

"We'll be safe," he said. "It a *tchindi hogan.*"

Wade frowned at him. "A what?"

"A devil house. See that hole in the north end? Some Navajo died here a long time ago. They knocked logs from the north wall and took him out there."

"Boy's right," Ellis said. "No warwhoop will ever go near this place again. Afraid the devils will get them."

Hunter tethered his horse and unsaddled. He stripped some kindling from the rotting logs that had been knocked out of the north wall, stopped in the lower door with these.

He found the circle of rocks in the center where the ashes of countless fires lay in powdery dust, and stacked his kindling here. Then he ignited it. Flames licked upward, turning the film of alkali on his face to a mealy shimmer. Then his eyes widened with the complete surprise of it.

The light revealed an enormously fat man sitting in the far corner like some gross Buddha, holding a four barreled pepperbox in one hand. He had a flat-topped hat jammed so tight it left a ridge of flesh just beneath the band. There were greasy channels in the deep furrows of his face where the sweat had run down to drip off his pink chin and make dark stains on his marseille waistcoat.

"George Mott, gentlemen. At your service."

Ellis let out a low whistle, "Had me spooked, Mott."

Mott shrugged. "Apaches burned out Tubac. I thought it would be safer out of the Territory."

"We didn't see any sign in front," Hunter said.

"I hid my horse in a gully at the rear," Mott offered. He smiled slyly at Wade. "The banker from Virginia, I believe."

Hunter saw the little pucker of muscle run through Wade's face. The lieutenant remembered Mott now, an agent for some Sante Fe mining interests down around Tubac. The man had been through Tucson several times. His little eyes almost disappeared in their pouches of fat as they licked back across the room to Hunter.

"I understood most of the officers in the Territory were resigning their commissions in favor of the Confederacy."

163

"Is that what you understood?" Hunter said.

"He was traveling with Wade," Hock Ellis said.

"Well." Mott's chuckle shook his great belly. "Perhaps you and I are the only Black Republicans in the house, Hock."

Ellis snorted assent, easing himself to a sitting position against the wall, pulling his holstered cap and ball around so it lay between his legs.

"We'll have to draw a Mason-Dixon line right through the middle of this room," he said.

The heat of the fire was reaching Hunter, and he unbuttoned his tunic. "As I remember, there was a sink behind this hogan."

"Sink's still there," Mott said. "No water left."

Hunter saw the desperation momentarily swallow the antipathy lying between the men. Wade lowered himself to a seated position, taking out a handkerchief and dismally wiping the grime from around his mouth. Mott looked at the pepperbox in his hand, put the gun away. As Hunter sat down, the jackknifing of his body shoved the manila envelope up out of its inside pocket till a corner peaked from beneath the lapel of his tunic. He saw three pairs of eyes swing to it.

"Orders, Lieutenant?" Mott asked.

"To Santa Fe," Wade said sardonically.

"My, my," Mott said. "I've heard an order was also sent for Fort Warren to destroy all the supplies they couldn't transport."

"Wonder what'd happen if them orders didn't reach Fort Warren?" Ellis said, turning wonderfully innocent eyes on Hunter.

"They'd leave without destroying the supplies." Mott's grin was cherubic. "The supplies would fall into the hands of the Confederates. It would practically give them Arizona."

"Them Johnny Rebs know about everything that's going on," Ellis said. "They must have an agent out to stop those orders."

"Or two agents," Mott said slyly, glancing at Wade.

"Or three?" asked Hunter, mildly.

Mott stared at him for a moment. Then a chuckle began to spread from the subterranean depths of him till the dank hogan was filled with great spasms of sound. Finally it settled back into the man and the hogan was quiet.

Despite Hunter's burning thirst, exhaustion bore heavily on him. He felt his eyelids drooping. The desire for sleep became overpowering. He drew on all his will to remain awake. He sensed the culmination of the whole thing coming.

Mott began snoring softly, fat chin sunk against his chest. Wade let out his breath and leaned back against the wall, closing his eyes. Again that urge to sleep hit Hunter. He heard Ellis stir, and felt his eyes snap open. But the station-keeper was only settling against the earth.

The fire seemed to fade out. Darkness gathered. Something cottony was closing in against Hunter. It was pain to fight it. Then something brought him awake again with that sick shock.

George Mott was staring across the fire at him with eyes sly as a weasel's.

Hunter shook his head, trying to clear it. At the same time there was a sharp whinny from outside, and the drum of excited hoofs. It brought Hunter instinctively to his feet, scattering the fire with a kick of his foot as he wheeled toward the door. He heard someone give a sharp cry as the coals hit and burned. Then he was plunged through the door with gun in hand.

He saw that it was his horse, running down off the slope with snapped reins. And even as he watched, the ungainly jackrabbit that had spooked the animal hopped off into the night.

Hunter went down the slope at a run. He

knew the horse was too jaded to run far. He saw it slowing up ahead of him, and slowed himself so as not to frighten the animal further. He reached it and caught the reins and began to soothe it. He was several hundred yards from the house. The stars were out and the night was dead-black about him. Then he heard the first soft sound from behind him.

Quickly he tied the broken reins and led the horse a few paces to a creosote bush, hitching it firmly here. Then he walked directly away from it, making enough noise so they could hear him. Whatever happened he didn't want the horse to be spooked again. And he knew about what was going to happen.

He reached a gully filled with the acrid taint of greasewood. He moved down this for a dozen yards till he came to a dead end. He started to crawl up out of it when he heard the sound again. It was nearer. Already the pitch-blackness just before dawn was beginning to dissipate. He knew how swiftly light would come now. He had another moment to act.

If he left the gully now he would be trapped out on the flats without cover when light hit. Yet he would be just as effectively trapped in this dead end if he remained. There was the faintest crackle of greasewood before a moving body. Then silence again.

He took off his cap and tunic. He bellied up against the bank till he reached a greasewood bush on the east lip of the gully. Pearly streaks began to drift through the blackness of the sky. He found an outthrust branch upon which to slide the arm of his tunic, wrapping the body of it around and pulling in the other branches till he could button it. Then he put his forage cap on the top branch. He slid back into the gully.

The pearly streaks were spreading out until there was no blackness left. He began to crawl up the other side of the gully. In another moment it would be light. There was more noise from the other end. He reached the western lip of the gulch. On the other lip across from him, the first of full dawn silhouetted the tunic, arm outstretched toward the sun. He grabbed up a handful of rocks and threw them across the gulch. They landed by the silhouette with a sharp crackling.

There was another vicious crackling of brush from the bottom of the gully, twenty feet down from the end, and the sudden blast of a gun. He saw the silhouetted tunic jerk. His Navy revolver bucked in his hand as he fired at the other gun flashes. He squeezed the trigger three times and then stopped. The echoes ran out into the desert and grew flat and small and died. The stench of black powder lay heavy on the air.

Finally Hunter edged on his belly through the bushes along the edge of the gulch till he came over the place where the fat man sat slumped in the sandy bottom. The front of him was soaked with blood, and his pepperbox had dropped in the sand.

"You're the only one?" Hunter said.

Mott's chin sank onto his chest. "That right, son. I saw you in Tucson when all the other troops had gone. I figured you were the messenger. I got out ahead of you. The Indian sign drove me here. I figured it would drive you here too. There was hardly another route you could take. You'd know the safety in a *tchindi hogan.* So I waited — "

The last left him on a sigh, and his eyes closed. In a moment, Sheridan Wade moved around a turn in the gulch, staring at the dead man.

"I thought you were the one, Wade," Hunter said.

Wade was staring dully at Mott, his shoulders sagging, his voice strangely dull.

"Just a banker, John," he said wearily. "I told you that. I guess I had some idea of

169

trying for the orders, if the agent didn't show up. I guess it doesn't matter now, does it?"

There was a rattling of greasewood behind Hunter, and Hock Ellis rose up, his cap-and-ball pointed at the lieutenant. "Maybe you'd better let a real Unionist take them orders the rest of the way."

Hunter turned, then silently pulled them from his pocket. Ellis opened the manila sheaf. Then his mouth parted in surprise.

"This is blank paper."

"The real orders are on their way by another route," Hunter said. "We knew the Confederates would probably have an agent out to stop them. I was supposed to decoy that agent."

He was watching Wade as he said it. The man stared at Hunter as if trying to understand something almost beyond his comprehension. His voice sounded weak.

"Then all the time — you only made me think — "

"Yes, Wade," Hunter said. "I had to let you believe nothing had changed. That you were still quality, and I was trash. I had to find out if you were the agent."

He saw the final understanding turn Wade to a defeated little old man. He tried to feel triumph. But Lucy and the past were too far away. He drew a heavy breath, turned to see Hock Ellis holding the papers out to him.

"I guess the things that make for quality or trash out here are a little different than they were back in Virginia," he said. "You've proved that to me as well as him, son. If these were the real orders, you'd be the man to take them. I owe you an apology. I'm only the second-best Unionist in the country. Kin I shake hands with the first?"

Six-Gun Bride of the Teton Bunch

Victor Bondurant opened the door without knocking and stepped in, closing the portal behind him and standing against it. Lamplight glittered across the sheriff's star on his hickory vest and caught the quick, perceptive flash of his vivid black eyes. The strange scars scoring his jaw had always given the narrow, calculating intelligence of his face an ineffably vicious look.

"Not knocking anymore, Victor?" said Hammer, from where he sat at the table.

Bondurant's flannel mouth began to curl at one corner, like a lazy snake into that slow mocking smile. His right hand lifted, from where it had hung above the white bone butt of the big Forehand and Wadsworth sagging with such studied casualness at his negligible hips. The light made a brazen flash on the twenty dollar gold piece held with ironic delicacy between his thumb and forefinger.

Hammer stared at it a long time before the expressions began seeping into his face. A strange pain flickered through his wide brown eyes, and a small muscle quivered into view down his heavy-boned jaw. His broad lower lip stiffened outward till the even line of clenched, white teeth was visible, and he drew a heavy breath through these that lifted his deep chest up against the soiled denim shirt he wore.

"It popped up down in Kemmerrer," said Bondurant. "Nearest we could trace it was to a saloon keeper who couldn't remember the drunk. Double eagle, Gordie, minted in 1882, only six hundred and thirty of them issued. Maybe you know the story." His voice had taken on a thin sarcasm. "The whole issue was allotted to the paymaster at Fort Laramie. The government made the mistake of sending it by stage from Cheyenne to Laramie. They sent a troop of cavalry under Captain Bill Bondurant to take it off the train and escort it through, but that didn't make any difference to the Jackson Hole Bunch. They were a wild crowd, Gordie. They drew the troops off and jumped the stage at Eagle's Nest Gap. Even got the money off before Captain Bill got on their tail — "

"Victor!" cried Hammer, unable to stand it any longer. He had stood without feeling himself rise. He had been over his books and his strong, spatulated fingers were pressed so hard on the ledger their tips showed white. He stood that way a moment, seeking some control, and when he finally spoke again, his voice was husky and strained. "When will you stop riding me, Bondurant? How many times do I have to tell you I don't know where that money is hidden — "

"And you didn't kill Captain Bill Bondurant." It was as if the sheriff had finished it for Hammer. Victor Bondurant walked across the room toward the bed, sending one quick sharp glance to either side that took in everything, and turned about, his eyes resting on Hammer again to study him from beneath the sardonic arch of his brows. "You know when I'll quit riding you, Gordie. When I find out where you have that money, and when I find something to convict you of murdering my father. Maybe Kelly figures you've paid your debt to society, spending ten years in jail for complicity in that robbery. I don't. And maybe the jury couldn't find you guilty of murdering Captain Bill. I do." He held the coin up, starring at it with the cruel little lights coming and going in his brilliant eyes. "It's inconceivable to me Kelly can be so easy on you, Gordie, seeing as he was the lieutenant riding stirrup to stirrup with Captain Bill at the time. Even close enough to hear what that man said at the tail end of the Jackson Hole Bunch when he turned and shot Captain Bill." His lips barely moved around the words, now, and his voice was hardly audible. " 'Ain't that nearly hell,' he said, Gordie, 'ain't that nearly hell . . .' "

The light threw Hammer's shadow across the wall in a warped, leanshanked, heavy shouldered copy of his figure, stiffening as he did, till the top touched the shadows in the rafters. His breathing formed the only sound for a moment, hoarse, strangled. He wondered how much longer he could contain himself. Bondurant's narrow head raised in a small, jerky motion, and his tongue made a sly flick across his mobile lower lip.

"If you didn't drop this coin in Kemmerrer, Gordie," he said, "that would mean one of the others was back, wouldn't it? Eden, maybe, or Makwith. If they were, what would you do, Gordie? 'Hello, Makwith, glad to see you back, thanks for leaving me there when my horse got burned down, I served ten years for it, but that doesn't matter, glad to see you back, we'll go and get the money now and split it up — ' "

"Victor . . ."

It came from Hammer sounding as if someone had their hands on his throat, throttling him, and one of Bondurant's sardonic brows raised in mock surprise. "You're trembling, Hammer." His laugh was short, harsh. "How you've changed since you were a kid. You didn't have such wonderful control over yourself then. So wild, so unbroken." He allowed his eyes to wander momentarily over the high-ceiled room, the heavy pegged furniture, the grizzly pelt before the stone hearth. "But then I guess it would take that kind of a change to get what you've got here. Not many men could come back and build a spread like the Big Dipper with everybody just waiting for one wrong move. Little outside money must have come in handy on the rough spots, ah, Gordie — "

Hammer's move toward Bondurant contained a spasmodic violence, but was halted abruptly by the sound outside the house. It came sharply through the door, in a lull of the wind, the thud of hooves, the creak of saddle leather, then the portal shook to someone's fist. Hammer's lips twitched stiffly about the words.

"Come in."

Edmond Kelly had the stiff, mincing walk of the inveterate horseman whose girth had grown with the years, but who still retained the lean, handy legs of a man used to the saddle. His fleshy face was whipped the color of raw beef by the wind, and the furrows in his jaw turned pale white when he tucked his chin in with a characteristic gesture to give the whole room one swift, lashing glance from his glacial blue eyes. He tugged off one rawhide glove and beat his palm against the leg of his corduroys to remove some of the numbness.

"Fortunate you're here, Bondurant," he said. "Hammer's cut my fence again and half a hundred head of E Kay stuff has drifted into that chasm in the Snake."

"Again!" said Hammer, stung to thoughtless reaction. "You know that storm drifted it down last month, Kelly, you said so yourself — " and then the import of it struck through his anger and he stopped, staring at Kelly, the breath stirring his heavy chest more swiftly. Kelly's foreman had come in. Lister Birgunhus was an immense Swede with tremendous hands made more for the huge battle axe of his Viking ancestors than for the curved butt of the Frontier he packed. His blonde hair hung tousled down about the shoulders of his thick plaid mackinaw, and a long pale mustache dropped into a dirty yellow beard.

"We thought it was an accident last time maybe," he rumbled. "But we saw the wire this time, Hammer. It had been cut and pulled aside."

"I've tried to be decent with you, Hammer," said Kelly, his words coming out in clipped, angry gusts. "I wasn't any happier than the others to have a jailbird for a neighbor, but I tried to give you the benefit of the doubt. I've overlooked a lot of things, all along, but this snubs the dally." He turned partway to Bondurant, moving his hand in a vicious gesture. "I want you to do something about this, Sheriff."

Bondurant's smile curled up one corner of his lips. "Some legal action might be taken if you have proof it was Hammer."

"The fence is cut, my cattle are dead at the bottom of the cliff, what more proof could you ask?" snapped Kelly.

"That's only circumstantial," Bondurant murmured.

Kelly bridled like a spade-bitted horse. "Circumstantial, hell! You and half a dozen others know Hammer has wanted that south forty of mine for a winter shelter ever since he came here. How many offers for it has he made me in your presence? How many of his Big Dipper beef have we found drifted

178

over there through that fence?"

"That's still not strong enough for me to do anything, Kelly, you know that," said Bondurant, flipping the coin.

"Then I guess it's my hand." Kelly's voice had lowered to a tense, restrained scrape, and he took two mincing steps at Hammer, till their faces were but inches apart, and his protruding girth touched Hammer's belt. "What are you going to do about it, Hammer?"

Hammer's big hands had closed. "I didn't cut your fence, Kelly, but I'll go out and repair the cut like I did last time."

"That won't quite be enough, Hammer. Do you think I mean to go on playing this kind of game forever. You cut it and I'll let you patch it up and you cut it again. How could you possibly conceive that this would get you the pasture? Just because I lose a few head of cattle and some of yours drift through? That's such a childish way, Hammer, I can't quite believe that's your real motive; this offer to patch the fence is so childish, as if that would end the whole thing."

"What else can I do."

Kelly moved his face closer. "You can get out, Hammer." It was so unexpected that Hammer felt himself draw up, unable to answer it, and Kelly's next words struck his face on a hot breath. "I told you I'm not chewing this hay over a third time. If you can't think of anything else to do but patch that fence, I can. And I'm doing it. You're getting out, Hammer, one way or the other, and if you won't go of your own accord, I can always force you."

"Don't be a fool, Kelly — "

"Don't call me a fool," snarled the man, flushing, and his hand flashed up to crack twice against Hammer's face, backhand and forehand. The spots showed red in Hammer's pale face, gradually disappeared into the pallor again as Hammer stood there with his whole body trembling like an aspen in the heavy wind. He felt the terrible, driven desire for violent reaction but he could see them all waiting for that; Kelly bent toward him with that one hand still held up; Birgunhus grasping one glove with the other ready to bare his own gunhand the instant Hammer moved; Bondurant's brows arched in hopeful expectance.

For a moment Hammer could not see with that black wave of violence sweeping up in him, and all the years of careful deliberate, terrible restraint threatened to be smashed. Without actually seeing it, he was aware of his own Remington in its holster with the gunbelt wrapped around the scabbard, lying on the table, and his right hand twitched. Then gradually, before his awesome exertion of will, that blackness receded, and Kelly's waiting face swam into view before him again. Bondurant emitted a rueful little breath, looking at the coin as he flipped it.

"Maybe you're wrong, Kelly," he said. "Maybe you can't force him."

II

The snow had hidden the drift fence in most places, piling up in haunted white mystery, but cattle had trampled it down about the cut section, and two or three posts stuck up here in shorn loneliness. They kept their horses heavy on grain during the winter to stand the cold up here, and the shaggy steaming flank of Hammer's roan held a padded resilience as his leg slid across it, dismounting. He stood staring at the cut fence, trying to consider the possibilities in the light of a cold calculation that came hard to him, with that terrible, frustrated rancor still gnawing at him. Yet he felt a dim satisfaction at not having allowed Kelly to force his hand back there. It would have been the worst thing he could have done, with Bondurant just waiting for some overt act on his part to jump him, it was what he had fought against and guarded against so many years now.

He turned to his pack animal and unslung the bale of bobwire, unrolling it in the snow. He could find no clear motive for anyone deliberately cutting the fence. If Kelly really wanted him out, perhaps the man had opened it in hopes of engendering a clash which would result in Hammer doing something which would put him in Bondurant's hands. Yet that was not consistent with Kelly's attitude during these years. The man was too blunt for something like that. Hammer had torn off the old, rusty wire, and was pounding the third brad into the east post when the sense of another presence stole over him. He turned slowly, to see her.

It was Irish hair, blue-black as a Colt barrel, hanging in a long, curling, untrammelled bob about the milky line of her neck. There was something nebulously sensual about the small crease which formed in the plump flesh of her chin when she tucked it in that way, and her heavy-lashed eyes seemed to hold some deep, mysterious, slumbering capacity in their dark blue depths. It had always inspired a strange awe in Hammer to look into them, that way, and the words came from him in a hollow whisper.

"Carey Shane."

She wore a heavy canvas mackinaw with a sheepskin collar and a pair of man's blue jeans, and she dismounted like a man, with a lithe, casual swing of one leg, her eyes on him all the time. She bent forward to study his face narrowly, taking in the grooved lines which had formed about the thin restraint of his lips, the weathercreases at the corner of his eyes which imparted to them such a withdrawn, calculated look.

"You've changed, Gordie," she said, in that husky, whispered way he remembered so poignantly.

"Bondurant was right, then," he said. "Makwith is back."

A dim, harried look passed through her eyes at the name, and she dipped her head in a short nod. "The old spot in the park. He'd like to see you."

"Isn't it sort of dangerous there," he muttered. "They detailed a troop of U.S. cavalry to police the park in '86."

She shook her head. "We haven't even seen them. You know nobody ever comes in those hills north of Old Faithful."

He shrugged, and mounted. They reached one of his Big Dipper line shacks on Jackson Lake in a couple of hours and he turned the pack animal into the shed behind. Then they followed the shore around to the Snake again, and took the river north toward the park, cutting across to Belcher River and following it up through Silver Scarf Falls where a slate grey water ouzel hopped unconcernedly about on the slippery rocks and dove into a foaming pool. Carey had kept sending him those covert, sidelong glances all afternoon, and finally he could not retain it.

"So you stuck with him," he said, at last.

Something tightened the planes of her face. "He's my husband, Hammer," she said, and the simplicity of it would have struck him harder but for the sense of something else moving behind her words, something she could not quite hide from him. Up past the falls they turned west from the river through a saddle in pine-covered slopes and dropped into the geyser area. They passed small pools of boiling vari-colored mud and a small geyser spouted steam on their left. Soon the ground began to tremble perceptibly beneath their feet.

"That's Old Faithful," muttered Carey. "She goes off about every hour. The cabin's near enough to shake each time."

They left the trail and cut into meadows of snow into deep stands of blue spruce.

The cabin stood in a dell, hidden from all sides by this heavy timber. Legend held John Colter had built the shack when he first discovered Yellowstone and brought back stories which caused the park to be called Colter's Hell. The structure looked old enough for that, with its blackened logs. With a quick, unreadable glance at Hammer, Carey dismounted first, and turned to push open the door. He was close enough behind her to hear the crash of a chair inside, and then could see the man who had jumped up from where he had been sitting, hands gripping the worn oak stocking of a rifle so tightly the bones protruded whitely against the gnarled flesh.

"It's just Carey, Makwith," said the woman in a pleading way.

Makwith Shane lowered the gun reluctantly. He was gaunt to the point of emaciation, and his straggly mane of black hair, shot with grey, only accentuated the ravening, wolfish appearance of his face. There was no flesh to fill the starved hollows beneath his prominent, Indian cheekbones, and his eyes gleamed bloodshot and feverish from their deep, skeletal sockets. It was such a violent change from the laughing, reckless, vivid youth he had known that Hammer could not quite hide his shock, and Makwith saw it.

"All right, all right, what did you expect?" said Makwith viciously. "A stinking government man on my tail all the way up from the Red River and nothing but the lousiest crowbait in Texas for horseflesh and a damn whining woman nagging my tail off twenty-four hours a day — " he broke off, a strange, cunning light flashing through his eyes, and his narrow, gaunt head dipped in a sudden, obsequious way — "hell, Gordie, I shouldn't pop off like an old squaw on an occasion such as this, should I, I'm sorry, hell, I'm sorry, after thirteen years and I jumped down your throat the first minute, it was just you surprised me, that's all, here, sit down — " he lifted the chair back on its feet, shoving it toward the table, and turned toward Carey — "make us some coffee, will you, honey?"

Hammer cast a glance at Carey, still not quite seeing how it was, and then took the chair. Makwith leaned the rifle against the stone fireplace and took a three-legged stool across the plank table, bending forward to put his elbows on the rough pine boards and study Hammer. His mouth twisted in a warped grin, revealing yellow, decaying teeth.

"I understand you're a big rancher here-abouts, now, Gordie. I have to hand it to you. It must have been an uphill grade."

186

"It was," said Hammer, glancing at the greasy leather chivarras on the man's skinny legs. "Texas?"

"Yeah." Makwith's laugh was harsh. "Mex leggins. They all wear 'em down there." He jerked his head at a flat-topped Mormon setting at the end of the table. "Utah, too. Oh, we've been traveling, Gordie." He bent forward sharply, eyes strange and bright on Hammer's face, speaking swiftly. "That's why we couldn't get to you, Gordie, I would have sprung you, believe me, I would have moved heaven and earth to get you out, but God they wouldn't let me be, I had to keep moving all the time, Carey and me been on the bob ever since. Thirteen years, Hammer, running all the time, why in hell did you have to pick a soldier to burn down — " he stopped abruptly, seeing the mistake of that in Hammer's face, and held out a bony, grasping hand placatingly — "ah, I didn't mean that, Gordie, I know it wasn't your fault, it was dark and you were jumpy."

Hammer's lips worked faintly against his teeth, and he held himself from answering with an effort, back stiff against the chair. Carey came over with the coffee pot and some tin cups, staring from one to the other in a wide, dark way.

"All right," said Makwith, waving his hand

at her. "Gordie and I want to talk. Get out."

Carey's lips pouted. "But Makwith — "

"You heard me," snarled Makwith, half-rising. "Get out!"

"It's cold outside," said Hammer. "I think your wife has a right to hear whatever you and I have to talk about, Makwith."

For another moment Makwith remained out of his chair, face twisted in that wolfish snarl. Then servility returned as his glance swung to Hammer.

"Sure, Hammer, sure, what could I be thinking, you see how jumpy I am, hell." He poured a cup of coffee. For a moment the spout touched the rim of the cup, making a small, staccato rattle. Makwith jerked it up with a guilty look. He shoved the cup to Hammer, poured himself one. He took a quick, furtive gulp, watching Hammer over the rim of the cup. There was a palpable effort to the casual sound of his words. "I guess it would have been nigh onto impossible to make a go of it without that money to tide you over the rough spots, hey, Gordie?"

"What money?" said Hammer.

Makwith's laugh held that same furtive effort. "You never used to be a joker, Gordie."

"Neither did you," said Hammer.

Makwith sobered abruptly. "I'm talking about the fifty thousand golden eagles, you know that, now quit hiding things in your poke, I'm serious. I had my ear to the ground. It came over the grapevine, the things you had to buck up here, Bondurant, and the way Edmond Kelly and his bunch tried to squeeze you out at first. I didn't call on you then because I knew you'd need it, but now you're sitting on top of the horse, and I'm the one who needs it, Gordie."

"Needs what?"

"The money, my share," said Makwith impatiently. "There was four of us, wasn't there? Eden is dead now so we split his fourth. Has Dee Sheridan hit you for his yet? The last time I heard he was up in the Tetons somewhere."

Hammer bent toward the man, studying the gaunt, ravaged face. "Are you trying to tell me, Makwith, that you think I have the money."

"Think?" Genuine surprise lit the man's bloodshot eyes momentarily. Then a sly, growing malignance turned them a strange yellow tint. He leaned forward on his elbows. "Gordie, don't act like this, even if you're joking, I'm in no mood for it, can't you see how bad I need that money. You was the one got those bags off the stage, we all know that, I was up on the rimrock holding them with my rifle. I saw you do it."

"And the bags were on the back of my horse when Bill Bondurant shot it from under me," said Hammer.

"Sure, sure, and they wasn't there when we came back next day and found the animal," said Makwith. "I never did understand how you found time to cache them bags."

"I didn't have time," said Hammer. "The horse slid off in a gully. I hadn't even got to my feet by the time the troops came up."

"But the money was gone, Gordie, the troops didn't find it, we know that — "

"Someone else must have doubled back for it," said Hammer. "They've been dropping those eagles here and there ever since. One showed up in a bar in Kemmerrer a little while ago. Did you come through that way, Makwith?"

The man took a quick, sharp little breath, straightening up. "You mean you think I got — " he cut off, slamming both palms flat on the table so hard it trembled and driving himself to his feet that way, his voice rising to a shrill stridor — "Listen, Gordie, I told you not to talk this way, I know you got that money and I want my share. The others'll want their share, too."

"I haven't got it."

"You have," shouted the other, rage turning his face livid.

"Makwith, please," said Carey, catching at his shoulder.

"Let me go, you damned trollop," screamed the man, jerking his arm free and letting it fly back to smash her across the face. Carey stumbled backward with a sick cry and crumbled against the stone fireplace.

"Damn you, Makwith," roared Hammer, kicking his chair back so it would not trip him as he rose, but his knees were still bent when Makwith whirled back and grabbed the front of his open mackinaw, pulling him down across the table with a violent jerk.

"I guess that would make you mad, wouldn't it?" shouted Makwith. "You was always sweet on her, wasn't you, Gordie. Well she's mine, by God, and I can do anything I want with her — "

With his chest against the planks, Hammer twisted over in an effort to free himself, and the weight of his body upset the table. Makwith released Hammer, allowing him to fall on over with the table, and then jumped at him as he sprawled across it between the legs. Makwith struck him, screaming like a

191

crazed animal, that greasy hair hanging in matted tendrils down in front of his eyes, lips pulled back from those rotting teeth, eyes filled with frenzied rage.

For a moment Hammer was filled with the same blinding rage, engendered doubtlessly by seeing Makwith strike Carey that way, the same rampant emotion he had known as a kid, and he was as abandoned as Makwith, shouting crazily at the man as they rolled across the upset table like two wild animals, biting and kicking and slugging. They came up against a leg and it snapped off beneath their weight, allowing them to roll off on the floor. Hammer caught Makwith in the mouth with a heavy blow that knocked the man partly away from him, allowing Hammer to get on his knees. Then, crouched there, seeing the terrible animal rage which gripped Makwith, realizing how it blinded a man, Hammer brought all the deliberate, careful control to bear which he had developed during these last years, stifling his own red anger in its cold fist.

Makwith threw himself on Hammer again. This time Hammer shifted his head aside in a swift, calculated way, avoiding one of the man's clawed hands, and his own hand shot up to grasp the other. With this leverage, he twisted Makwith to one side and used the man's own momentum to pull him on in, jabbing for Makwith's groin with his free fist at the same time.

The man emitted a sick, spasmodic groan, and lost all volition. Before he could recover, Hammer jabbed him there again. Then he released the incapacitated man and allowed him to roll over on his face on the floor. Hammer stood there, chest heaving, looking down at Makwith for a moment until he became aware of Carey's eyes on him. She was still slumped against the fireplace, holding herself up by a clawed grip on the rough stones, and there was a strange, twisted wonder in her face. He stared at her a moment, then he wheeled toward the door.

"Hammer — " Makwith's voice stopped him, and he turned his head over one shoulder to see the man, still sprawled there on his stomach with his arms hugged across his groin, one knee lifted to twist him partway over so he could look up at Hammer, and his voice shook with a hoarse, bitter, agonized hatred — "There are other ways to get that money. I could have used them first, I didn't have to give you this chance, but now there are other ways, and by God before we're through, you'll wish to hell you never saw a double eagle in your life!"

III

Snow came on the wind, and to Hammer, wading through it from the barn to his house, there was something vaguely sinister about its nebulous, powdery touch, sifting insistently against his face and sticking his eye-lids shut. He shook his head in a small, growing irritation, stumbling on the stone steps of his front porch, pawing for the doorhandle. A thin sliver of yellow, as tall as himself, appeared before him, quickly growing into a larger rectangle. Partly blinded by the snow, he could not comprehend it for an instant. Then he realized he had opened the door to a lighted room.

"Crazyjack?" he called, thinking perhaps that one of his crew had come in from the line shack for something. But the ramrod did not answer, and he pawed his eyes free at last to see the room was empty. Then its round, yellow gleam caught his eye, lying on the top of the table beneath the sputtering camphene lamp. It should not have shocked him so. Yet it did, somehow, filling him with the sense of small, chill fingers spidering his spine. With a muttered oath he stepped to the table, picking the coin up. Then, insidiously, the face seemed to rise before him, the vivid black eyes filled with that cunning, waiting intelligence, the odd, haunting scars grooving that sharp, vicious jaw, the mocking, fluid, curling smile.

"Damn you, Victor," he said, in a guttural voice.

"Victor Bondurant?" asked the throaty voice from the doorway.

Hammer had not realized how tense he was till he whirled that way. Carey Shane stood there, blinking snow-fringed lids, taking off her mittens. Hammer felt the little muscles twitch in his cheeks, and he took a heavy breath, striving for relaxation.

"Is he still riding you, Hammer?" she said, compassionately, coming on into the room.

He gripped the coin, a speculation sending its cold shaft through his mind suddenly, and his eyes narrowed, "I don't know."

"That's the reason you've done it," she said.

"Done what?"

"This change," she said. "I saw it at first, and didn't recognize it. I saw it again tonight, with Makwith. For a moment there, when he first jumped you, it was what you used to be, Gordie, so wild and abandoned, without any control. Then, suddenly, that control. I guess you've had to, haven't you, with Bondurant riding you, all of them riding

195

you, just waiting for one wrong move — "

His hand kept opening and closing on the coin. "I guess so."

She came up to him suddenly, one hand on his chest. "Why, Hammer, why do they do it, why can't they let you alone, haven't you proven your sincerity by now, can't they see what it was by now? You were only a wild orphan kid running in the wrong kind of company, they've made mistakes too, won't they ever realize how many times over you've payed for yours?"

"Bondurant still thinks I killed his father," said Hammer.

"How can he be such a fool?" she said hotly. "It was so dark and confused and so many shooting there."

"It's that expression the man used just before he shot Captain Bill Bondurant," Hammer muttered. "You don't hear it much up here. More to the south, Kansas, or Oklahoma. Some say Sam Bass used it. There were two or three troopers right behind Captain Bill. Edmond Kelly was one. They all heard the man call it. 'Ain't that nearly hell,' he said, and then shot Captain Bill."

Her lip formed that rich petulance, and light rippled blue-black across the angry toss of her hair. "That doesn't cinch any saddle. Just because you knew Sam Bass down on the Red River. They haven't any right, Hammer — "

"It doesn't matter," he muttered. Then he raised his eyes to hers. "I'm not the only one who's had a rough time. How did you get out?"

She shrugged uncomfortably. "You know how Makwith drinks. It put him to sleep."

He slipped the coin in his pocket to catch her shoulders. "Why do you do it, Carey? Surely, you can see, by — "

"He's my husband!" she blazed, her chin snapping up. Then, with her eyes meeting his, he saw the tears forming in them, and suddenly she was in his arms, sobbing against his chest. "Oh, I don't know, Hammer, maybe I don't love him anymore. You can see how he's changed, he's not right in the head anymore. He gets those rages, you saw him, he drinks so much now, he's so sick, Hammer, in the mind, in the body. He does need me, doesn't he, tell me so, Hammer, he'd be dead without me. I just had to make my choice, that's all. Maybe I don't love him like I used to, how could a woman, but I can't leave him now — "

He tightened his arms around her, seeing for the first time all the hell she must have endured these last years, knowing the same rended emotions he had felt so long ago when he had first realized how he felt about her, and how he could never have her as long as Makwith was alive.

At first he thought the camphene lamp had flared up, to flicker the shadows across the wall that way. Then he realized the source of light was coming through the opened door. The shrill whinney of a horse, muffled by the snow, reached him. Carey pulled away, tear-stained face turning up to his, and then whirled in his arms to stare out the door.

"Your barn, Hammer," she gasped. "It's on fire!"

The drifted snow clutched at his feet with every step he took and threw a blinding white blanket before his eyes and fell in small clouds from his shoulders with every violent movement of his body. His other horses had started screaming now, and one began kicking at the walls as Hammer reached the door, catching the edge and throwing his weight outward against it to heave the portal open. With a bursting roar, flames licked redly into his face, and he staggered back shouting in pain.

"Hammer, Hammer — "

"The fire's all along the front," he cried to Carey, "my back door's locked. The loft is the only way left. Find me that ladder. I can't see. It might be out by the pig-pen."

Pawing at his singed brows and burned face, he went after the sound of her pounding feet in the direction of the building, only to smash headlong into a splintery wall. It dazed him, and he had to hold the planks to keep from falling.

"I've got it, Hammer," cried Carey, and he could see dimly from one tortured eye now, as the woman appeared from the powdery snow, dragging the heavy ladder. He helped her stand it against the building, and then climbed up, tearing open the loft door and bellying over into the hay. The flames had eaten through cracks in the loft floor, and he gagged on the odor of smoldering hay. The ladder on the inside was already burning and he had to hang and drop. He went to his roan first, fighting its head down in the stall to tie his bandanna about its eyes, battered against the sides by its violent thrashing. Finally he got it backed out of the narrow confines and headed toward the rear door.

He kicked the bar from its sockets and put his shoulder into the door, swinging it open. Carey was there to catch the roan as he came through, and he tore the bandanna off its head and wheeled back in after the next animal. It was a black stud he had rented from Kelly to service two brood mares, and it had already smashed the bottom of its closed box stall out with its wild thrashing.

"Ho, boy, ho, big boy," he called to the beast, trying to keep his voice soothing, but the moment he unlatched the gate and swung it open, the animal turned on him, screaming and rearing up. He dodged in, fighting to avoid its vicious front hooves and get the blind on, but the stud was in a blind frenzy. It broke forward before he could pull its head down, smashing out the open gate and running headlong toward the flames.

Hammer had just stumbled free of the stall when the horse, feeling the heat of the fire, wheeled back this way with a crazed whinney and charged down the aisle.

"Hammer, watch out," he heard Carey scream, and then his whole consciousness was thrown into the shuddering impact of the animal against him, and he had a dim feel of spinning off its shoulder and crashing into the side of the shattered stall and falling. It was all blackness with no relative objects to give him any sense of motion, yet it was there, regardless, that nauseated sense of spinning, round and round and round. He heard hoarse groaning, and his feet seemed to be getting hot. Then his shoulders twitched, and he realized someone was tugging at them. The groaning turned into muffled, animal sounds as he tried to help them, his face buried in the dirt and hay.

"Gordie, Gordie, try to get up," sobbed Carey, "You're too heavy to carry and it'll be on us in a minute, please, Gordie, please . . ."

Things were coming back more sharply now, and he heard the crackling roar of the fire behind him, and understood that heat on his feet. He managed to get his hands and knees, then, with her help, to rise. Carey pulled one of his arms around her shoulder, and together, the two staggered out. Carey must have opened the pig-pen to let the pigs out, for they made dim running grunting shapes all over the compound, and the roan was trotting in a frightened, nervous circle farther out. Free of the blazing barn, Hammer stopped and turned to look.

What framework of the front end was left, formed a bizarre, charred pattern that appeared momentarily in the crimson holocaust, and the rest of the building would be gone in a few moments.

The wild scream of those brood mares and his pack horse came to Hammer through the crash of falling timber and roar of flames, and his throat knotted up with a small, inarticulate sound of pain as he made a vague move back toward the barn.

"Gordie," said Carey, catching him, "you can't, it's hopeless, now, you'd only burn with them!"

He realized she was right, and stopped, big figure sagging wearily. Then another realization crept through, insidiously, and he turned his burned face toward her, twisted now with a strange pain.

"What's the matter, lose your nerve?" he said.

She stared blankly at him. "What?"

"Why didn't you just leave me in there?"

"Gordon, what are you saying?"

"Other ways?" His voice held a note of hysteria now, and he backed away from her in revulsion. "Sure there are other ways. Plenty of other ways. He'd started using them even before I saw him there in the park, hadn't he? I should have known it the moment Bondurant came with that coin. I should have known Makwith was back and starting in even then. It was him who cut that fence."

"Fence?" She took a step toward him, trying to read his face. "What are you talking about, Hammer, what fence?"

"Makwith," he shouted at her in a sudden fit of rage. "He wants me on my knees where I'll have to give in to him. He was the one bargaining up there in the shack, and he wants to turn the kack around. You can't deny it. He cut that fence to bring Kelly down on me. And he sent you down here to hold me in the house while he burned the barn. You can't deny that."

"No, Hammer, no," she sobbed, jumping forward to catch his arm, "don't be a fool, I told you, he's back in the shack asleep, how could you believe I'd do a thing like that — "

"I *do* believe it," he told her, tearing loose. "He needs you? You're damn right he needs you. To do all the dirty work he can't do. You make a good pair. You always did. I spent ten years in jail for the two of you. Makwith wasn't the whole reason I ran with the Bunch. Now get out, Carey. Don't touch me again, I'd be afraid of what I'd do." His big work-roughened hands were opening and closing spasmodically, "Get out, and by God you'd better hope we never meet again!"

IV

Crazyjack stumped heavily around the living room, doing unnecessary little things like straightening a tattered rug that didn't need it and moving the box of Remington flat noses from one end of the mantle to the other. He was an old ranny as grizzled as a bighorn's antler with a patch over his right eye and a bald pate that shone like a slickhorn. The Big Dipper could not support a large crew yet, and though Crazyjack was no more ramrod than the other two men, the combination of age and experience had always caused Hammer and the others to consider him in that light.

"Colter's Hell, Hammer," he growled, knuckling the grey stubble on his furrowed jaw peevishly. "I don't see why you have to pick this time of year to go breaking brush up north."

"Do you think I've got that money?" said Hammer, bent over his bedroll.

"Don't be a jackass," snorted the old man.

"They think I have, Crazyjack, and they won't stop riding me till I prove I haven't, Bondurant or Makwith or Kelly or any of them, and the only way I can prove that is to find out who has got it," said Hammer. "Somebody must know where it is. Those double eagles haven't been popping up by themselves all through these years. With Makwith ruled out, that only leaves Dee Sheridan. Makwith said Dee had last been heard of up in the Tetons. I know a few of his old pastures."

"Why not let me trail along then," said

Crazyjack. "With the cards stacking up the way they are, it ain't too safe for you to be running around alone. I keep thinking of that Bondurant."

Hammer's face lifted, and he stared for a blank moment at the fireplace. Then he tucked his chin down again, jerking the tarp around his bedroll. "I need you here. I've fixed it with Leese to give you power of attorney. You can draw on my account in Jackson to pay next month's grain bill if I'm not back by then, and the mortgage. Take that stud back to Kelly and don't let the shoats lose any weight."

He drew the last lashing tight around the tarped roll and rose and stepped to the table, lifting his Remington off and unwinding the belt from around the slick leather scabbard. He opened the box of flat-noses on the mantle and began stuffing the forty-fours into the cartridge loops on his belt. Crazyjack's voice was somber.

"It's funny, Hammer, but this is the first time I'll have seen you wear that."

Hammer paused, his eyes taking on that blank lack of focus. "I didn't want to pack it for fear of what might happen, Crazyjack. I hoped never to use it again."

The old man made a vague, snorting sound and stamped over to scoop the tarp off the floor. Together they went outside. Crazyjack slung the bedroll on the roan behind the saddle and lashed it tight for Hammer. Then the two men turned to each other, clasping hands. Without speaking again, Hammer turned back to slip the ground-hitched reins over the animal's neck and climb aboard . . .

He reached Jackson that evening, halting his tired roan in the slushy snow before the Hoback Saloon. He had talked with ranchers and fence riders all the way in without hearing anything he could use, and was beginning to feel a discouragement. He shoved through the batwings of the Hoback and moved through the sticky sawdust spread on the floor toward the bar, almost reaching it before he recognized the ponderous blond man bellied up to the mahogany. Lister Birgunhus must have seen the expression on the barman's face, for he turned with a glass of beer in his hand. His eyes caught on the toe of the holster protruding from beneath Hammer's mackinaw. He set the glass down.

"Please, Hammer," said the bartender. "I just got new lamps put up."

"Forget it," said Hammer, moving up to the bar. "I understand you've got in some new Grandad."

"Yeah," said the barman vaguely, moving

to get the whiskey without taking his eyes off them.

"What are you doing so far north?" Hammer asked the Swede.

Lister wiped foam carefully from his mustache, eyeing Hammer warily. "Repping for Kelly."

"I thought the limit of his drift was way south of here," said Hammer.

"A few E Kays were found in the Bar D stuff up in the Tetons," said Birgunhus. "I had to come after them. Bar D boys are busy cutting sign for some high-rider's been working their stuff over."

Hammer took the glass from the bartender and twirled it slowly to hide his mounting interest. "Just one?"

"They don't figure any more," said the Swede. "Only a few head gone at a time. Got his pasture narrowed down to Teton Pass. Even spotted him there last week. They say he forks the biggest lineback ever foaled — "

"Hammer," called the barman, "don't you want the Grandad?"

But Hammer was already to the door, pushing through, because nobody else would ride a buckskin that size, or choose Teton Pass in the wintertime. He swung aboard his roan and turned it down the street. A man came from the livery stable across the way and watched him ride out . . .

The pass lay west of Jackson, and Hammer began climbing a few miles out of the town, leaving the barren crowds of aspen quaking along the banks of the Snake and rising into the snow-laden spruce and pine. A luteous moon rose from behind the phalanxes of barren rock-ribbed peaks and threw the drifts into blinding relief. It was close to midnight that Hammer pulled over a ridge above timberline, passing through a short talus saddle in the granite crest. There was a slight turn in the saddle which put his profile toward the direction he had come. He could not actually see the slope he had climbed. It was only a dim sense of movement in the bluish shadow of a snowbank.

He halted his horse below the saddle and dismounted, crunching through a frozen surface back to where he could overlook the slope without being seen from below. He waited a long time before the movement came again, much farther up this time. It was farther to the north than it had seemed the last time. By that line of direction, Hammer estimated it would strike the top a few hundred yards down where another saddle cut through the sharp ridge. For a moment, he had the impulse to go on, and had even turned back for his horse. Then he wheeled back, tugging at his right glove. He could afford to spend the time it would take to make sure.

He traversed the ridge on his side, keeping below the top, and had his glove off and stuffed in his pocket by the time he reached the saddle. He glanced wryly at the hand, flexing the thick, spatulated, rope-burned fingers stiffly. They had once been so slim and supple. He drew a breath between his teeth, wondering.

Then it came, the small scuffling sound from the saddle above him, and he wheeled up that way, moving toward the cover of a granite uplift ribbed with frozen snow. He had not quite reached it when the man appeared in the saddle.

They saw one another about the same time, and had both done the same thing, and then stopped, and it came from Hammer in a hollow, strained way. "Bondurant!"

The sheriff's mocking eyes dropped to Hammer's hand, and a smile curled the corner of his lips. "I wondered who would have been left in the kack this roundup."

Hammer glanced involuntarily at his hand, still gripping the butt of his gun. He lifted it away, flexing calloused fingers, then raising his eyes self-consciously.

"Maybe sometime we'll find out," grinned Bondurant. He had been leading his big half-Morgan mare and he pulled her in to him. "Lucky you kept your temper smothered with Kelly, back at your house, Hammer. You have an amazing control over yourself. He was just waiting for one wrong move from you, with me there."

"You didn't seem so eager," said Hammer bitterly.

"I wasn't," said Bondurant. "I was glad you controlled yourself, Hammer, though I don't see how you did it. I don't want to haul you in on some minor charge of Kelly's. When I get you it's going to be for good."

He was still smiling when he said it, that lazy, cynical smile with no rancor apparent in his face or voice. It was worse than if he had evinced his bitter hatred. It lent the words an infinite deadliness. The old frustrated anger was clawing at Hammer, and he did not speak until he could retain an even tone to his voice.

"Why did you follow me this time?" he said.

"I thought perhaps you were on the way to get another sack of double eagles," said Bondurant. "With your barn burned out you'll need some extra cash to tide you over, won't you?"

"Damn you, Bondurant — "

The shot cut Hammer off, loud and clear on the thin mountain air. Frozen snow kicked up with a hard, crystalline sound to the right of him. The roan screamed in startled panic and wheeled to run, striking a snowfield on the slope behind and sliding down up to its belly. Hammer had his Remington clear out this time, and threw himself toward the saddle through which Bondurant had come. The sheriff had already ducked back behind the rocks there. They crouched together, straining to see the southern ridges above them.

"Been talk of an owlhooter cutting into Bar D stuff up this way," said Bondurant. "One of us could keep him busy here with my saddle gun while the other got out the other end of this cut and tried to work in behind him."

"You know your rifle better than I do," said Hammer, and had already begun to worm deeper into the saddle until he could move in a hidden crouch to the east. Bondurant had opened fire by the time Hammer reached the other end of the saddle. He found a gully that led him down to timber between high snowdrifts, and once in the Douglas fir, he moved swiftly across the slope, through furrowed trunks standing so thickly that his elbows were constantly scraping against the old man's beard growing in parasitic malignance on the trees.

His breath steamed whitely before his face. The shots had ceased, and it was so quiet the soft, incessant crunch of his feet began to irritate him. In the open spaces between timber, he sometimes had to crawl on his belly through the snow to keep under cover. He reached some pines with his pants and mackinaw soggy and frosted down the front, and realized he had passed beneath the saddle through which he had crossed the ridge.

He began working up toward the higher ridges on the south side of the saddle. The firing started up again, first from Bondurant, to the north, and then above Hammer, so close it startled him. His palm was sticky with sweat from gripping the gun so long, and he wiped it against the mackinaw under his armpit. He reached timberline and waited for the next shot. It came from a group of frozen rocks near the crest. If it were Dee, he would be too wary to stay in one place long, and Hammer stayed there. Bondurant's answering shot came. Then, after an interval, the sheriff must have showed himself purposely to draw this man's fire, for it came even nearer this time, almost down at the edge of the rocks on this side. Hammer shifted south in a lateral line, and when he was behind the man, took a gully up out of timberline that shielded him till he could reach the scattered rocks on the crest. He saw the base of the first jagged granite uplift ahead and rounded a curve in the gully and looked up to see the man squatting in a niche with a Ward-Burton in his hands.

"I thought so," the man said, and the weapon made a deafening crash.

A terrific blow struck Hammer's left arm, spinning him partway around and carrying him back against the bank of the gully. Pinned there for that instant by the impetus of it, he saw the man snap open the gun bolt.

"No, Dee, no," he screamed. "It's Hammer, can't you see," and then saw the man snap the bolt shut, and after that, it was only his instinct for self-preservation, jerking his Remington up and squeezing the trigger. Dee Sheridan stiffened, his hands twitching spasmodically, and when the Burton went off, it was pointing skyward. He hung there a moment, coughing in a hollow way. He dropped the rifle, a blank look passing through his eyes, clawing at the rock to keep himself erect.

"Well ain't that nearly hell," he said, then, and fell face forward on the rock, and slid down the rough surface to Hammer's feet. Hammer dropped to his knees, turning the man over. Sheridan's shirt-front was torn from sliding across the rock, and soaked with blood already from the hole Hammer's .44 had made in his chest. Then the sharp scrape above raised Hammer's head. Bondurant stood atop the rock, staring at Dee Sheridan.

"Well, ain't that nearly hell," Bondurant said, in a soft, unbelieving voice, and shook his narrow, dark head, "Well, ain't that nearly hell."

"How did you get in so quick?" Hammer said in a strained voice.

"I was moving in on him," muttered Bondurant. He squatted and slid down the rock on his heels, never taking his eyes off the man. "Who is it, Hammer?"

"Dee Sheridan," Hammer told him. "I guess he didn't recognize me."

Bondurant squatted there on his heels, gazing at Sheridan in that blank way. "I hate to believe it. After all these years, I hate to believe it."

Hammer shrugged. "Dee was just as close to Captain Bill as I was, and he was working that Ward-Burton as fast as he could snap the bolt."

Sheridan stirred feebly, opening his glazing eyes to stare up at them. "Captain Bill Bondurant," he said, and giggled in a weak hysteria. "Sure." He started to cough, and blood came in little spurts from his mouth, dribbling over his chin. "Didn't recognize you, Hammer, you've changed so, sorry, sorry — " his head began to weave from side to side — "thought you was some more of them Bar D hands. I was getting tired dodging them. Guess I was a fool to start the smoke-thrower that way but I was getting tired dodging them — "

"Dee," Hammer said huskily, tugging at his shirt. "Somebody's been passing that money. Was it you? They picked up a double-edge in Kammerrer last month. Did you go through there?"

"Money?" Lucidity entered Sheridan's eyes momentarily. He tried to laugh again, failed. "Don't be loco. Think that witch would give me any of it?"

"Witch? You mean Makwith and Carey have it? It was Makwith who doubled back and got it off my horse — "

"Makwith, hell," snorted Sheridan. "He don't know where it is any more than you or I."

"Then who? What do you mean?"

"You know what I mean," he said feebly, and seemed to rouse himself for a final effort, raising up with a strangled, gurgling sound. "There's only one person in the world knows where that money is. Carey Shane!"

215

V

They had buried Dee Sheridan beneath the
snow back in the Pass, and had come across
his horse while getting their own animals,
a buckskin at least seventeen hands high with
a black line down its back, the only kind
of animal Dee would ever ride. Bondurant
was leading it now, behind Hammer, and
with the strange growing feel of the man's
eyes on him, Hammer could not help turning
in his saddle.

"Ain't that nearly hell," said Bondurant.
There was bitter disappointment to it.

"You'd rather I had killed your father,"
said Hammer.

"I would," said Bondurant. "It would make
this easier."

"What?" said Hammer, and was turning
once more to look at the man when he felt
the rump of his roan slide to the left.

"Look out, Bondurant, you're shoving me
off," he shouted, reining the horse hard to
the left. The animal's hooves made a swift
scrambling sound against the frozen rock
face and for a moment Hammer thought it
was all right. Then that sense of something
thrusting at the roan's rump again, and the
head of Bondurant's Morgan knocked into

Hammer's elbow. The roan whinneyed in shrill fear, and its feet went from beneath it. Twisted in the saddle for that last instant, Hammer saw the satisfaction lighting Bondurant's vivid black eyes, and triumph on his curling, mocking lips. Then Hammer was going down amid the wild screaming of the roan and the crash of dislodged rocks and his own helpless shouts. He threw himself inward off the animal, but Bondurant's horse was in his way, and he struck its shoulder, clawing vainly at its steaming, slick hide.

His own mount was out from under him now, its heavy, hairy form in view for a last time, flailing through the steep slope of frozen snowbanks and disappearing abruptly over the edge into the sheer drop, its screams cut off sharp for a moment, then coming back in piercing echo from the other wall of the canyon. Hammer's own hoarse shouts drowned that, in his ears, as he felt his hands slip down the Morgan's leg and claw at the frozen snow surfaces. His torn nails crunched through the crust only to sink in slush beneath. He felt himself sliding down the steep slope faster and faster.

He caught at icy rocks and bellowed hoarsely with the agony of his weight coming against his wounded arm, and could not retain his grip. He swung his good arm out in a wild effort. His right hand crossed more jagged rocks, and he clawed at them wildly, and his fingers slipped on over their adamant surface, flesh ripped and torn, blood forming a crimson trail through the snow as he slid on down.

Then he felt the earth go out from beneath him, and heard his own terrified scream ring across the canyon and strike the opposite wall and echo back. That first release sent a clutching nausea through his gut, and then, for an instant, there was no sensation. Pain caught his leg as his foot struck something. Rocks ripped at the front of his mackinaw again, and his hands clawed spasmodically across them, once more in vain.

Something forced his feet together and his descent ceased abruptly. With his feet pinched in and no leverage there he would have fallen backward. His hands pawed blindly, catching at a granite outthrust. The weight of his body bore on his shoulder, and his twisted position tore at the muscles.

Somehow he managed to hang on, seeing that he had slipped into a shaft formed almost vertically in the canyon wall by faulting. His hands were clutching corerocks exposed in some earlier glaciation, and his feet were jammed together where the fault narrowed. Below him yawned hundreds of feet of empty space; above the sheer frosted rock wall.

He heard the soft neigh of a horse, then the clump of its hooves, and he knew he could not be far below the lip. He waited for what seemed an endless period, to allow Bondurant time to leave, the blood congealing on his ripped hands in the cold, his left arm stiffening up, a chilled ache adding its agony to the throbbing pain of the untended bullet wound.

Finally he could stand it no longer, and began to seek a new handhold higher up in the fissure. He found more jutting quartzite, and pulled himself up, painfully, a few feet at a time, till he reached the end of the fissure, where the vertical face became that slanting snow-covered slope. There he had to belly over and squirm carefully through the slush which he had caused sliding down, digging sometimes five minutes before he could find another rock for a higher handhold. Finally he reached the trail and lay there on his stomach, a terrible lethargy gripping him.

It was a bitter fight for him to force his body onto his feet. Then he turned eastward and began stumbling down the trail. He knew there was a Bar D lineshack at the east end of Teton Pass. If he could make that . . .

* * *

He had no measure of time. He did not know how long he had been staggering down the steepening trail. He lost count of the times he fell on his face. When he heard the horse snort from ahead, he did not recognize the sound, and kept right on going. Then he was aware of its dim, shying movement before him, and he opened feverish, red-rimmed eyes to see the buckskin trotting away.

"Bucky," he sobbed huskily, because Dee's horse would always have that name, "Bucky, come here boy, come here you moon-eyed bunch-quitter, oh damn you, Bucky — "

He finally reached the beast and after three tries managed to climb heavily aboard. Then he turned the animal toward the Hole and free-bitted it, knowing a dim gratitude that it had gotten free of Bondurant. It took a long time for the mutation of that thought in his reeling head, but slowly it began to change from gratitude to wonder. What if Bondurant had deliberately released the horse, to make better time? It sent a dull shock through Hammer, and he straightened up, tightened the reins and gave the buckskin his heels.

It had begun to snow again when he finally reached the valley; he had taken his left arm from the sleeve of his coat and hugged it to him beneath the mackinaw for warmth, and now it was so stiff he could not move it. It was the fear, driving him now, that caused him to skirt the yellow pinpoints of light from Jackson and head on through the growing storm to the north. He followed the frozen bank of the Snake through Togwotee Pass to Jackson Lake. With the waters gleaming silver beneath a frigid winter moon, he skirted the lake until it ended in the Snake again. Again there was no measure of time. It was all that endless plodding through snow-robed spruce marked at shoulder height with old scars from the previous spring where the bucks rubbed velvet off their antlers.

He slept in the saddle at intervals, and lost the river several times that way. With the rising sun, he grew giddy, and was biting his lips and shouting at himself in an effort to retain lucidity. The arm felt swollen and throbbed unmercifully, and the infection filled him with the sense of coming delirium. This was why Dee had always ridden a buckskin; a man following his kind of trails needed a horse with bottom, and a lineback like this one never wore out.

He struck West Thumb's turquoise waters late in the afternoon and turned westward.

He passed Black Warrior Springs, bubbling from beneath its snow-crusted shelf, melted snow constantly dripping off into the boiling water. He passed a series of small geysers, dimly aware of their hissing eruptions, and then struck Belcher and crossed into the ridges northwest of that.

Bondurant's Morgan stood hipshot in the snow outside the shack, and it was the first thing Hammer's snow-blinded eyes discerned as he topped the last ridge and dropped down the slope. Then he saw that the door was open. He half-fell from the buckskin and lurched inside. It was a moment before he made out Makwith Shane lying on the floor.

The gun must have been fired from but a few inches away, for there was not much left of his face. Hammer sent a feverish glance around the room, then turned to stumble out. He searched the trampled snow about the shack till he found the line of footprints leading back around the corral and into the timber of the slope. Reaching the top, he dropped down the outer slope, into a milky haze that grew thicker as he went lower. Soon he could not see ahead of him, but could still make out the tracks in the snow.

"Carey!" It came from ahead — the harsh voice of Victor Bondurant. Hammer stopped in his tracks. "Come back here, you can't get away up there."

"You shot Makwith." It was Carey's voice, farther away.

"He was a fool to put up a fight. I told him," answered Bondurant, and Hammer was moving again, toward the sound. "There's no need for anybody getting hurt, now."

"Do you think I'm stupid," she cried. "You'd kill me as soon as you got that money. It's been you all along, hasn't it? You weren't after Hammer because you thought he shot your dad. You wanted those eagles. It was you burned his barn."

"All right," he answered, and that plea had left his voice, and it was only the cold, vicious, calculating intelligence, now. "Maybe I did. Maybe I cut the fence too. I always figured Hammer used that money whenever he struck a rough spot, like the big storm in '88. Kelly bucked Hammer in the first years, but when he saw how clean Hammer was keeping his slate, he began slackening up. Even took a second mortgage on Hammer's place when the bank wouldn't. I thought if I could get Kelly climbing Hammer's frame once more, Hammer'd have to turn to the eagles again. But Hammer was a hard man. When that failed, burn him out. He did have to start after those eagles then, didn't he, even though he wasn't the one who knew where they were. Now are you coming, Carey, or am I getting you?"

"Nobody's getting her, Victor," said Hammer, as a rift in the mist opened up around Bondurant, standing in the soggy buffalo grass ahead. The sheriff wheeled, and Hammer pulled his right hand from beneath his arm where he had held it till the last instant so the fingers would be warm and supple and ready. "You wondered who'd be left in the kack," he said. "Here's your chance to find out."

Bondurant's swift recovery from the shock of seeing Hammer was characteristic. "Yeah," he answered, and went to unskin his iron.

Hammer's fingers made a faint slap against the slick black top of his holster, and then their sibilant scratch, and he was out first, with the Remington bucking in his hand. The high metallic whine of a ricochet followed the explosion of the shot, and Bondurant's shout of agony. The bullet must have struck the sheriff's gun, for as the mist was swept back across Bondurant by a shift of wind, Hammer saw the man's weapon fly into the air and fall to the ground.

He fired again at the last dim sense of Bondurant there in the shifting haze, and kept running on forward, emptying his gun at the spot where the sheriff had stood. He reached the man's gun, lying in the buffalo grass, and plunged a few feet farther into the milky stream without finding Bondurant. Then a rumbling rose from beneath him.

"Hammer!" It was Carey's voice, coming faintly over the growing sound. "It's Old Faithful. Where are you? The geyser's going off!"

"Get out," he shouted at her, going on forward, and maybe it was memory of all those years Bondurant had ridden him, or maybe it was that terrible frustrated anger in him which he could not control this time, or stifle, driving him on, "get back up on the slope. He's in here somewhere and I'm not leaving till I get him."

He saw a vague movement in the mist ahead and stumbled up rising ground. The rumbling beneath him assumed the steady, thunderous roll of bass drums, and his whole body seemed to take on the throb of the earth. Then, almost before seeing the man, Hammer ran into Bondurant's form.

"Gordie?" said Bondurant, and there was something close to amusement in the rising inflexion at the end of the word, as if Bondurant had been waiting there. Hammer could not see the man's face, yet the way Bondurant had spoken gave him a vivid sense of that curling, mocking smile and those bright, intelligent, waiting eyes.

He felt himself caught, still running forward, and swung around by his own momentum, and then he knew the man *had* been waiting, right there, for his horrified eyes stared over the lip of a yawning pit into the hissing white malignance of the geyser's mouth.

Instinctively, his hands clawed out to clutch Bondurant's canvas mackinaw. The sheriff had to throw himself backward to keep from being yanked off by Hammer's weight, and this pulled Hammer's body partway back over the lip. Bondurant kicked and beat at Hammer, trying to free himself. Legs dangling into the heat of the steam, Hammer allowed himself to slide down Bondurant's legs till he was belly down on the dead grey rock forming the crater's cone.

Bondurant jerked one foot free to kick him in the face. He had to lean back to free the other foot, and Hammer released it suddenly. Bondurant staggered back in order to keep his balance, and this gave Hammer an instant to squirm farther up on the lip till his legs no longer dangled over. The incessant, throbbing rumble rose to a defeaning roar beneath him, and the steam rose in a new cloud out of the geyser behind.

"Gordie, Gordie," he heard Carey's voice, somewhere way out there, as if in a dream, "it's going, Gordie, oh my God, where are you," and then Bondurant had recovered himself and was lunging back at Hammer.

In a violent spasm, Hammer reached his knees, and saw Bondurant's outthrust hands shift upward to catch his shoulders and thrust him backward. Just before those hands reached him, Hammer dropped back onto his belly. Without Hammer's shoulders there to stop him, Bondurant went right on over, shouting something as his feet caught momentarily on Hammer's prone form, and then his shout changed to a scream of agony that became indistinguishable from the hiss of steam.

Hammer lay there on his belly, staring blankly into the pit. The ground shook with a new spasm and the steam shot up from below in a great white cloud. Gasping with the insufferable heat, he scrambled erect and stumbled down the cone with the steam roaring out behind him and scalding the back of his neck. He was almost to the bottom when Carey came running through the hot mist.

"Get out, you little fool!" he screamed.

"I couldn't stay back there," she sobbed, catching him, and whatever else she said

227

was drowned in the last gargantuan roar. The ground shook so beneath them they could barely stand. Boiling water spilled over the lip of the crater and then the column of steam became water, rising higher and higher into the air. Staggering away, Hammer felt the boiling splash of it on his bare neck and hands, and heard Carey gasp with the pain. He threw an arm over her back and pulled her partly toward him, trying to shield her with his body. Running, they finally gained the rim of buffalo grass outside the milky fog. Here they sagged into the grass, sobbing with exhaustion, and gazed blankly at the hundred foot column of water with its unfurling flag of steam. Finally, it began to die, and the westerly wind dissipated the steam, and the rumbling ground sank to a sullen mutter. Tears still sticky on her cheeks, Carey knelt before Hammer, clutching him with one hand and passing the other over his face in small, maternal gestures.

"I thought . . . I thought," she muttered. "Bon— Bondurant — "

"He won't get the money, now," said Hammer heavily, studying her face. "It was you, all along, then."

"Not all along," she told him. "It was Eden who doubled back after the money. We had all planned to meet on the Green, you remember. But three of the troopers followed Eden into the park. His horse went out on him near Old Faithful here and he had to cache the money because it was too heavy to carry on foot. When he finally joined us, he didn't say he'd gotten the money. He planned to have it all himself. But he never got the chance. Makwith shot him in an argument over cards down near Santa Fe. Makwith was so drunk he fell asleep soon after that, and Eden told me where the money was before he died. I knew turning the money over wouldn't alleviate your sentence any; you'd been sent up for complicity in the crime, and for one of us to give back the money would only be further proof of your guilt. Yet, I was afraid to tell Makwith about it. He would have started right out spending it, and those coins would have been a clear trail right to our door."

"But those coins that did pop up," he said.

She shrugged. "I had gotten a few of them from the cache, and there was times when I just had to use one. That last one in Kammerrer. We were down to our last old boot, and Makwith was crazy for a drink. I was afraid he'd do something dangerous if I didn't get him one."

"How did Dee know you had found out

where the money was?"

She shrugged. "He saw me use one of the coins about a year ago. Tried to force the location out of me. I threatened to tell Makwith that Dee had made advances or something. Dee was afraid of him. We got separated last March."

"Then the bulk of it is still up here?"

She nodded, rising to her feet. "In an extinct old geyser about five miles north."

He stood too, drawing in a deep breath. "I feel as though a great load had been lifted off me, Carey. That money's haunted me for thirteen years now. Bondurant had convinced everybody in Jackson Hole that I knew where it was. To know that I can turn it back now, and have them off my neck, and ride down the road without feeling I'm being watched . . ." He trailed off, gazing at her a moment. Finally he spoke, "Makwith — "

"I know, Hammer, I know," she said, taking the step that brought him against her, and her face against his mackinaw.

He put his arms about her, and they stood that way a moment. "Maybe this is the wrong time to say it, Carey, but you know I've always wanted you," he said.

"It seems I've been torn and rent all my life, Hammer," she said. "I knew what Makwith was, but I couldn't help myself, whether he was good or bad, right or wrong, I couldn't help myself, I had to ride his trail. And then you came along and it was even worse. As much as I loved Makwith, you did something to me, and that twisted it around even more. I think it was the worst the other day, when I came on you mending that fence. I couldn't love Makwith the way I used to, after all these years, and yet I couldn't leave him, and then, to see you again like that . . ." She halted, breathing heavily, and when she spoke again, it held a strange, new quietude. "And suddenly, for the first time in my life, now, Hammer . . . I feel whole."

"I haven't much to offer," he said. "But it's all there, down at the Big Dipper, if you want it, Carey."

"I want it," she said. "I want you, Hammer."

Lunatic Patrol

Waiting for him to do something was the worst. The silence was bad, and the emptiness, and the endless snow, fighting us with that soft, inexorable insistence every foot of the way. But waiting for him to do something was the worst.

"What a stupid organization, the Mounted Police," he said. "They send a sergeant-major like you five hundred miles after a man, with orders to bring him in, alive and well, and half the time you Mounties come back crazier than the man you haul in. You have to feed him and nurse him and keep him happy, like he was a baby, and all the time he's just waiting for your first slip so he can kill you and get free. And even when he does make the break you have to keep yourself from killing him."

I thought: *Maybe you think I don't want to kill you?* I squatted by the fire, kneading the grease and water and dough together for the bannocks, gritting my teeth, keeping my face turned away from him. *Maybe you think I don't want to, Dobrois. More than anything in life.*

He waited a moment for me to answer him, and then laughed. "Oh, you don't have to humor me any more, Graham. I've got the manacles on, haven't I? You don't have to try and keep it from me. I know you think I'm crazy. *Voilá!* Tell me what keeps you from doing it, then, Graham. After you've been goaded and baited and maddened twenty-four hours a day the whole three-hundred-mile run by some man you think is crazy, what keeps a Mountie from killing him? An ordinary man couldn't stand it. They say Constable Walsh was as crazy as the man he brought in last year. Yet he brought him in alive."

It was hard to realize he was unbalanced; he talked so rationally, so intelligently, even if there was that sly undertone to his words. But all I had to do was turn enough to see his eyes. I had seen the same thing in a trapped wolf's eyes. Cunning. Waiting. That was it. Waiting. He was waiting. I was waiting. The whole world was waiting. . . .

233

"All right," I said, and my hands shaped the kneaded dough into the frying pan with quick, jerky gestures. "All right. Not one prisoner has died on this patrol since 1904."

"Ah." His voice was mocking. "Tradition. That's it. The Force. Bigger than one man. Or all men. But why say *this* patrol, Graham. You won't offend me, I assure you. Why not the lunatic patrol?" He stopped a moment, and I could feel him watching me. "I don't think that's it, Graham. Maybe that's part of it. But not enough. Not enough to keep you from killing me when you want to so bad you cry in your sougan at night — "

"Never mind." My grip on the handle was so tight it hurt as I stood the frying pan face up toward the fire to brown the bannocks, and I was driven to it, somehow. "You're a sick man, Dobrois, that's all, and I have no right — "

"Ah, a sick man. *Voilá!* That's even better than a homicidal maniac. That's the best one I've heard." Dobrois's face was mostly beard, and all I could see of his mouth was the shadowed white line of his teeth showing in that artful grin. Then the grin faded, and he frowned. "A sick man, *hein?* It seems somebody told me that before. Or a sick mind. *Oui,* that was it, a sick mind. It wasn't you, was it, Graham? *Non*. Somebody else. Some girl — "

"Shut up!"

The dogs stopped their restless whining, staring brightly at me now instead of Dobrois. The echoes of my shout rang down the somber lanes of black poplars that were so stunted by the short summers up here north of Lac la Martre. There was a surprised look on Dobrois's face.

"You're touchy about that, Graham? What is it? Your pet theory? A sick mind."

My teeth were grinding again as I stared at him. Surely he must know. He was just baiting me. Then I smelled the bannocks, and whirled to pull the frying pan away from the fire. They were burned on top. My hands shook, scraping the crust away, spilling the ashes over my caribou-hide leggins. He was still frowning when I carried the folding tin cup of tea and the bannocks over to him.

"Somebody told me," he said. "A sick mind."

"Don't tell me you can't remember. Don't try and make me believe that, Dobrois."

The tone of my voice brought his eyes to my face, and they were as guileless as a baby's. "Remember what, Graham?"

"Ben Shovil down on the Moose Jaw, for instance."

"Non, non." His voice was sharper. "Why do you keep insisting I murdered him? I'm not the lunatic, Graham. You are. I never knew any Ben Shovil."

"Or Laurent Duprez?" I was bending tensely toward him. "Or Jean Fontaine, or — "

"Or who, Graham? Go on." He was watching my face with a certain, growing calculation.

I couldn't believe he didn't remember. It was so inconceivable to me that it shouldn't be in his mind, as bright and bitter and hateful as it was in mine. I shoved the tea and bannocks at him and caught the sudden cunning flash of his eyes, and tried to jump back from it. But the tea was already in my face, scalding and blinding. I heard my own shout of pain as I jumped backward, fumbling beneath my parka for my Webley. Then I stopped, without pulling the gun out. Vision had returned to me and, holding my free hand over my burned face, I could see him through my fingers, still sitting cross-legged where he had been, the empty cup held in his hairy, manacled hands, grinning slyly up at me.

"What's the matter, Graham, *hein?* What's the matter?"

* * *

South of Lac la Martre, the noise we made only seemed to accentuate the silence, lying as thick and intense and malignant as the snow, all about us. This was the lonely, empty country that had driven Dobrois mad, and so many others brought back on the lunatic patrol. The spruce runners on my big Cree police sledge made their monotonous crunch through the slush, and when I thought I could not stand it any longer I would shout at the dogs.

"Mush, Eric, mush — "

"Whoa, Eric!" shouted Dobrois. "Whoa, whoa!"

"Shut up, Dobrois. Mush, Eric — "

"Shut up, Dobrois," the half-breed mocked me. "Whoa, Eric!" Then he threw back his shaggy head to laugh wildly. I couldn't help the spasmodic way my hand went out toward him. The frozen fingers of my mittens touched the lazy-board, and I stopped myself, hoping he couldn't hear the small, strangled sound I made. How many times had I reached for him like that? How many times had I wanted to kill him?

"*Nous irons sur l'eau* — " He had started the song again, staring straight ahead with a crazy smile on his face and muttering in that maddening sing-song voice. "*Nous y*

237

promenar, nous irons jouer dans l'île — "

"Dobrois, stop that!" I shouted at him. He turned abruptly, that vacuous leer on his face.

"What's the matter, Graham?"

Jogging beside the sled, I tried to find any calculation in his face, and couldn't. His eyes were bright and empty, and he began to gibber the song again.

"Dobrois, where did you learn that song?"

His smile was guileless. "The *chanson*, Graham? I don't remember. I think I heard a girl sing it. Celia? *Oui*. Celia, I think."

He *did* remember! At first I thought it was the runners across the ice, that shrill, broken sound. Then I realized it was me. The desire to get my hands on him swept me with such a bitter force I couldn't see for a moment. *You do remember, you dirty cross-breeded liar! All that was just baiting me, before. "Where did I hear that, Graham? I don't remember. Some girl? Oui." All baiting me, and* . . .

Maybe it was Dobrois's shout that brought me out of it. He was jerking from side to side in the sled as we ran through a stand of stunted poplars, laughing as the cariole rocked dangerously.

"Dobrois," I yelled, making a grab for the bobbing tail-line. "Dobrois, stop that.

You'll tip the sled! Whoa, Eric, whoa — "

My grab at the line missed, and the cariole rocked over on the other spruce runner, swinging the stern around to pull the whole team into the trees. Eric rammed head-on into a spruce, the other dogs piling up behind him. I heard his agonized howl as the over-turning toboggan smashed in on the whole yapping, snarling bunch of them. I ran up to heave the heavy police sled off the dogs, tearing at their writhing, furry bodies to free Eric. Either the weight of the other dogs had done it, or the sled itself; Eric lay there with both hind legs twisted under him, look-ing up at me, and his big dark eyes knew how it was, just the way I knew.

I must have been cursing even then. I whirled away from the lead dog, my head jerking from side to side until I saw where Dobrois had been thrown out of the sled. He had rolled out of the cariole and brought up against a snow-bank, and was sitting cross-legged there with that empty grin on his face.

"Whoa, Eric," he said, laughing inanely, "whoa, whoa — "

"Damn you, Dobrois, I'll have to kill that dog. You've broken his back legs, and I'll have to kill him, do you understand? I'll have to kill him, kill him, kill him — "

With my hands around his neck and his heavy, stinking body jerking and fighting against me, I stopped myself, realizing it wasn't Dobrois that had driven me this far. It was still in my mind, somewhere, *Nous irons sur l'eau, nous y promenar* . . . But the other was there too, coming up through my terrible blind passion — "a sick mind, Graham, a sick mind, and he's not responsible. No matter what he does, he's not responsible."

It was a moment before Dobrois could get back his breath, choking and gasping. Finally he managed to sit up again and the blood returned to his face. He looked up at me where I stood above him, and I could see no anger in his face, not even pain now. Just that blank leer. He raised his manacled hands, shaking them till the chain rattled, and giggled at the sound, like a baby amused with his rattle.

"Whoa, Eric," he babbled. "Whoa, whoa . . ."

I stared into the darkness, feeling the strange, breathless fear that rises in a man, sometimes, when he is wakened abruptly in the night. I lay sweating, my fists clenched in the heat of my blankets, fighting the reasonless panic.

"Graham," it came again, and I realized

240

that this time I hadn't dreamed it. I grabbed for my Webley where it lay by my side, and rolled over, pulling out the sougan till I could sit up with my legs still beneath the blankets. I could see him now. He was still in his own blankets, dog-chain holding his wrists to the stunted poplar.

"Graham," he said, "my neck hurts. What happened?"

"Go to sleep."

"I want some tea."

"You had your tea."

"Graham" — his voice was soft with cunning, and I realized some lucidity must have returned to him — "Graham, I want some tea. If you don't get me some tea I'll start yelling and cursing and wake up the dogs and cause a hell of a *veillée*. You've got to take care of me. I may be crazy, but you've got to take care of me like I was a baby and feed me and nurse me and make me happy, and if you don't — "

"All right, Dobrois, all right!" In desperation, I got out of my blanket roll and began to build a fire with numb hands. When the tea was made, I had to unhitch his dog-chain so he could raise up and drink. He kept rubbing his neck. He asked me again what happened. I didn't answer, and that speculative light came into his eyes.

"Did I try to get away, Graham? Why won't you tell me? It feels like somebody choked me."

"You know what happened."

"But *non*, I don't."

I studied his face. "You really don't remember?"

He shrugged. "The last thing I remember is throwing tea in your face before we went to bed this evening." He laughed suddenly, slyly. "Does it still hurt, Graham?"

I couldn't believe it yet. "That wasn't this evening. That was two days ago. We're thirty miles south of Lac la Martre now."

His surprise seemed genuine enough and he rubbed his neck. "Two days? You're lying Graham. You just don't want to tell me what happened."

"You smashed up the sled and broke my lead dog's legs and I had to shoot him. You didn't even try to get away."

He studied his handcuffs a long time, then he looked up at me, laughing craftily. "Never mind, Graham. Next time it will be different. Sooner or later I'll get away. It's a hundred miles more, and you've only got four dogs left, and you're about to crack under the strain. How much longer do you think you can stand it, Graham? Where do you think Constable Walsh cracked? The first day? The

242

twentieth? They say he was as crazy as the man he brought in . . ."

He trailed off, chuckling, as he saw how I was leaning forward. I tried to relax, unable to reconcile this lucidity with his periods of utter idiocy. I didn't know enough about insanity to tell if it was logical. Yet, if he really didn't remember upsetting the sled . . .

I lowered my head so he couldn't see I was watching him, and then began to hum the song: *"Nous irons sur l'eau, nous y promenar . . ."*

"When were you on the river, Graham?"

It wasn't the reaction I had wanted, or expected. "The river?"

"That's an old *voyageur chanson,*" he told me innocently. "I didn't think many white men knew it. The rivermen used to sing it when they poled their York boats up the Athabaska. Where did you learn it?"

"Don't you know?" I said.

Again his surprise seemed genuine. *"Sacre bleu,* how should I?" He began to sing it, waving his manacled hands back and forth to the time. " 'We shall go on the water for a boat ride, we shall play on the island — ' "

"Will you shut up!" I whirled on him, fists clenched.

He chuckled, and that cunning was in his

eyes. "Is it just the strain, Graham, or is there something special about the song?"

"Never mind." Trembling, I turned around and walked stiffly to the team, and unhitched my butt dog from where I had chained him to the tree. "Morning star's coming. No use going back to sleep now."

"Where did you learn the song, Graham?"

I had myself under control now. "Where did *you* learn it, Dobrois?"

He hesitated a moment. "I don't know, exactly."

"Or don't remember?"

"It seems to me a girl was singing it."

"And she said you had a sick mind."

His head raised. "How did you know?"

"And you weren't to blame, no matter what you did. You had a sick mind, and you weren't to blame — " I clamped my mouth shut over it, dragging the reluctant butt dog to the sled and attaching the heavy moosehide traces to the toggles on his collar. I went back to get the next dog and was unhitching his chain when an agonized howl from the sled whirled me about, my hand on my Webley. Dobrois stepped back from my big Chipeway butt dog, grinning at me. The animal was lying on its side, tugging feebly at the traces, howling in dismal pain. I saw his right forepaw, and couldn't help the way my gun came up.

Dobrois grinned at it. "You can't kill me, Graham, remember? You're not a man. You're a policeman. Tradition, Graham. The Force. You shouldn't have told me how Eric got his legs broken. It gave me ideas."

"Get in the sled," I said, and my voice was shaking. *"Dobrois, get in that sled."* The gun was trembling in my hand, and he saw it, and climbed into the cariole. I got some *babiche* lashings from the birch-bark rogan in the bow and tied the breed in till he couldn't move. Then I went over to the other side of the fire and retched.

"Does it make you sick, Graham?" he said. *"Mon dieu,* I never wanted to kill a man that bad."

It started to storm before noon. I had been forced to kill the butt dog, and soon the drifts were piling up so heavily in front of us that my three remaining dogs were unable to haul the heavy sled without aid from me. Finally we struck a slope, and I got them going at a fair pace.

"Cha, you *klis, cha,"* I cried, turning them left from a bank in front of us.

"Eu," shouted Dobrois from the sled, *"eu!"* And the dogs turned right again.

"Shut up, Dobrois," I called desperately.

"Cha, cha, cha — "

"Eu, eu," laughed Dobrois, and the dogs turned right once more, and went head-on into the drift before I could turn them away. Dobrois lay in the cariole, laughing gleefully as I shoved the heavy sled out of the bank and undertook to untangle the dogs. A trace had caught in one of the toggles, and it was a maddening job getting it out with my frozen hands. Finally I finished and went back to the sled, getting a Hudson Bay four-point from the bow. Dobrois watched with bright eyes while I cut a strip from the blanket. Suddenly he began to sing.

"Nous irons sur l'eau, nous y — "

It was the blanket that stopped him. I jammed a wad beneath his teeth, trying to hold it there and tie another strip over his mouth. But he spat out the first wad and bit me. I yanked my hand away, shouting hoarsely.

"Nous irons sur l'eau," he howled, jerking his head from side to side and laughing crazily, *"nous y promenar — "*

I wanted to kill him. I had both hands on the edge of the rocking cariole, gripping it so tightly I couldn't feel the pain of my bitten hand. I was trembling as violently as the sled, and the tears began to slide down my cheeks past my mouth before they froze.

God, I wanted to kill him!

"Nous irons jouer dans l'île, nous irons jouer dans l'île . . ."

I was still crying when I had finished gagging him. The storm had grown more violent, and the dogs were so exhausted by now that I fastened myself into the harness and pulled with them. In the white, swirling snow and cutting ice I couldn't tell when night came and only stopped when I could run no farther, seeking an uplift of some kind so I could pitch camp in its lee. By the time I found the rise, all I could do was throw myself down with the dogs and lie there, still in the harness, with the snow piling on top of me.

Finally, moving in a stupor, I managed to get up and cut myself loose. I groped through the snow till I found some timber, chopped off some higher branches of the stunted spruce and stumbled back to camp.

Then I went to get my Marble axe from the cariole. There was snow on Dobrois's face, and I wiped it off, and then was sorry I had, because I could see his eyes. He lay there motionless in his tight bindings beneath the snow-mantled musk-ox robe, the lower part of his face hidden by the gag. But the way his eyes were fixed on me, I knew he was grinning, and they were filled with that cunning intelligence, and I knew it had started once more.

Going back to the wood, my whole body was taut with a sense of waiting for Dobrois to do something again. He was bound and helpless in the sled, yet my jaws ached from gritting my teeth, and waiting.

I chopped up the branches, then put the axe aside to get my knife and carve away the wet outer wood. I shifted a little to get more shelter from the rise above, and built the fire. I was bent over the first blaze, shielding it from the snow, when I thought of the axe. There was no reason to think of it that way. But I did.

"The cariole was coming apart, Graham," he said, when I looked up and saw him standing close to me. "I've been working my way out of that *babiche* all afternoon." And then he yelled hoarsely and swung at me with the axe held in both manacled hands.

I hadn't been able to throw myself back far enough, but when his body struck me, it wasn't the way he had gauged the blow, and I screamed with the stunning pain as the blade struck my cheek at an angle instead of cleaving my skull. The best I could do was roll blindly aside beneath his next blow, still gripping the knife in one hand. The axe struck the snow beside my head with a dull thud, and I tried to catch his arms while they were still down there.

"I waited, didn't I, Graham?" he panted, struggling back up. "All the time you had to run while I was resting, and I waited. Two hundred miles, Graham, and pulling the sled yourself these last days, and I waited. And now you're so tired you can't even fight me, and I'm going to kill you, Graham, I'm going to kill you — "

I could see that lucidity was leaving him, as it must have left him when he murdered Shovil on the Moose Jaw, and the others. He tore free of my feeble graspings with a wild shout, and the cunning was swept out of his eyes by a maniacal lust. He rose up, straddling me for the third blow, and I knew it would be the last. It was all I could do to lurch up beneath him and paw groggily for the chain on his manacles. He pulled back to tear my hand away, and it threw him off me with my fist still around that chain, yanking me across his body as he rolled to the side.

I was over him now, holding his arms above his head with the grip on the chain. My free arm rose with the knife. He must have seen my expression, because his scream held a sudden, animal fear.

"*Non,* you can't kill me. You can't!"

The palisaded walls at Fort Simpson stood on the island at the mouth of the Laird, and the river was frozen over enough so that I could drive my sled across to where Inspector Arden and a few of the others were waiting for me at the edge of the ice. The welcoming twinkle left Arden's blue eyes as he saw the mess the axe had left of my face.

"You've had a rough time, Graham."

I fumbled beneath my coat for the patrol sheet, not wanting to talk about it now. "Your original report had three people murdered in district D. I found a fourth."

We kept check on the white settlers, and the paper contained a list of the people in my district. Arden's glance ran down the line, lips forming the names which were crossed out.

"Fontaine, Duprez, Shovil — " He stopped on the fourth one, and the blood drained from his weathered face. "Graham — you've got Celia Manette."

"He found her by the river." It came from me in a hoarse, driven way. "She was singing that French *voyageur* song her father always sang when he was drunk. She even tried to argue him out of it. She told him he had a sick mind and wasn't to blame for what he did. She promised him we wouldn't kill him — "

"Dobrois confessed?"

"No." I hardly recognized my own voice. "He doesn't remember any of them. I thought he did at first. I thought he was baiting me. But he has periods in his right mind, and then he goes out of his head completely."

"But if he didn't tell you," asked Arden, "how do you know? The song, I mean, trying to argue him out of it."

"It was the same thing she told me, Arden." It tumbled out of me hoarsely, almost incoherently. "I was up at her cabin when I got the orders to report down here for my patrol sheet, and we both knew it meant the lunatic patrol, and she told me. A sick mind, she said, and he wasn't to blame for what he did. No matter what he did, he wasn't to blame. She made me promise, Arden. She said it would drive me crazy if I didn't remember. It was the only thing that kept me from killing him. No matter what he did, *she* wouldn't blame him. He had a sick mind, and *she* wouldn't blame him. She'd want it *this* way, wouldn't she? She wouldn't blame me — "

"Of course not, Graham, of course not." He had his hand on my arm now, and there was understanding in his face. He had been on the lunatic patrol, himself. "Celia would be proud of you."

Dobrois had been brought up in time to hear Arden. "Celia?" he said.

The inspector turned to stare at him. "You really don't know?"

Dobrois had been lucid these last few hours, and he shrugged, grinning. "Know what?"

Dully, I felt Arden's sinewy hand tighten on my arm. "Celia Manette was going to be Graham's wife, Dobrois."

"*Bon*, Graham, *bon*." Dobrois's face was as guileless as a child's. "When is the wedding going to be?"

Chuck-Wagon Warrior

When the fire was going good, Larrup shoveled hot coals across the sheet of corrugated iron on the ground and put three skillets on to heat. The roundup crew was already drifting in. Rigger came from the Texas brush on a played-out cutting mare. He was twenty feet away when Larrup began to smell the rancid bacon grease he smeared on his long yellow hair.

"How's the new belly cheater?" Rigger grinned.

"You want me to cook your dinner or stop and gab?" Larrup asked.

"You must be better'n the other cook, you're sure ornerier," Rigger chuckled. He got off the mare and began hunting through the pockets of his jacket. "Looks like I'm out of makin's, Larrup. Got a quirly?"

"I chaw," Larrup said.

Rigger sighed disconsolately. Then a strange expression came to his gaunt face, and he stared around the clearing. At this moment, Skid rode from the brush. He was the ramrod of the Double Crown, tall and dour and slack as a piece of old hemp.

"Skid," Rigger said. "I didn't realize it when we pulled in this morning. This looks like the place Charlie disappeared."

Skid gave him a sharp glance. "Shut up," he said.

Larrup glanced up. This was the first time he'd heard them mention the cook he had replaced. Somehow he sensed that it was connected with the strange tension he had felt in the whole crew. But the anger pinching the edges of the foreman's eyes stopped Larrup from asking. He turned before Skid caught his glance, and began pouring water in the coffeepot. He'd cooked in enough roundup camps to know when it was better to mind his own business.

Before the pot was full, Wrangatang rode in. He was the wrangler, a tattered kid of seventeen with a face older than his years. He watched Larrup set the coffeepot down and bank a shovelful of coals on its windward side.

"Old cook used to put the pot right in

the fire," Wrangatang said slyly.

"He musta learned to cook in a sheep camp," Larrup told him.

"Sure, Wrangatang," Rigger mocked. "Don't you know any belly cheater worth his salt never cooks right in a wood fire?"

Wrangatang glanced around the clearing. "Speakin' of belly cheaters, ain't this where the last cook disappeared?"

"I said shut up, damn you!" Skid's voice cracked like a whip and the towheaded wrangler jumped a foot out of his saddle.

Then the foreman hiked one long leg over the slickhorn and slid from his lathered bluetick roan. He took his Stetson off by the brim and beat it absently against his leg as he frowned around at the brush.

"Got a quirly, Skid?" Rigger asked.

"Roll your own," the foreman said irritably.

Larrup went methodically on with his work, taking it all in. He got a double handful of dough from the sourdough keg and rolled it out on the tail gate of the chuck wagon, skillet-size and rawhide-thin. Then he flipped it into the skillet, setting this back on the bed of coals, putting a lid on, and shoveling more hot coals on top.

When he was at work, the fluid skill of his movements seemed to rob his lean body

255

of its awkward look. His face was as brick-red as his hair, spattered with freckles, and the professional crankiness of a chuck-wagon cook was belied by the wry quirks that kept coming and going at the tips of his mouth.

He spooned pinto beans from a glass jar into the second skillet, and while he was slicing bacon rind and garlic into it, Silent Joe Smith and Dally rode in. Silent Joe Smith dismounted and began to unsaddle.

Rigger sidled over to him. "You got a quirly, Joe?" Silent Joe Smith heaved his saddle off and carried it to the chuck wagon. Rigger spat after him. "Forget it. You really must have a dirty back trail if it keeps you that clammed up."

"Slack off, Rigger," Dally told him. "We all got a right to our past."

Rigger frowned. "Makes me sour when I run out of makin's."

"At that rate, you should be a reg'lar lemon," cackled Wrangatang.

Rigger picked up a handful of dirt and flung it at him. It almost hit the two riders coming out of the thickets. George Adams led, a ponderous kettle-gutted man, the boss of the Double Crown. His Prince Albert and satin lapels and his Stetson was bone-white and his grin looked like a campaigning politician's.

"Appears as how our new cookie knows the ropes," he chuckled expansively. "Any man that can have chuck ready before them Mexicans bulge in is fast. Yes sir, holy fast."

Larrup hardly heard the man. He was looking at Adams's niece.

Roma Adams sat a fiddle-footed mare right behind her uncle, and the wind had blown her blue-black hair into impish curls all about her flushed face. There was a puckish mischief to her snapping black eyes and full smiling lips.

George Adams got off his big Choppo horse with a loud squawk of rigging.

"Came out to see how the tally books were filling up, Skid. Can I have a look?"

The foreman took a couple of beef books from his hip pocket and went over to Adams. Roma slid off her fiddling mare and came smiling to Larrup.

"Charlie always had some pun'kin candy."

It was so much like a little kid he had to grin. "Ain't got none of that. We can mix up a batch of Charlie Taylor to put on that pan bread."

"I'll wait around on one condition," she said; "that you tell me how you got your name."

He got a jug of molasses from the shelf and took the plug out. Then he gave a hitch to his belt.

"Larrup is what they call molasses up in Deaf Smith County," he said. "They make it so thick if you got your hand stuck in it you couldn't pull it out. When I was a little button, I fell into a big vat of larrup Pa was making out back. It was like trying to pull me out of cement. Menfolks came from miles around to help. It was just like a house-raising. Whole families camped on the place for nights on end. There was horse races and square dances and everybody got drunk as grandpa at the fair. But nobody could pull me up. Be too big a waste to pour all that molasses out. They had to eat buckwheat cakes for six months before it got low enough so's I could be pulled free."

Her chuckle dipped her chin in, digging a satiny furrow in the soft flesh beneath her jaw. He was so taken up with looking that he didn't realize how long he'd been holding the jug upside down.

"Feels like something's clogged it up," he said, shaking it. "You lived with your uncle all your life?"

"Dad and Mother died three years ago," she told him. "Uncle George was appointed executor by the courts. He'll keep the ranch going for me till I'm of age."

He sat the jug down disgustedly. "A six-hitch team couldn't drag this larrup out. We'll have to be satisfied with prickly-pear jelly."

She smiled. "You're even better than Charlie."

He gave her an oblique glance. "What's all this mystery about Charlie?"

All the humor left her. "He just disappeared," she said darkly. "About a week ago. He was going to roast a bull's head for Enrique and Toro. They were the first back from roundup. Charlie wasn't anywhere around. The whole crew beat the brush for him. Not a sign."

"That's sort of funny," he frowned. "Toro said he'd get me a bull today for some fresh beefsteaks if I'd roast its head for him — "

He broke off at a sudden great crash from out in the brush, and Roma whirled, eyes widening mischievously. "Sounds like they're coming now," she giggled.

Larrup could hear them shouting a long time before the bull finally burst out of the thickets. Both the Mexicans had their ropes on it, and the beast was hauling them in its wake like two feathers in the wind.

"Hola," shouted Toro. "Get out of his way. We can't hold him."

The crew scattered. The bull saw the chuck wagon and veered that way, yawning and heaving on the ropes. Roma started to run from the wagon, but tripped and fell.

"Get up, Roma," Toro bawled. "We can't stop him — "

Roma rolled over, shaking her head dazedly. Larrup saw she would never make it. He lunged out after her. The bull looked big as a house coming down on him. He caught the girl under the arms and threw himself backward with her. They rolled beneath the wagon as the bull thundered by, hooking vindictively at a wheel.

Sprawled beside Larrup under the wagon, Roma looked at him with fluttering eyes. A shaky laugh escaped her.

"I guess you saved my life."

His grin was embarrassed. "I'd like to do it every day."

Part of the fright had left her, and she managed a faint smile. "I'd rather try something a little less strenuous."

"How about a buggy ride some night," he said. "The moon's wonderful this time of year."

She tried to look shocked. "You pick strange places to ask a girl something like that." Then she sighed wistfully. "Strange place or not, you're the first man who's even asked me in a long time."

He frowned at her. "I should think they'd be lined up at your door."

"They're all afraid of Uncle George," she

said disconsolately, and then started to get up.

He saw that the whole crew was still fighting the bull out in the clearing, and caught her arm.

"Why does your uncle keep you on such a tight string?" he said. "Does it have anything to do with what's going on here?"

On her hands and knees, she looked at him sharply. "You feel it too, then?" she said.

"Feel what?" he asked.

"I don't know." She shook her head helplessly. "Just something. The crew's so jumpy. Everything's so strange."

"Roma," called Adams. "What are you doing?"

Larrup looked up to see that the noise had died down, the crew having finally thrown the bull in the middle of the clearing.

"I was telling her how I got my name," he said.

Adams frowned at him, then snorted. "How did you?"

Larrup climbed from beneath the wagon, giving a hitch to his belt. "Harks back to when I was up in Wyoming, cooking for the Hearts and Sevens outfit. All the boys kept ragging me about being slower than molasses in January. I got tired of it and told them I'd race a jug of molasses just to show them. The ramrod and me took a jug of blackstrap up to the top of a big hill. The ramrod poured the molasses out. As soon as it started running down, I started running too. The whole crew was waiting at the bottom to see who come out first."

"Who beat?"

"The molasses."

"Aw, now Larrup," Wrangatang said. "You know molasses won't run downhill."

Adams came over to the wagon, staring down at Roma with a strange smile. "Now that's not what you were talking about, my dear. Tell your uncle the truth."

She had climbed from beneath the wagon, and she dropped her eyes, brushing uncomfortably at her dirty clothes. "We were just talking about Charlie," she said in a low voice.

"Charlie." It left Adams in a whisper. He sent a glance at Skid, and then tried to hide it. He began to get red. "I guess you and I better go home," he said.

Roma looked up swiftly. "But Larrup was going to put some Charlie Taylor on a piece of pan bread for me — "

Adams tucked his chin in, the smile spreading over his face like oil. "My dear," he said softly.

Larrup saw fear steal through Roma's eyes. She turned and went to her horse. Adams followed, mounting his own animal. Without looking at any of them, he followed her out of the clearing, still smiling at her back.

"Poor little gal," Dally said.

Larrup looked at him. "How's that?"

Dally turned away, coiling up a rope. "Nothin'."

Toro had stepped off his bronc out by the bull and was winding up his rope. He slung the rope on his horn and waddled toward the chuck wagon, a huge tub of a man in suede *charro* pants and knee-high *mitaja* leggins. He hooked a spoon from the wreck pan and dipped up a taste from the pot by the tail gate. His eyes rolled heavenward.

"What ecstasy! I never like gringo cooking till you come, Larrup. Now I don't ever want to see a *tortilla* again. Look here, Enrique! We got the spotted pup for dessert tonight."

The other Mexican was still sitting his whey-bellied stud. "Untrammeled," he said.

Toro frowned at him. "What?"

Enrique looked surprised. "Perspicacious?" he asked.

Toro shook his head. "No, no."

Enrique looked desperate. "Pyrolisis?"

Toro shrugged helplessly, turning to Larrup. "Enrique, he only know three word in English, but nobody they understand them."

"His ma must have married a dictionary," Rigger told Toro. "You got a quirly?"

"Last time Toro give you some of that Mexican tobacco, you was sick all night," Wrangatang mocked.

Rigger swept a tin plate off the tail gate and flung it at him. Wrangatang ducked, thumbing his nose. Skid was watching Larrup, who had gotten the spade from the wagon.

"What you going to do with that?" the foreman asked.

Larrup was poking around for a soft spot in the ground. "Dig a hole. I promised Toro I'd roast the bull's head."

"Sure, Skid," Toro said. "You wrap the head in the grass, fill the hole with hot coals — "

"Let's just have steaks," Skid said.

Toro's mouth sagged open. "You ain't going to throw away the greatest delicacy of all?"

Larrup found a soft spot and sank the spade in, but Skid came at him in a whipping walk. "I said you ain't going to cook it."

Larrup looked up inquiringly. "It's hard to believe you're telling me how to cook."

Skid grabbed the spade and tore it from his hands. "You ain't roasting any bull's head."

Larrup came to his full height. The quirks were gone from the tips of his mouth. His voice was barely a whisper.

"Give me back my spade."

Skid turned to toss it in the chuck wagon. Larrup lunged forward, grabbing it. The foreman tore the spade loose and swung it at Larrup.

Larrup doubled over and drove a fist deep into Skid's belly. The spade passing over his head and air leaving Skid made the same whistling sound. Skid bent double into Larrup. The cook hit Skid in the face. This straightened the foreman like a reach pole and pitched him over backward. He hit hard and lay still.

"Now," Larrup panted. "I'm going to roast that bull's head if it's the last thing I cook for this outfit."

Larrup got into Eagle Pass about ten that evening. He left the horse he had ridden at the livery stable, where the first Double Crown hand to hit town could pick it up. He found out the stage didn't leave till noon the next day, so he got a room at the Mexican inn on the plaza. He was still so mad he wanted to go back and whip Skid all over again. He'd burned his hand roasting the bull's head, and that didn't help either.

He had left without bothering to get his time from Skid. A man couldn't whip the foreman and still stay on with an outfit. Especially when he didn't want to stay anyway. At least he tried to tell himself he didn't want to. But the picture of Roma Adams kept floating through his mind. And he still couldn't help wondering why Skid had made such a fuss over roasting a bull's head.

Next morning he got up early and had *eggs al rancho* and coffee strong enough to smell in Mexico City, and then wandered down the river. He sat down on the shelving bank with the willows clattering softly in the wind, still unable to get Charlie and Roma and Skid out of his mind. Mostly Roma. Then a shadow fell across him and he jumped with surprise and looked up to see the girl sitting her fiddle-footed mare there.

"They told me at the inn you headed toward the river," she said. She stared at him a moment longer, lips parted, and then swung off, ground-hitching her reins. He was on his feet now and she took a step toward him and then stopped self-consciously.

266

"Oh, Larrup," she said. "Don't go — "

She trailed off and her parted lips and the wistful plea in her eyes gave her a little-girl sweetness that pulled him toward her till they were not inches apart.

"I wish I didn't have to," he said.

She caught his arm, face upturned. "I felt so lost when I heard you'd gone. You're the only one who ever paid any attention to me around there. All the other hands are even afraid to speak with me for fear of making Uncle George mad."

"It's more than that, isn't it?" he asked.

Her eyes widened. "What do you mean?"

"You're afraid."

She stared at him a long time before answering. "Yes," she said, with a little catch to her breath. "I guess I am."

"Of what?"

Her curls bobbed with the helpless toss of her head. "I don't know, Larrup."

"Your uncle?"

Surprise lifted her brows. "What makes you say that?"

"Don't try to tell me you like him."

She avoided his eyes. "He's my uncle, Larrup. I shouldn't say anything like that. He's taken care of me — "

"Like your own mother," Larrup said cynically.

"All right — " she shook her head angrily — "so he hasn't been everything he could. It's a big ranch. He's been busy."

"Not too busy to make you do exactly what he wants."

She was near to tears. "Oh, Larrup, let's not talk about him. It isn't only Uncle George. It's everything — Charlie disappearing, the crew so jumpy — "

"I couldn't come back to the outfit now," he said.

"I'll talk with Uncle George," she said. "I'll talk with Skid. Surely, they'll — "

"You know they won't," he said.

Her lower lip began to tremble. "You're leaving, then?"

"I didn't say that."

Her voice rose in wild hope. "You're staying, then."

"Do you think I could go away — now?" he asked softly.

"Oh — Larrup — "

Her whole body seemed to lift toward him and it was the most natural thing in the world for him to take her in his arms and kiss her. Afterward he held her against him and felt the trembling of her body. Her face was buried against his shoulder, and it muffled her voice.

"I guess I didn't really know how badly

I needed somebody," she said.

"You've got somebody," he told her. "Let's go back to the inn and get my gear. I'll go back to the ranch with you and make a stab at it, anyway. And if they won't sign me on again I'll camp in the brush right outside your window and they won't be able to drag me out with six teams of circle mules."

Her face was radiant as she walked back with him, leading her mare. They came around the inn from the rear and found a buckboard in the plaza with a Double Crown painted on its side. George Adams stepped from the inn door, his face wreathed in that campaign grin.

"Looks like my niece preceded me with the good news," he chuckled.

"What good news?" Roma asked.

"Oh." Adams pursed his lips, and the grin faded. After frowning a moment at the girl, he turned to Larrup. "The hands have quit. They've all got the bellyache from the slop Toro tried to cook. They're sitting down there at the roundup and they won't eat till you come back."

"How about Skid?" Larrup asked.

"Skid is going to apologize."

"What for? Me whipping the tar out of him?"

Adams's chuckle shook his expansive belly.

"Did you ever see such a man, Roma? Get your gear, Larrup. I'll even give you a raise."

They took the wagon road cutting north from the river, with Roma's mare hitched to the tail gate and trotting along behind. Before they were out of town, Adams turned to smile benevolently at the girl.

"And how did my little niece happen to be in town so early this morning?"

Her chin lifted defiantly. "I came in for the same thing you did. To get Larrup back."

"Did you now?" Adams's smile broadened without gaining humor. He looked strangely at Larrup. "And you went down to the river to talk it over."

"I was telling her how I got my name," Larrup said.

Adams lost his patience. "I thought you already told her."

"I didn't get to finish."

Adams gathered his good humor with palable effort. "How did you get your name, Larrup? I mean really."

Larrup gave a hitch to his belt. "It harks back to the days I was cooking for the Corkscrew outfit up in Deaf Smith County. We'd made a camp near the edge of a cliff. This hand named Rawlins choused a beef in for me to butcher. When he dabbed his rope on, the beef ran right over the cliff. Rawlins couldn't cut loose when he went with it. Nearest thing at hand was my jug of molasses. I dumped it over the edge, and it was so cold that there larrup froze just as it got to Rawlins. He grabbed it and climbed back up. Saved him from a horrible fate. Ever since, they been calling me Larrup."

Adams guffawed and the horses whinnied and Roma looked up at Larrup with shining eyes. He knew he'd stay on the Double Crown now if he had to whip the foreman every day before breakfast.

They reached the roundup camp in a couple of hours. The whole crew seemed to erupt from the clearing as soon as the rig broke brush.

"Enrique!" Toro bawled. "Larrup, he's back. Now we have spotted pup and son-of-a-gun in a sack. I'll never have to eat that terrible greaser food again."

"Untrammeled," Enrique grinned.

"No, Enrique, please."

"Perspicacious?"

Wrangatang was hanging on the edge of the wagon and bouncing it up and down, Dally ran around doing rope tricks, and Silent Joe Smith sat over by the fire looking mysterious. At last Larrup saw Skid, standing by the chuck wagon, slapping his hat absently against his rawhide leggings. Larrup swung down and Roma started to follow him.

"You take the wagon home, Roma," Adams said. "I'm going to stay and help with roundup for a couple of days."

"You said I could see Larrup," she told him.

"Not today, my dear. Can't you see he'll be too holy busy for little girls?"

She pouted defiantly. "I'm going to stay anyway."

Adams smiled and tucked his chin in. "My dear," he said softly.

She tried to meet his eyes, but at last her gaze dropped. She sent a helpless glance at Larrup, then shook out the reins. Adams turned to the crew, as the wagon rattled away.

"Let's hit the brush, boys," he said. "Today ought to clean up those pastures."

With a great creaking of leather and snorting of animals, they saddled up and lined out into the thickets. Only Adams and Skid were left. The foreman came over to Larrup.

"You don't need to apologize," Larrup said. "I can see it's eating you."

"I didn't stay back to apologize," Skid said. He slapped his hat against his leg. "Where's the book?"

"What book?" Larrup asked.

Adams grinned like a Cheshire. "You didn't think we brought you back 'cause your cooking was so good, did you? We couldn't have you running around loose with that book. Just give it to us now and everything will be all right."

"I don't know what you're gabbing about."

Skid put his hat on. "Then we'll try and make it clear — "

The crackle of brush cut him off. Rigger rode into the clearing.

"Forgot my tie ropes," he said.

Adams chuckled hollowly. "Well, now. Skid was just apologizing to Larrup. Weren't you, Skid?"

"Yeah," Skid said. He caught a look from Adams, and went on to get his roan and Adams walked over to the horse Wrangatang had roped for him out of the remuda. The two men rode out together.

Absently, Larrup got the molasses jug down and upturned it, trying to unclog the neck. But he couldn't do it. Rigger came around the corner of the wagon carrying his short tie ropes.

"Got a quirly?"

"You forgot. I chaw."

Rigger sighed disconsolately. "Was Skid really apologizing?"

273

Larrup glanced up sharply to see a quizzical light in the yellow-haired man's eyes. "What's going on, Rigger?"

The man shook his head. "I don't know, but it's something funny. There's something between Roma and her uncle. Looks like she's afraid of him."

"Would it have something to do with Charlie?"

Rigger frowned. "I been thinking on that. Funny how Skid got upset about you digging a hole to roast that bull's head. Charlie was going to roast a bull's head for the Mexicans the day he disappeared."

Larrup and Rigger looked at each other with the same revelation growing in their eyes. Then Larrup turned to get the spade from the chuck wagon.

"I went ahead and roasted the bull's head after I licked Skid," he said, staring around the clearing. "I was mad. I didn't dig the hole as deep as I would otherwise. I found a soft spot over by that coma tree. Like somebody had already dug it up."

"The place Charlie dug to roast his bull's head," Rigger said. "Somebody's filled your hole in too."

Larrup started digging. He had to go deeper than he had dug to roast his bull's head. They uncovered a man's hand. There was

274

a big gold ring with the initials CM engraved on it.

"Charlie Malloy," Rigger said. "That's his ring, all right."

Larrup turned away, sick at his stomach. Then there was a crackling of brush, and Skid and Adams rode into the clearing.

"We figgered that's what was going on when Rigger didn't come back out," Adams said.

Larrup's lips were white around the edges. "Why did you do it?"

"Charlie got hold of the tally book," Adams said. "He threatened to expose us. Skid had to shoot him. The crew didn't have time to get rid of him any other way. We had to dump him in the hole dug for that bull's head."

"Only we couldn't find the book on him," Skid said. "We figure he hid it somewheres on the chuck wagon. And now Larrup's found it."

"But I ain't — " Larrup protested.

"It don't matter," Adams said. "History repeats itself. You've dug a hole too."

Rigger and Skid and Adams all pulled for their guns at once. Rigger got his free first and shot Adams off his horse. Skid got Rigger in the leg and Rigger flopped over on his face. Larrup threw his spade at Skid. It hit the ramrod's roan and the horse reared up and pitched Skid off its rump. Skid hit rolling and Larrup saw that he didn't have time to get Rigger's gun. He darted behind the chuck wagon with Skid's first shot eating into the wagon bed a foot behind him. He reached the lowered tail gate and started heaving everything in the wreck pan at the foreman.

With pots and pans and skillets flying all around his head and clanging off his shoulders, Skid didn't have much accuracy. He threw up an arm to ward them off, shouting in that black rage.

"Come on out and fight like a man, damn you."

Larrup found he was out of things to throw. Skid straightened up, blinking his eyes, and started to line up his gun. In desperation, Larrup caught the molasses jug by its long black strap and heaved it. Skid tried to fire and dodge at the same time.

The bullet went wild. The jug met his head and he pitched over backward with broken crockery and black molasses pouring over him, lying still when he hit. Larrup ran out to Rigger, who was holding his leg.

"Forget about me," grunted Rigger. "Look what came out of the jug."

There was a little book, rolled up, lying in the pool of molasses by Skid's head. Larrup went over and got it.

"It's a tally book," he said. "That's why the jug was stopped up. Charlie must have rolled the book up and stuffed it in there."

"Look under June the seventeenth," Rigger said.

Fingers sticky with molasses, Larrup found the page for the seventeenth. "Thirty-one steers and ten heifers and three calves," he said.

"That's way off," Rigger said triumphantly. "I made a count of my own that day. We was all working the same pasture and I tallied off over sixty head. That's what Skid and Adams were doing. Giving a short count every roundup and running the difference across the border. No wonder they wanted the beef book. One look and any of us hands could see how far off the tally was."

Roma swung the wagon into the clearing and pulled up, staring wide-eyed at the carnage. "I was afraid something would happen," she said. "I went slow. Heard the shots — "

Her under lip began to tremble and she dropped out of the wagon and ran into Larrup's arms. He held her tight, telling her everything.

After that they bound up Rigger's leg.

His bullet had hit Adams in the shoulder, and the man was just coming round from the shock of that, and of falling from his horse. He tried to bluster, but he was too weak to be very convincing. They did what they could for the wound, and got him in the wagon.

Rigger's eyes lit up as they saw the Bull Durham tag hanging from the man's shirt pocket.

"Wait a minute now," Adams said.

"Don't make me shoot you again," Rigger grinned, pulling the tobacco sack and a book of cigarette papers from the pocket. "I just went through a lot for this quirly."

They tied up the still unconscious Skid, and put him in the back with Adams and Rigger. Then they started back to the ranch with Roma sitting beside Larrup on the front seat.

"Looks like you'll need somebody else to take care of you," he said. "How about a man that can cook?"

"If you'll tell me how you really got your name," she said.

"I was cooking for the Double Crown outfit," he said, hitching his belt. "This evil old uncle was swindling his niece out of her cows. The uncle got suspicious that I knew what was up, and set twenty killers on me.

All I had to defend myself with was this jug of molasses — "

"I know exactly how it ended," she said, snuggling over against him. "And ever since that day they've called you Larrup."

The Devil's Keyhole

PROPOSITION

A lot was happening in Downieville that winter night of 1857. A Sydney Duck had been caught pilfering from sluice boxes down on Goodyear's bar and was getting thirty lashes over in front of the St. Charles House. Poker Nye was reeling down Rogue Alley, pockets and hands filled with pokes of gold dust worth $30,000 which he claimed to have panned in one week up on Musketo Creek. The false-fronted buildings along Main Street were shuddering beneath the impact of the boisterous crowd of miners carrying Signora Biscaccianti and her grand piano on their shoulders to the hall where she was to give a concert. And in the Washington Bar, Glen Anders was getting drunk again.

He had panned enough out of the Yuba to buy a bottle, and sat morosely at one of

280

the unused short card tables over in the corner of the smoky, reeking room. There was a dissolute, bloodshot film to his strange, tawny eyes, and his face had a puffy, unhealthy look. Coppery streaks ran darkly through his hair, originally as bright yellow as his beard, curling like a Viking mane about the base of his neck.

When he first heard the movement beside him, and turned his head up to see the woman, he had only a drunken, befuddled impression of a stunning, Junoesque figure, red hair piled high on her head, flesh like rich cream. Her black velvet basque was laced tightly beneath deep breasts, and her green moire skirt rustled sibilantly with her slightest movement.

"They told me I'd find you here, Mr. Anders," she said. "I'm Opal Mason. I want you to build a bridge for me."

He made a snorting sound. "I don't like jokes when I'm drinking."

"You don't want to insult Miss Mason," said a dry, rustling voice at Anders's elbow.

He shifted his foggy gaze to see a narrow, drawn man, as if some inner smallness kept pinching him in. He had a sharp, jaundiced face, and the notch of the Sydney Duck in his ear — those freed or escaped convicts who had been flooding to California from the English penal colonies in Australia. Anders had seen this one around Downieville, and knew him casually.

"You'd better go out the back way, Dusty," he told the man. "They're whipping one of your brother Ducks over in front of the Saint Charles."

Dusty Warren stiffened, face going pale but a glance from Opal Mason held him. It brought Anders's attention to the other man standing behind him. An immensely tall man, with eyebrows peaked like a devil, and the pointed ears of a satyr.

"Sluefoot," he introduced himself, grinning blandly down at Anders. "Pike County, Missouri. Here to see that you give more careful consideration to Miss Mason's offer of a job. They tell us that before the Marestail, you used to be the best engineer in California."

"Yes," Opal Mason said, sliding into the empty chair at Anders's table. "That's why I've come to you. You know what an enormous demand there is for water, since they started hydraulic mining down around Nevada City. The local supply isn't enough to give those miners one quarter of the water they need. Last year, my father formed the Mason Water Company to bring water in from the outside by canals. Our source will be the North Fork of the Yuba. We've brought our ditches and flumes down as far as the Devil's Keyhole. We've tried three times to build a bridge across the Keyhole, and each time it's collapsed. The last engineers I had out there said it couldn't be done. You're our last hope."

Anders ran his tongue around the inside of his mouth, grimaced. "Why not bypass the canyon?" he asked, recalling the deep gash that some imaginative 'Forty-niner had dubbed "The Devil's Keyhole."

"Victor Robinson and some other speculators have formed a rival water company, with their source at the headwaters of the American. They've been trying to keep us from operating all along. Somehow they've managed to get control of enough of the land on either side of the Keyhole so we can't go around."

He nodded. "And if Robinson beats you to Nevada City, you go bankrupt."

Her chin lifted. "There are other considerations. Robinson's calling his outfit the Placer County Canal Company. You know what prices he and his speculators will charge. Half the miners in Nevada City won't be able to pay it."

"And you're a philanthropist," said Anders.

Her face hardened. "Our crews are made up for the most part of miners who were forced out of their diggings around Nevada City by lack of water. They wouldn't have pitched in if they didn't have faith we would charge no more than a fair price for the water when we got the canal dug."

Anders took a deep drink, wiped the back of his hand across his mouth. "And why did your father send you instead of coming himself?"

Her eyes dropped to the table. "He was killed in the last collapse."

Anders studied that hazily. Then he nodded gravely, saying in a thick, slurred voice, "All right. You've pulled all the stops. You've proved to me that the world will know immeasurable benefit by your philanthropic effort to get the water through. You've brought tears to my eyes with the well-timed tale of your father's death. I still don't want to build your bridge."

She straightened sharply in the chair, face flushed. Then she recovered herself, saying stiffly, "They told me you were a bitter man."

"Suspicious, too," he said. "Why should you want me — knowing what happened at the Marestail?"

"There are some people who don't think you were responsible for that mine collapsing," she said. "The court kept all your papers as evidence for that inquest, and they're still accessible down in 'Frisco. A couple of Eastern engineers were looking over them last year. They said the fault couldn't have been in your calculations. The stresses you figured in that shoring would have taken a maximum load twice as heavy as Garry Hill."

"That gives me great consolation," Anders told her sarcastically. "I still don't want to build your bridge."

"You're being very stubborn," Dusty Warren said, moving around till Anders could see him fully. Something sly was in his pale eyes as he smiled. "They say you studied in Europe."

"England and Italy," Anders muttered. "What's that got to do with it?"

"Like a doctor, or a musician." Dusty's eyes shone. "Man must really be tied up in his work when he goes to those lengths. They say you used to forget about eating and sleeping when you were on a job."

A wicked light rent the film in Anders's eyes. "Dusty — "

"Must be hell to have it taken away, when a man feels that way about his work. How long has it been since you've built a bridge, Anders? How long has it been since you've even seen one?"

285

With an inarticulate sound, Anders lurched to his feet. From the tail of his eye, he saw Sluefoot jump away, reaching for a gun. Anders swept his chair toward the man with a vicious backhand motion, saw it catch the Pike's feet and carry them out from under the man. As the floor shuddered with Sluefoot's falling weight, Dusty made a grab for Anders, pulling one of the slung-shots the Sydney Ducks had made so infamous in San Francisco.

Before he could strike, Anders caught the man's arm, swinging him around into the next table. Dusty crashed against one of the housemen who had been dealing cards there, uptilting the chair so the man had to jump to keep from falling. The Sydney Duck caught at the sliding chair, going to one knee.

Anders had already whirled to grab his bottle by the neck, cracking it on the edge of his own table.

The reek of rotgut whisky filled the room as it flooded over him, dripping onto the floor. Dusty rose up off his knee, staring fixedly at the broken bottle.

The other men at the next table had left their seats now, to spread away from this. Anders walked at Dusty, not slow, not fast, with the broken end of the bottle pointed at the man's face.

A hoarse, gusty sound escaped Dusty as he backed away, making some show of maneuvering in underneath the bottle, to strike at Anders with the slung shot. Anders did not try to circumvent it. He kept right on going with that bottle held in the same position. There was an insidious horror to broken glass that not even naked steel could match.

Still ducking and sidestepping, Dusty kept backing up, unwilling to lunge in. Finally the bar stopped him. Men had spread away on either side to leave him standing there alone. Anders halted in front of him, just beyond the reach of that slung-shot, with the bottle held at the level of his face.

"Now drop it, or I'm coming on in," he told Dusty. "You can't get me quick enough with that slung-shot to stop me from leaving you without a face."

There was no more sound in the saloon. The sweat stood out on Dusty's face like rainwater. His eyes flashed in the light. Anders thought he was coming in anyway. But the fear of that glass had entered his soul. The slung-shot made a subdued thud against the sawdust covering the floor.

As Anders stepped forward to kick it aside, he heard the rustle of feet against that saw-

287

dust behind him, and started to whirl around. The blow on his head set off an explosion within him that blotted the world out, and left nothing.

DEAL

Someone was beating a tom-tom when Glen Anders regained consciousness. It made a great thumping clatter. The reverberations seemed to knock his head from side to side. Then the rancid smell of old hay reached him.

He opened his eyes to see snow-covered timber swelling up on either side of him to meet a sky blue as a turquoise ring. He was lying on the hay. The clatter was the movement of the wagon beneath him. He rolled over to see Opal Mason sitting on a blanket, leaning against the other side of the wagon.

"You really stay on the other side a long time when somebody tucks you in, don't you?" she smiled. "How's the head?"

Face reflecting a surly anger, he reached up to feel the back of his head, without answering. He blinked up at the sky again. The sun was high over the ridges. Ten o'clock in the morning. He had been unconscious just about fourteen hours, then. He tried to figure how far into the mountains this wagon could take them in that time.

"We must be pretty close to the Devil's Keyhole," he said.

"Your head's clear, anyway," she smiled. "Another mile and we'll be there."

He studied her, trying to retain the anger, failing. "You didn't really want me that bad, did you?"

"I told you how much I needed an engineer, Anders," she said. "If you had believed me it would have saved you a bump on the head."

He shifted irritably in the rancid hay, grimacing at the taste of old copper in his mouth. "Haven't you ever heard the old proverb about leading a horse to water?"

"And not being able to make him drink?" she said. She tilted her head back, smiling secretively at the trees. "That may be true if the horse isn't thirsty, Anders. What if he hasn't even seen water for a long time?"

He turned angrily from her, and she let out a bubbling little laugh, saying, "You made the analogy, Mr. Anders." Then she sobered, studying him. "It's not a bad analogy, either. I saw your face when Dusty started riding you about how long you'd been away from your work. There was thirst in it, Anders.

My father always said the luckiest man alive was the one whose work could be as dear to him as food and drink. I guess about the unluckiest, when that work was withheld from him. Dusty couldn't have goaded you to such an anger unless you felt very deeply about it. I'm betting you'd give your soul to get your hands on a bridge again."

He would not look back at her. The little muscles bunched up along the ridge of his unshaven jaw. He was sitting that way when they rounded the turn and came within sight of The Devil's Keyhole.

It was an immense, tumbled gorge, so straight a man could stand at its lower end and see two miles through the notch to the next range of mountains, the rocks of its side so framed as to give it the shape of a keyhole. There was little timber to its massive granite walls, except for a pocket of scrub oak here and there, stripped naked by the winter. At the base of each wall was a talus slope grown over with larch and pine. The abutments for the trestles had been sunk into this slope, and the timber framework extended brokenly upward from these, to grasp mordantly at empty sky line the hands of a skeleton with some of the fingers missing.

The sight of the structure brought Anders

up a little in the wagon. For a moment, the film left his eyes, and they were filled with a sharp calculation. Then he felt the woman's attention on him, and turned angrily away from the bridge, trying to blot out the expression.

"I thought you weren't interested," she said.

"Damn you," he muttered.

"Don't swear at the lady," said Sluefoot softly, from the front seat. "She asked you to go up and take a look at it. Now, are you going, or do you want another lump on your head?"

The wagon track turning off the main road led up only as far as a group of rough log cabins sufficing for the construction camp. From here, a footpath led the rest of the way. Anders and Opal Mason followed it up, trailed by Dusty and Sluefoot. For the first time, Anders saw how the Pike came by his name. One of his feet was turned in, and dragged noticeably.

There was a crew of men clearing away the debris beneath the wrecked bridge, salvaging what materials they could. Overseeing them was a tall, bulky-shouldered man with a leonine mane of red hair and a great, curly beard. Even in the biting cold of the canyon bottom, untouched as yet by morning sun, the man wore nothing over his long-sleeved red flannels, allowing them to suffice for a shirt.

When Opal Mason came up, he turned to walk down from the crew. The woman started to introduce them, but Anders cut her off.

"Never mind. Yuba's worked for me before."

Yuba Carter's smile brought the tip of his tongue out, to flick at his upper lip in a sly way. "Why not tell her where, Anders?"

"If you're talking about the Marestail, she already seems well acquainted with that," said Anders heavily.

"Just like to keep the books straight," said Yuba.

"You didn't keep these books very straight," said Anders. "Who planted these abutments on stratified rock in the first place?" He kicked at the rock upon which the abutments had been placed, until a strip of softer rock chipped from between the stratas of granite. "No wonder your trestles pulled apart, with all the unequal settlement you got here. Who was the last engineer?"

"Yuba was," said Opal defensively. "He was the only one who would stay, Anders. I think you're making a snap judgment of his work — "

"Never mind, Miss Mason," Yuba told

her. "I'd defend my bridge if I thought it was necessary. But I don't think the man who built the Marestail could tell a baby how to build a doll house."

That little muscle twitched beneath Anders's cheek again. He stuffed fisted hands into the pockets of his mackinaw, speaking in a brittle voice. "Seems to me a decent engineer would have considered suspending his bridge, after his trestles came down three times."

Yuba started to answer, sharply, but Opal's voice blocked him off. "Where would we get the material? There isn't any cable for it this side of New York."

"I might be able to get you some number nine, Birmingham," said Anders.

Yuba spat contemptuously. "It would take a thousand strands of that to make the size cable we'd need. And where would we spin it?"

"Don't have to spin it," Anders told him. "Some of the best bridges in Europe are hung with parallel wires."

"Where'll we get beams long enough?"

"Strap them together. Pine has enough shearing resistance for that."

"You dismiss it damn' easy," said Yuba. "Like it was only pine and wire we had to worry about when it comes down. There's going to be men working out there in the middle of that bridge, Anders. How can you be sure it won't be another Marestail?"

Anders felt the blood drain from his face, till it held a sallow, puffy pallor. The crew had gathered around them, now, and there was a sullen, muttering shift among the men at Yuba's words. Yuba's deliberate, constant reference to the Marestail had put Anders at the edge of his control, despite himself. He spoke in a savage voice.

"You talk as if you knew how to build a bridge, Yuba. I wouldn't have much faith in a man after his trestles collapsed three times. You couldn't qualify for engineer when you worked for me. Where did you get your papers for this? Ditch-digger's U?"

It was an insult Yuba could not shrug off, before the men. He made a guttural sound, deep in his throat, and lunged toward Anders. The engineer tried to sidestep, but his feet would not move fast enough. He stumbled, and Yuba came into him.

"That'll do," said Sluefoot sharply. "Unless the both of you want to spend the rest of the winter without ears."

Still against Anders, Yuba turned to look at the lanky Pike, leaning against the abutment, a Peterson five-shot held in his hand.

"Go back down to camp, Yuba," said Opal.

"I want to talk with Anders."

Yuba's glittering eyes crossed Anders's face before he turned away. Anders had never seen such naked hate. Then the man turned to swing down the narrow trail. Small muscles twitched spasmodically through Anders's body as he tried to relax.

"You aren't in very good shape, are you?" Opal asked with an ironic smile.

"Listen," he growled. "Any day I can't take Yuba — "

"You couldn't have taken him today," she said. "One quick move and you start stumbling all over. I'll bet you haven't got any more wind left than an empty sack. You must have been lapping up that rotgut for a long time, Anders."

He lowered his eyes, moving his head from side to side in sullen anger. "The Marestail was a long time ago."

"Two years," she said. "A man can get pretty near the bottom in that time." She shrugged. "Never mind. A few weeks of hard work and no liquor and you'll be as good as new."

"What makes you think I'll stay?"

Her smile held indulgent triumph.

"I saw your eyes, Anders. You'd give your right arm to get your hands on this job."

He met her eyes fully, for the first time.

"All right. I'll stay. On one condition."

"Yuba? I didn't think you were that small."

"I don't want you to fire him," said Anders disgustedly. "Just call off your dogs the next time he asks for it, and let me have him."

She looked surprised. Then that indulgent smile tilted her lips, becoming a rich, throaty laugh, that stirred things deep at the base of him.

"It's a deal, Anders," she chuckled. "It's a deal."

DEFEAT

Those first days were hard for Anders. The labor itself was grim, dawn till dusk, with the temperature often far below zero, the canyon iced-over, wading through snow up to the knees. He was in no shape for it, and it was torture. He was soft and short of wind and his mind would not handle the figures in the swift, efficient way he had known so long ago. He found that mind filled with things he had not thought of in years. Shearing stress and modulus of elasticity. Ultimate resistance to tension when the strength is not axial; the specific gravity of water and pine, granite, and cast-iron.

He sent Opal's agent to a man he had used in San Francisco when he was working at the Marestail, and through him they got the Birmingham wire from a suspension bridge that had not been completed down near Marysville. They had already used straps on the trestles, so Anders did not have to send out for them.

He sensed the doubt and uncertainty of his crew, but they kept in line as long as they were working on solid ground, constructing the piers from which the cables would be suspended. When they were finished, a line was shot across the chasm with the first wires attached. The wires were bound together and strained by their own weight in the dip proposed for the bridge. The completed cable was mounted in saddles atop the piers. On the morning that work on the platform itself was to begin, the trouble came.

Anders had been sleeping in the engineer's shack with Sluefoot, while Yuba had taken to bunking in one of the shacks housing the men. Anders came out that morning and wound his way up the side of the cliff, shivering in the bitter cold. It still cost him a great, labored effort to climb this trail, making him realize every time he did so how sadly out of shape he was. But his eye was clearer, even now, and some of the fat had melted from around his middle.

He was beginning to feel the old eagerness, the old inspiration, at seeing this thing take shape beneath his hands. It was a feeling inexplicable to the person who had never known it, a sensation akin to that felt by an artist, a composer, an inner fire that caught up a man and allowed him to lose himself in the work.

He found the men gathered around the piers at the top of the cliff, and turned to Grenfels, telling him, "Get the jury rig ready. We're going to lower the first section of beam this morning."

Grenfels was a big Swede with cropped hair and a square, bucolic face. Some of these men were hired help, but many were miners forced out of the Nevada City area by lack of water for hydraulicking. Grenfels had been part owner of a coyote hole south of Virginia City. He shifted booted feet uncomfortably beneath him, his cheeks drained white by the cold, and refused to meet Anders's eyes when he spoke.

"I don't know, Anders. If these piers are the same kind as that bridge at San Felipe, and it gave way beneath a platoon of soldiers — "

"What the hell does a pick-and-panner

like you know about any bridge at San Felipe? That was ten years ago, in Spain." Anders faced to Yuba. "You been filling these men with fancy ideas?"

Anders looked over the sullen, furtive group of men, some unwilling to face him, others watching him defiantly. He knew the Marestail was in their minds, and that logic would not suffice here. He could quote facts and figures all day and fail to make a dent in the prejudice that Yuba's insidious suggestions had formed.

"I never sent any man out where I wouldn't go myself," Anders told them. "Put that jury rig on the cables, Grenfels. I'll tie in these first sections myself."

They slung the ropes over the cable up by the saddles, from which hung a temporary platform. This was loaded with tie-rods and cast-iron straps and the necessary tools. Anders stepped aboard, and they slowly allowed the jury rig to slide down the dip of the cable. He gave a nod when he was at the right distance to drop the first section of the main beam, and they halted the platform.

There was a wind coming up the canyon, and the cables were creaking mournfully as they swayed. The gorge yawned a thousand feet beneath him, an awesome, tumbled abyss, ice gleaming on its rocky walls in the early morning light. He knew a sudden sharp giddiness, and swung his eyes quickly from the sight. There was an insidious reluctance within him to release his grip on the ropes, but they were making ready to lower the first section of beam out to him now. He had to remove his gloves to work. The chill bit into his fingers like an icy knife.

He fumbled bolts and tie-rod up off the floor of the platform, and raised up to start fastening the rod in place to the cable. The platform itself was shaking and trembling in the wind now. He had to chip ice from the cable before he could get his bolts in place. It was really a job for two men, at the least. He was reaching up to slip the tie-rod onto its bolt when his foot slipped.

He dropped the rod, caught wildly at the ropes, hearing the sharp gasping sound from the crowd of men watching. He hung there for a moment, watching that tie-rod turn over and over as it fell into the canyon.

He lowered himself to the platform again and crouched there, trying to down the nausea in him. Then, with a soundless curse, he got another tie-rod, and climbed back up to put it in place. He finished this, and dropped back to the platform, giving them the nod to lower the first length of pine beam. Its end crashed down onto the platform. The straps and rod connections were already bolted in place, and all he had to do was hitch up the tie-rods.

It was a bitter, maddening battle, out there on the swaying, buffeted platform, but he finally got the beam connected. Then he climbed up to attach the tie-rods on the other side. He saw that his grim battle was winning them over, however.

They dropped the next beam out to him. He finished this, then they swung the tie-beam out. When he had this in, he raised his head to see them watching him. Grenfels was standing the closest to the edge, eyes on those beams, and Anders knew what was in the man's mind.

As more beams and rods were added, the weight of the structure itself would increase. Inevitably, the men would have to put their own weight on those beams, during the course of their work. Actually, the suspension bridge's own weight was a much smaller factor than the weight of a bridge supported on trestles. But these men had never worked with suspension before, and had already seen their trestle bridge collapse three times. Anders realized the proof had to be graphic. He stepped off the platform onto the beam, hanging to the tie-rod.

"There," he shouted, above the buffeting roar of the wind. "You've got a shearing strength of over four tons to the square inch here. The whole bunch of you could line up on this beam and she wouldn't go down. What are you afraid of?"

Yuba cupped his hands to his mouth. "What about this wind? It's going to play hob with your stresses. Get enough oscillation and you'll pull the platform apart."

"I've already accounted for that," shouted Anders.

"Yeah — on paper," called Yuba. "The Marestail shouldn't have collapsed, on paper, but she did."

"Damn you, Yuba," shouted Anders, wheeling to make his way right down the beam toward the men. "There isn't a chance this — "

There was a groaning sound as a new blast of wind caught the platform. One of Anders's hands slipped on the icy cable. He shifted his weight wildly, trying to catch a new grip. There was a shriek beneath him. He felt solidity fade from under his feet. His hands came free of the cable and he was falling.

The beam had sheared free of its strap under him, and swung in toward the cliff as he fell. He felt his feet strike it, and knew it would be his body next, and then he would be gone from it.

He grabbed wildly for the timber. He felt the square, biting edges of it, hugged it into him. The timber finished its quarter arc, slamming in against the wall of the canyon.

He felt himself sliding down its length, and tightened his grip, groaning aloud with the pain of splinters eating at his hands. He got his legs twined about it, then, and stared upward.

Twenty feet above him the beam was tied into the piers on a swivel connection, planned so the beam could rise and fall with the movement of the bridge. He knew the connection would hold, but the wind was buffeting at him, and he was beginning to swing like a pendulum against the rock face.

Grenfels and the others had gotten a rope and were lowering it to him. Hugging the beam with one hand and his legs, he freed the other hand to catch the rope, swing it around him, caught it up in a hitch. Slowly, painfully they began to pull it upward. He was surprised to see Yuba among the others hauling on the rope.

Then, abruptly, Yuba slipped and fell into

Grenfels. The rope slid from Grenfel's hands. Anders felt himself drop, saw it jerk the rope from other hands, felt his chest swell with the breathless anticipation of going on down.

Then, from behind, Sluefoot appeared. Yuba was down on his knees, blocking off the others in his struggle to keep the rope. Sluefoot kicked him in the stomach, doubling him over and knocking him completely free of the press. Then the big Pike turned to grab the rope himself. Anders hung against the cliff, holding tight to that hitch, his shirt wet with sweat in a temperature near zero.

When they finally hauled him over the edge, he crouched weakly on his hands and knees, regaining strength. Yuba was on his feet, holding his stomach, those eyes glittering balefully at Sluefoot.

"I won't forget that," he said.

"Why, now," drawled Sluefoot, grinning. "You were fouling up that line so much they would have dropped Anders."

"They should have," snarled Yuba, transferring his anger to Anders. "Any man who'd risk a crew's life on that kind of a bridge. I told you a suspension wouldn't work, Anders — "

Anders got groggily to his feet, breathing

heavily. "That beam has a maximum resistance to shearing of nearly four tons a square inch, Yuba. How in hell — "

"Sure, sure, I know," said Yuba. "You had it figured all out on paper. Paper figures don't do much good when you're out there a thousand feet above the ground. What if the whole crew had depended on your figures, Anders? You'd have fifty more men to add on that hundred who died in the Marestail cave-in — "

Anders lurched forward, grabbing at him in rage. "Damn you, Yuba, you know that's not the truth. Something was faulty with that beam — "

"Something was faulty with the engineer, you mean," Yuba said hoarsely. "Take your hands off me, Anders."

"Not till you quit putting things in these men's minds," panted Anders.

"I'll put something in your mind," Yuba told him, grabbing at his arm.

Anders tried to pull away. His reflexes came too slow. Yuba caught his arm, swinging it up to sink a fist in his belly. Anders went down, doubled over. He rolled it off on a shoulder and came to hands and knees, trying to regain his feet.

He thought he had been fast, but Yuba reached him before he had balance. He bent forward, hugging arms in to his head like a bear. Yuba's blows battered against this shield, then one tore his arms apart, rocked his head.

He saw Yuba's belly, struck with all his strength. Yuba grunted. He waited for the man to double over and uncover. Another blow rocked his head. The whole world spun and he was on his back again, realizing dimly, unbelievingly that his blow to Yuba's belly had not even stopped the man.

For the third time he started to get up. He tasted salt, dripped blood the color of claret. Yuba came in with his boots while Anders was only on his knees. The first kick caught Anders in the ribs. He did a flip-flop. The second one tore at his shoulder, rolling him over and over. He tried to come to his knees again. The third kick caught him still trying, slamming into his face, and he sank to the ground.

He tried to get up again, could not move. He heard Yuba's heavy, panting breath, right above him, heard the muted scrape of the crowd's feet, surrounding him. He lay sodden and inert, muscles unable to answer his will, and wanted to cry because he could not get up and smash the man's face in. He had not known such utter, humiliating defeat since the Marestail.

It was Sluefoot who helped him down to one of the cabins. Opal came, in a few minutes, with Dusty Warren. A sly grin broke across the man's narrow face as he saw Anders's condition.

"You should of waited a few more weeks before tackling him," Dusty said. "You didn't think seven or eight hikes up that trail would get back reflexes you'd taken years to lose, did you?"

Opal turned angrily on Dusty. "You don't have to kick a man when he's flat on his back, do you? Get out, both of you. I want to talk with him."

When they were gone, she got a cloth from a shelf, dipping it in the water butt by the door, and sat down on the edge of the bunk, wiping off his bloody face. He lay with his eyes closed, body stiff with humiliation.

"Grenfels told me what happened," she said. "Do you think the wind was really the cause of that beam slipping?"

"I can't see how it could be," he said. "I know it couldn't shear the beam, and I don't see how it could have pulled free of the strap. Those bolts were tight when I checked them. Something else — "

He trailed off, sinking defeatedly back into the bunk, and was silent for a time. Finally he said, in a husky voice, "I suppose they won't try again."

"You've lost their confidence," she told him. "There's talk among a lot of them about quitting."

"Instigated, no doubt, by Yuba."

Through the damp rag, he felt angry tension stiffen her hand. "I didn't expect that from you. Can't you even take a beating decently?"

"I looked at him in the same light before we fought, if you remember," he said.

"Just because he worked for you on the Marestail," she said hotly. "Maybe he was right, to begin with — "

He caught her hand, pulling it off his face, to surge up angrily. "And maybe I was right, when I didn't want to work for you in the first place — "

"Let go," she said, trying to twist free. It brought her deep breasts round against him. He felt the tremor shake his body, and his arm went about her without any conscious volition, pulling her whole upper body down to him.

Her lips were stiff as her body in that first moment. Then the sand leaked out of her and her body melted against him, her lips flaring like ripening fruit. It was a stark, elemental moment, that left them both breathing heavily when she finally pulled away.

They stared at each other a long time without speaking. With an abrupt motion, she rose and walked over to face the wall.

"Never mind," he said, swinging his feet to the floor. "I'm going."

She spoke in a muffled little voice, still faced away from him. "I don't want you to, Anders. That isn't it at all."

"Is it that you couldn't love a man who built the Marestail?" he asked. She whirled toward him, denial in her parted lips, but he would not let her voice it.

"I can understand, Opal. A woman must have faith in the man she loves. I guess I haven't given you much reason for faith." His shoulders sagged. "Maybe it *was* in my calculations. Maybe Yuba was right."

"Anders — " she held a hand out to him — "no — "

A knock on the door brought startled surprise to her face. Then, in a low, trembling voice, she asked who it was. Sluefoot answered, saying Grenfels was with him.

Anders opened the door. A twenty-foot pine beam lay between the men, one end

309

sunk in the snowdrift piled up against the cabin wall.

"Thought you might like to see this," said Grenfels. "I couldn't understand why that beam would fall either. Couple of others and I pulled it in, matched it up with the other beams of the load. It was three inches short."

Anders frowned. "Those iron straps covered six inches of the beam-end. If it had sheared off it would have been six inches short."

Sluefoot pursed his lips, nodded. "Don't need no engineer to figure that out. The short end had been sawed right where the bolt went through. Enough solid wood left to hold under ordinary circumstances. But if any weight at all was put on it, and the beam got to yawing around in the wind, that'd pull it right out of the straps."

Anders was still frowning at them. "Who do you figure set it up like that?"

Grenfels shrugged. "The strap would cover the sawed section. That's why we didn't spot it when we carried the load up this morning. All the straps had already been bolted in place."

Anders stared at them questioningly. "The possibility has been in my mind a long time that Yuba could have been planted by Victor Robinson's Placer County Canal Company to see that this bridge didn't get built across the Keyhole."

"If he was," grinned Sluefoot, "he must have figured his job was done. A lot of the men have quit already, and he was one of them."

Anders turned to Opal, and she was smiling now. "We'll get you another crew," she said.

Sluefoot shook his head dubiously. "That's easier said than done, Miss Opal. When those men get back to Downieville with news of what happened up here under Anders, there won't be a laborer you could hire for his weight in gold."

"There's still miners," said Grenfels. "They know what kind of prices they'll have to pay if Placer County gets their canal through first. I'm going down to Nevada City, Miss Opal. I'll get you a crew."

Sluefoot watched the man head off down the hill toward the barracks to get his duffel. Then he turned and walked to his bunk, dragging out his own duffel bag.

"Back in Pike County they taught me to always look ahead. I saw you was heading for real trouble up here, and seeing as you didn't pack one, I meant to give you this. I guess I didn't get it to you in time. Maybe you'll still be able to use it."

Anders looked at the old Colt conversion Sluefoot fumbled from the duffel bag, and felt a new warmth for the immense, droll Pike steal up his spine.

"What'll I do with it, now that Yuba's gone?"

"When he hears you're going to start again, he's liable to be back," said Sluefoot, pressing the butt of the gun into his hand. "This time, he won't be able to stand back and use your reputation to break things up. This time, he'll have to come loaded for bear."

COMEBACK

After that they were racing against the winter. The ice was already beginning to break up on the larger rivers, and the snow had melted in the lower valleys. In a few weeks, spring would bring its torrents down the canyons, and if they weren't ready to take that water clear into Nevada City, all their work would be in vain.

Grenfels brought his crew back, all miners, now, men who had been waiting in the lower camps for the thaw so they could go back to work. They weren't as skilled as the other crew had been, but they had more heart,

312

for this water meant their very existence to them.

Anders pushed himself to the breaking point. But the Spartan existence was having its effect on him. He was still young enough so that even the driven exhaustion of the daily grind could not hold back the change that was taking place. He could climb that trail from camp to bridge without being winded, now. The fat had melted off his belly, his face was no longer puffy and sallow, it was hard and lean and burned dark by the sun. His eyes and mind were clear, and he had lost that sullen defensiveness.

They finished the platform and flume across the chasm on the very day that a man brought down word of the river's final break-up, with the water ready to divert into their ditches whenever they wanted. Another crew had already finished the ditches and flumes on down into Nevada City, so they were ready.

The night before the dikes were to be opened, the crew got together in one of the cabins and threw a party. Up to now, Anders had kept close guard on every phase of the job, knowing that Placer County was not through trying to stop them. Tonight, however, the only men he could persuade to stand guard on the bridge were Grenfels and

Dusty Warren. He put Grenfels on the same side as the camp and Dusty on the other.

He himself walked the night out, jumpy with expectancy, making a constant tour of every approach to the bridge, the Colt conversion Sluefoot had given him in his belt. Opal brought him coffee near dawn. They were too jumpy, too exhausted to talk much. After a while she went back to try and get a little sleep.

Then vague dawn light peeled blackness off the rock faces, exploring the depths of the canyon with hesitant fingers. The bridge was beginning to sway with morning wind as he crossed its fifteen-hundred-foot length to give his remaining coffee to Grenfels. The man was staring through the dense, black timber toward the south.

"Placer County?" asked Anders.

"I guess we're all thinking about them," said the Swede. "I hear they haven't got their ditch through yet. We've beat them."

"Martin will open the dikes at six this morning," said Anders. "Water'll hit here pretty soon afterward. If Robinson's Canal Company means to do anything, it'll come in these next few minutes, Grenfels. I'm going down to the barracks and try to get a few more men up here to watch with you."

He went back over the bridge, eyes red-rimmed from lack of sleep. There was nobody at the other end.

His hand dropped to the Colt, and he whipped from one side to the other, searching the timber here for what could have happened to Dusty. At this moment, there was the thud of feet from the trail, and he saw the man panting up toward him.

"Underneath the bridge," Dusty gasped at him. "I think they're planting dynamite. I was starting down when I saw you."

"You stay here," Anders told him, already running down the steep trail. He had his gun out now.

In order to work on the piers from under the bridge, they had made a footpath to the shelf down there, cutting off from the main trail. There was a sharp turn from the trail into this path, rounding a granite boulder higher than a man. Anders took it on the run and came face to face with Sluefoot, almost crashing into him.

"Dusty said some Placer County men are down here," Anders shouted, trying to get around him on the narrow trail.

That lazy smile unfurled Sluefoot's lips. "He's right. Fact is, one of them is standing behind you right now."

Anders started to wheel instinctively, but Dusty Warren's voice stopped that. "Come any farther around and you'll get this slung-shot on your head."

Sluefoot pulled his Paterson Colt, saying, "You can drop your own gun, Anders. I gave it to you so you wouldn't pick one up that might hurt somebody. There ain't no powder in the shells."

Anders could not help lowering his eyes to the conversion. With a muted, growling sound, he dropped it onto the trail.

"You've been working for Placer County all along, then?" he said.

Sluefoot grinned. "It was easy for me. Nobody knew me in this section. And Dusty had forked for Opal's dad in 'Frisco. Placer County wanted more than one card up their sleeve."

"You sawed that beam?"

"Yuba did. The men were just waiting for you to make a slip. Yuba figured it wouldn't take much to make them lose faith in the suspension bridge. He would have been right, if Grenfels hadn't found that sawed beam. The crew didn't stop to figure how it was that your weight could shear a beam that had resistance of over four tons the square inch. They just thought it was Anders of the Marestail at work again."

"Why did you bother to save my life when that beam failed?" Anders asked.

"Opal was coming up the trail," Sluefoot told him. "She would have become suspicious at the way Yuba was fouling up everybody on that rope. We didn't think it was necessary to kill you then. We thought you was finished here as it was." The grin left his face. "But now things are different. We waited till this last minute so there wouldn't be time for anybody to put up another bridge after this one came down. And you're going down with it, Anders, just to make sure there ain't a slip-up."

Sluefoot cocked his gun. At first, Anders thought the sharp, clicking sound following that was an echo. Then he heard the woman speak.

"I've got mine cocked too, Sluefoot. Shoot him and I shoot you."

It snapped Sluefoot's head upward, as if his eyes were trying to focus on something back of Anders, taking them from the engineer in that moment. Anders lunged forward, knocking the gun aside with a sweep of his hand. Sluefoot tried to dodge the other blow, but Anders brought it through his blocking arm into his belly. Sluefoot draped over his fist like a wet rag.

Anders wheeled away from his falling body, to see Dusty Warren standing in his original spot, slung-shot gripped impotently in one

317

hand, with Opal standing farther back along the trail, an old Springfield musketoon in her hand.

"I couldn't sleep, Anders," she said. "I — "

"Hold them here," he whipped out at her. "They wouldn't have decoyed me down here unless something was meant to happen up on top."

He went up the trail to the piers as hard as he could run. He swung around one pier, the entire length of the bridge leaping into his vision, with Yuba crouched about twenty feet out, over a bundle of dynamite sticks.

Anders's feet raised an unholy rattle on the wooden flume as soon as he left solid ground, in his run. Yuba jumped to his feet, match in hand still unlit, and grabbed for a gun. But Anders's running passage had started the bridge to oscillating, and its back-swing pitched Yuba over to the other side, just as he gained his feet. It gave Anders time enough to reach the man before he could get the gun out.

He went bodily into Yuba, grasping for the gun. Yuba tried to jerk it free, and his swinging hand struck a tie-rod. He cried out in pain as the gun flew from numbed fingers, spinning off into space. Anders shifted for a blow, but Yuba recovered himself, grappling Anders and heaving him back.

Anders stumbled backward across the ten-foot breadth of the flume to the other side. The planks were only three feet high on the sides, and he would have flipped over if he hadn't caught a tie-rod. He held himself there a moment, bending outward from the rod, toward Yuba. The other man was in a crouch at the other side, nursing his numb hand. They stood that way a moment, on the swaying bridge, with the cables creaking above them, each man waiting for the other to leap.

"You seem to favor dynamite," Anders panted. "Is that what you used at the Marestail?"

"The Marestail caved in because you're a lousy engineer," snarled Yuba.

"This job has given me a chance to add things up, Yuba," said Anders. "A company calling themselves Sierra Gold started tunneling into the east side of Garry Hill as soon as the Marestail Company went bankrupt from that cave-in. Victor Robinson was rumored to have controlling interest in Sierra Gold. Were you working for him then, too?"

Yuba spat, a vicious look twisting his mouth. "So maybe I was. So maybe Robinson had spent too much money prospecting around Garry Hill to lose it when somebody else found the gold and hired you to sink

319

a shaft. It won't do you any good to know it, Anders."

Anders tried to find some emotion, with this realization, after so many years of bitter ostracism, that he had come face to face with the man who had ruined him. But he could feel nothing. He only knew that he had to get Yuba off the bridge before the water came. He lunged away from the side at the man.

At the same time, Yuba jumped toward him. Anders dodged in under an outflung arm, striking for the body. Yuba blocked it, counterpunched. It was all so fast that the men were moving with instinctive reaction now. And the engineer's reflexes were different from what they had been that first time.

He did not even know how he blocked Yuba's counterpunch. He only knew that it rolled off a shoulder. He saw the surprise on Yuba's face. That was blocked off by his own fist, rocking Yuba's whole head back. He went on in, punching again, until Yuba was up against the side of the flume.

Here the man caught a tie-rod, jack-knifing both legs up between them, and then straightened them viciously. It was something even Anders's new responses could not block. It shoved him back off balance to go rolling down the splintery planks of the platform. He came to his hands and knees the same way he had that first time, with Yuba coming in right on top of him.

He saw Yuba's foot before his face, ducked aside. He had a contorted glimpse of the surprise of Yuba's face again, as the kick missed. Anders caught the leg while it was still off the ground, heaved against it.

The whole bridge shuddered with Yuba's toppling weight. Beyond the man, Anders saw the first torrent of muddy water leaping out of the ditch onto the bridge. There was a wild, untrammeled force to it that would sweep them helplessly along if it caught them down here, probably spilling them right over the edge of the flume.

Anders tried to scramble erect, but Yuba caught him. The man had not seen the water, and took the trembling to be caused by their struggle. Anders slugged at his face. Yuba rolled aside, hooked a leg behind Anders' knee, pulled him off balance. They both rolled heavily into the side of the flume.

Stunned, Anders had a distorted view of Yuba's rage-twisted face swinging down against him, one fist raised to finish it. Anders rolled his head aside in the last instant, heard Yuba's fist go into the planks with a dull knocking sound. He came up beneath the man, getting to one knee. From here, supporting Yuba's whole weight with one arm, he struck the man in the belly, blowing his cork in a last, violent effort.

Yuba staggered backward, a sick look to his face. The bridge surged upward beneath Anders, rising like a wave before the forces of mass in motion, and he knew the water must be right behind. He leaped for the side, grabbing at a tie-rod. The wild water caught at his feet, swinging him with it. But he had the tie-rod, and hung on grimly, kicking desperately till he found the solid edge of plank beneath him.

Yuba was in the center of the flume when the water caught him. An awesome terror blotted that sick look from Anders's blow off his face, as the water caught him up. He disappeared for an instant, then bobbed up like a cork, arms flailing, mouth open to scream. Water filled it and he went under again. This first rush of uncontrolled water was spilling over the sides by the gallons as it swept down the flume. The next time Yuba came up, he was spilled over the edge in one of these waves. His hands caught for tie-rods, slipped off. He turned over and over as he fell, a thousand feet down.

Slowly, painfully, up on the side, out of the main current, Anders made his way down the bridge, going from one tie-rod to the next, feet constantly slipping off the edge beneath the buffeting of that spilling water. He was near exhaustion when he finally reached the piers, where Opal was waiting with the crew. They had Sluefoot and Dusty backed into one of the piers, with guns on them.

Anders gestured wearily at the riotous water racing across the bridge. "There it is. Nevada City will have enough water, at decent prices."

"And Glen Anders is back in the engineering business for good," she smiled, a young, glowing look to her face.

"I guess I owe a lot of it to you," he said.

"You can pay me back."

"You got another bridge to build?" he asked.

"There are other things beside bridges, Glen."

He stared into her eyes, seeing what was there, and when he finally spoke, it was in a low, husky voice, that none but they could hear.

"I guess there are, Opal. Would you turn away, now, if I kissed you?"

"Never again, Glen."

"Then let's get away from here," he said. "I'm going to make you prove that."

Saddlemates

In the deep creek bottoms, firelight caught the mottled leaf pattern of the near brush, turned the lower trunks of white birch to bleached bones, made a flickering uncertain visage of the face. There was a raw, harsh masculinity to the long, belligerent jaw, a sense of infinite sun and wind and broad untrammeled space to the obliquity of wind-burned cheeks.

The man had been squatting like this a long time, watching his pot of coffee come to a boil, when the sound of a horse caused him to rise. It brought the rest of his body into view with a dim flash of age-whitened ducking jacket, a brazen wink of shells in a sagging gun belt. The horse was a bay, with a coat red as wet blood. The rider was a woman, swinging off and turning to come forward confidently.

"Sorry I'm late, Garry — " she started, then broke off, staring at him.

"You've got the wrong Hackett," he smiled. "I'm Nye."

The puzzlement had not left her great, dark eyes. "Garry didn't tell me he had a brother."

"Not brother," said Nye. "Father."

Her black hair swirled angrily against the shoulders of her jacket when she tossed her head. "Did you talk Garry out of coming, or something?"

"I just came a little ahead of him, that's all. I couldn't help seeing your note the other day, asking him to meet you here, at this old corral. Why don't you ever sign your notes, Pony?"

She had a large, lush body, something sensual about its slightest movement, as she turned partly away from him in a sullen, pouting way. "Go on, preach your sermon. I've heard them before."

"I just wanted to meet you," he said. "Garry's told me about you, and he's been coming into Buffalo Bow a lot to see you since we started hiking hay up on the Buford place."

Crow's-feet formed their myriad tracks at the corners of his gray eyes, giving them the sense of strangely shy, painfully gained wisdom. But as he studied her, the wry speculation left his face, replaced by a haunted, almost tortured luminosity to his eyes. She turned back to him, a disturbed frown on her face, as she saw the look.

"And now that you have met me?"

"Aren't you a little old for Garry?"

"I thought you weren't going to preach?"

"I can't help wondering what you see in him — a kid, a shabby, penniless hay-hiker like him, so rough — so — "

"You don't seem very proud of your son," she murmured.

"More proud than you realize. Only I don't take my pride in the same things you would."

"Maybe he has a way with women," she said huskily, moving toward him. "Maybe he gets it from you. If I am a little old for him, maybe I should have seen you first, Nye Hackett — "

He moved back sharply, searching her face for the mockery. But her faint smile held no derision. All he saw in her eyes was the candid, provocative smolder.

They were still looking at each other when Garry rode into the firelight. He stopped his horse, staring at them, and it would have been difficult to tell him from Nye, in this vague illumination. His face held the identical raw masculinity in the long prominent bones of jaw and brow, his body was formed of the same driving, rawhide lines.

"Why didn't you ask me, Nye," he said; "I would have introduced you."

"I did ask you," Nye told him soberly. "If you'll remember."

"So you sneak around behind my back like I was a kid."

"Now Garry," placated the woman.

"You sound quite motherly in his wagon," Garry snapped, wheeling toward her in the saddle. "Did you get some amusement from discussing me while I wasn't here?"

"You're acting like a fool!" snapped Pony.

"I'm glad to know what you think of me," he told her. "I wish I'd found out earlier."

Firelight caught the hot, ruddy flush of his face as he swung his horse out beyond the corrals, and then he was gone into the underbrush. The woman turned an arched brow to Nye.

"He's got a hot head."

"He was cocked for it," Nye told her. "He and I had an argument about this before I left."

He turned and went for his own horse, hitched to a bar of the old, unused corrals here.

The moon had lifted a saffron sphere over the Owl Creeks, but Nye found it was still a dark ride through Paintbrush Gap. It was a tortured, winding gorge, walled high with escarpments of sandstone. Suddenly, however, he was up against this wall itself, and it took him a few minutes of milling about to realize he must have turned off the main cut into a box canyon. It required a long time to trace his way back into the Gap. The mouth of that spur canyon was so narrow and so blocked with buckbrush that it would be hidden to anyone coming down the main trail.

This did not remain long in his mind, however, as he broke free of the Gap onto the road leading toward Buffalo Bow. Ahead the lights of town started winking their seductive invitation. He pulled his horse down, reluctant to go on, now. He had hoped to catch Garry before the boy reached Buffalo Bow. With a savage little shake of his head, he reined his black mare, Tar Baby, on once more.

The towering, timber-shrouded hills pushed the buildings of Buffalo Bow in against each other along the main street like driftwood piled along the line of high tide. The usual Saturday-night crowds of cowhands filled the streets and the saloons lining the avenue.

When Nye found the boy's horse, among half a dozen others at a tie rack, it was still steaming, and he figured he was only a few minutes behind Garry.

The boy was still standing by one of the dry, potted palms near the entrance, surveying the bar somberly. Nye tucked a hard hand under one elbow.

Garry turned sharply, overhead lights flashing blankly against the surface of his eyes. Then all the defiance leaked out of him.

"I guess a drink wouldn't have helped much anyway," he said, not meeting Nye's eyes. "I guess I was hoping you'd come."

"I'm glad you were, son," said Nye. "You know I wouldn't deliberately set out to humiliate you."

"I'm sorry, Dad," said Garry. Then he shrugged helplessly. "But I just couldn't help feeling the way I did — "

"Of course you couldn't," said Nye. "A man's always a little sensitive where a woman's concerned. Can we forget it now?"

The boy grinned broadly. "Sure. Sure we can."

"Let's go get these whiskers off our jaws, and some grub in our bellies. Maybe we'll feel more like drinking then."

Their walk was jaunty, out through the

swinging doors, and to the barber-shop, a few doors down.

A lone customer was just rising from one of the chairs, and Garry brought to a halt like a viciously bitten horse. Nye saw a tall, spare man, a hint of gray at the temples of close-cropped black hair, a mouth that formed a humorless line across the gaunt bones of his jaw. There was something sardonic about the way he tilted his head at Garry.

"Think she'll like you any better with a shave?" he asked.

"It always struck me," said Garry, "that a man who was sure of himself didn't have to ask questions."

"I'm sure of myself," said the other. "That's why I hope you give heed to what I said last time. I don't want to see you with her again. Or hear of it."

Garry looked at the sheriff's badge on the man's vest. "You're in an enviable position. Bring that tin star in on whatever you want."

"I told you I never mixed my public duties with my private affairs," said the sheriff. "If I did anything concerning you, it would be personal. Very personal." He turned to slip his coat and hat from the rack. Wheeling back, he allowed his eyes to touch Nye's briefly. "You look like a more sensible man than your brother," he said. "Why don't you keep him out of this trouble?"

He did not wait for an answer, shouldering by them, slipping on his coat as he went through the door.

"What's the sheriff's name?" asked Nye.

"Means," said Garry, slapping his battered Stetson on the rack.

"You and him having a little play over Pony?"

"I don't know," said Garry sullenly, dropping into the barber's chair Sheriff Means had just vacated.

Nye could see both barbers watching the sheriff across the street, now. Then it was the pair of cowhands, veering around Sheriff Means with more than the usual respect for the law. In the illumination of oil lights on the facade of a saloon across the street, Nye saw a group of idlers turn to watch Means. It brought Nye's attention, for the first time, to how high and square the man held his shoulders.

"The sheriff seems to attract a lot of interest," observed Nye, turning to seat himself in the empty chair.

"It's a busy town," muttered the barber, blotting it out with the hurried rattle of his clippers.

Nye leaned back, closing his eyes, but had not yet relaxed when the clippers stopped.

The metallic abruptness of it brought Nye's eyes open. He heard the chair creak beneath the sharp, forward inclination of his body, with sight of the man now in the doorway.

His fustian of robin's-egg blue was padded heavily to accentuate shoulders already remarkable for their breadth. He stood chewing on a black cigar and staring after the sheriff with his heavy brows drawn in so tight by his concentrated scowl that they almost hid his eyes.

Sheriff Means had gained the walk across the street and turned southward, disappearing at last in the deep shadow beneath an unlit overhang. At this moment, Pony Adams came into view, pulling her bay into the hitchrack of the saloon across the way. She was beyond Garry's vision, leaning back as he was in his chair. The man at the door did not look at her either. He seemed to realize how he was masticating his stogie, and removed it from his mouth with a vicious sweep of one arm, turning inside the door to spit at a brass cuspidor. This brought his glance onto Nye.

He did not try to hide the surprise widening his sensual, blue-lidded eyes.

"Well, Nye Hackett," he said, finally, "when did you break out of jail?"

Nye felt the planes of his face go tight.

"You always had a poor taste in jokes, Bob."

Bob Kordes smiled. "I'm not joking, Nye. You sure couldn't have gotten out any other way."

Nye was aware of Garry's quickened attention, now, and said it in a careful, controlled way. "I've been out of jail fifteen years, Bob. I thought you'd know."

Kordes shrugged. "I've been up here for a long time, Nye. How would I know?" He tipped his head backward: "Benny."

The man had been blocked off by Kordes's immense body. He moved into view, taking Kordes's coat as he shrugged out of it. There would always be such men with Kordes, these small, nervous men with narrow faces and eyes that never seemed to focus on any single object and the restless, servile hands to take his coat or light his cigar or do whatever else he needed.

Kordes let his sleepy glance touch Garry indifferently. "Your son?"

Tension had stiffened Nye's hands beneath the barber's sheet. "That's right."

"I thought Debbie was bringing him up," murmured Kordes.

"She left him with the Carters," Nye told him.

"What a happy childhood," snorted Kordes. "A ma who didn't want him and

333

a pa up for murder."

Nye saw Garry's body draw up beneath the barber's chest. He felt the taut, bleak reaction filling his own face, felt the old, raw temper of his youth surging up from the coals of it that had never quite died, a temper he had spent the last twenty years trying to drain out of himself. Kordes belonged to the past, that youth — maybe that was why he could touch the emotions of it so swiftly.

"You want to be careful you only came in for a shave, Bob," said Nye, gripping the arms of the chair tightly. Then he saw the expression in the man's eyes, and the intent, and knew he would not be able to block his own reaction to it any more than he could stop his breathing.

"You're the one who wants to be careful," Kordes told him. "I'm not Halloran, Nye. I'm not unarmed, and my back isn't turned."

Nye put his boots on the floor and lunged out of the chair with the sheet still on him, grabbing Kordes by the lapels of his marseilles waistcoat with both hands. "Tell my boy you never said that, Bob, or I'll knock it back down your throat and all your teeth with it."

Kordes tilted his head back slightly. "Benny."

It brought movement from the other man

in a swift, habituated response. As he took one step aside to get from behind Kordes, Nye jumped at Benny, catching him before he had even gotten to the tails of his coat far enough off the butt of his gun to draw it. Nye's lunging fist to the solar-plexus carried Benny back against the wall. The man groaned, doubling forward to hug his middle. Nye caught him by one shoulder and spun him around, kicking him out the door. The man stumbled across the sidewalk and went face-first into the mud of the street.

Nye was already turning back. Kordes had faced about to see the finish of it, without making any other overt move. Garry was still sitting in the barber's chair, but his gun was in his lap.

"He wouldn't have done anything," Garry told Nye.

"He wouldn't have anyway," said Nye thinly.

"Why should I?" said Kordes. His face seemed unruffled, but small, violent little lights kindled in the heavylidded somnolence of his eyes. He glanced at his cold, battered stogie, held it out without looking toward the barbers. One of them took it from him, tossing it in the spittoon. "There are always men like Benny to do it for me," Kordes told Nye. "There will be another one. Sooner or later. You know that, Nye."

Nye and Garry walked southward from the barbershop, silence driving its stiff, uncomfortable wedge between them. Garry was the first to break it, an effort in his voice.

"That's why you didn't want to come to town?" he said. "That's why you didn't want me to see Pony."

"It's why I didn't want to come to town," Nye told him. "I found out Kordes sat a fancy saddle in politics here the third day we were pitching hay for Buford. I'd hoped to make a stake and get away before something like this happened. I just didn't want to get mixed up with him again, Garry, that's all."

"You knew Kordes back in Waco?" asked Garry, rhetorically. "He knew Halloran?"

"Halloran worked for him. Another Benny," said Nye. He saw the boy looking at him with twisted brows, and he turned to Garry, finding his voice filled with a swift, bitter intensity it had not known in years.

"Garry, I can see what's on your mind. It wasn't like Kordes said. You get your hot head from me, all right. When I came on Halloran and your mother — in our own home — " he shook his head, lips working in a restrained, barely perceptible pain — "I don't know exactly what happened,

336

but Halloran wasn't unarmed, Garry, and his back wasn't turned, you've got to believe that."

Garry met his eyes. "I believe it, Dad," he said levelly. "I didn't mean to probe. I figured you never talked much about it with me because you wanted to forget it. I never heard the straight of it from the Carters. They said something about 'unpremeditated'. Was that why you got off with such a short sentence?"

"They dragged in something about the 'unwritten law,' too," shrugged Nye. "Maybe you and I should have talked it out. Life won't let you forget a thing like that, I guess."

"Like Pony?" asked Garry. "Does she look that much like Mother?"

Nye turned to him in surprise, and Garry smiled faintly. "I couldn't help seeing the expression on your face, Dad. The way you were looking at Pony when I first came on you by the corrals in Paintbrush Cap. You always get that expression when something reminds you of Mother. Hurt, like. Tortured." He caught at Nye's arm. "You can't judge Pony that way, Dad. Just because she looks like Mother."

They had stopped, and Nye saw now that Garry had noticed the bay where Pony had hitched it before the saloon across the street.

"It's more than looks, Garry. It goes deep. I've got to say it right out, now. Part of the reason I didn't want you to see Pony was that Kordes was here in Buffalo Bow. The other part was Pony herself."

"Don't say anything, Dad," Garry told him. "Her horse is over there. I acted like a fool out by the corrals in Paintbrush. I've got to apologize."

"You're just getting sucked in on something, Garry," said Nye swiftly, grabbing the boy's shoulders. "I know Kordes. The pattern's too old. That sheriff's dead body will be dumped into the Pecos, and it'll be soon. I've seen too many men marked for killing. The whole town's waiting for it!"

The boy was struggling to free himself. "What's that got to do with Pony? She doesn't even know Kordes."

"Was she that careful — to tell you?" said Nye. "They were so particular not to look at each other tonight, too. I've never seen a pretty woman go by without Kordes looking at her. If she's been in town a day, he knows her. They're building something, kid, and it's bad — "

Garry was working harder to get away. "Dad, let go, you're talking crazy."

"Face it, kid. You're just a two-bit hay-hiker that never got beyond the fourth grade. You don't even talk her language. She has a reason for seeing you and it's tied in with Kordes and Means and the whole setup here — "

He had hoped to shock the boy into some sense with the brutal frankness of it. He saw the shock, in the boy's hurt eyes. But it did not bring the reaction he wanted. The expression faded in those eyes, seeming to withdraw into the boy till only a blank, empty surface remained.

"I'm going to see her, Nye. Don't try to stop me. Don't interfere any more. I might forget you're my father."

Nye watched the boy's figure move down the street till it disappeared in the crowd before the saloon. He did not know when he finally moved. He had the sense of buildings, a sidewalk. Men. At last there was a bar before him, a drink.

He began to take in specific detail. It was some rotgut layout down near the west end of the main street, cramped, reeking little hovel with dank sawdust on the floor and half a dozen short card tables planted around the tinny piano at the rear. The pianist was banging out *The Cowgirl's Lament*, and the man next to Nye at the bar was singing it happily under his breath:

> *"My mother she's dead in a lonely grave,*
> *My father he ran away.*
> *My sister she married a gambling man,*
> *And I've been led astray . . ."*

Nye's body rocked with a slap on the back, and he could not stop his impulsive, angry whirling motion. It brought him eye to eye with the grinning, flushed man next to him.

"A drink, my friend," said the man thickly. "Let me buy you a drink. You look low enough to eat off the same plate with a snake."

"I guess so," said Nye.

"You're the brother of that young buck who's locking horns with the good sheriff over Pony Adams."

"Father," said Nye. Then his eye caught the glinting star the man wore. "And you work for Means?"

"Deputy Sheriff Quintin Cameron," grinned the man. "I'd be sheriff if my tastes didn't get so liquid. I'd be mayor." He shrugged tipsily. "What's the difference? Maybe I'm happier looking down the neck of a bottle." Some drunken instinct sensed Nye's suspicion, and Cameron turned quickly, patting him on the shoulder. "Come now. Just because your son and my boss are looking across the fence at each other doesn't mean that we should act like two strange dogs. Let me buy that drink and we'll sing together."

In an ugly mood, Nye tried to get drunk, and couldn't. But Deputy Cameron could. And the drunker he got, the more talkative he got. Finally Nye realized he was ignoring a precious mine of information. Cameron must have felt his intensified attention, for he wiggled his head from side to side, smiling wryly.

"You are wondering about the combination of spirits and an officer of the law," he said, in pompous inebriation. "It's the truth, Hackett, that in any other town they wouldn't let me wear this badge a day. They've been hunting six months for somebody to replace me, but they haven't found a man yet who would take the job, drunk or sober."

The bibulous humor was swept from his face sharply, and he put his elbows on the bar, staring blankly into the mirror.

"Do you know what it's like to live with a walking corpse, Hackett? That's what it is. I don't work with him. I live with him. I have to. I can't live with anyone else in this town. Once a man's marked down with Means, he stands as lonely as Means himself. Some men take to drink because they're thwarted, Hackett. Some because they're down. I took to it after about three months of waiting, day by day, to see John Means murdered where he stood beside me — "

He trailed off in a shallow, whisper way, and Nye stared at him, vaguely shocked by this unexpected glimpse of the man's deepest sources.

"How did it start?" he asked softly.

Cameron glanced at him. Then he spat on the floor, brushing sawdust over it with his foot. "Kordes, of course."

Nye listened quietly to the old story of how Kordes had gotten his grip here through control of the gambling and saloon interests when the town was a rail end. When the Union Pacific pushed on, and a more solid class of people began to form the town, a movement started to halt the corruption which had run rife under Kordes's hand.

One of the few honest officials left in the local government was Sheriff Means, who was sponsoring a petition to the territorial legislature to have Buffalo Bow put under the jurisdiction of the federal courts, as Laramie had, in order to clean it up. Patently, if this petition, and the evidence Means was gathering, ever reached the territorial capital, Kordes would be through here.

"How is it Kordes hasn't burned Means down before this?" murmured Nye, twirling an untasted drink.

"Kordes can't afford to make a martyr out of him," mumbled Cameron. "Things are too close to cracking for that. Shoot him down on the streets and there's liable to be a vigilante committee show up at Kordes's hotel. You saw how Means walks alone. He knows Kordes is afraid to touch him. Even rides out on posse. The Shane Brothers have been operating down around Rocker Junction, and Means has gone after them two or three times lately. He knows Kordes can't dust him off and keep clean of it too."

Nye left finally, hearing Cameron's raucous singing for a block down the street. He was busy now trying to finish the pattern of it. A beautiful woman cultivating a shabby, penniless hay-hiker half her age. A meeting-place in a canyon with a hidden cutoff. A sheriff who had to be gotten out of the way.

He had the impulse to take a hotel room, filled with the sense of deserting the boy in a crisis if he left town. But the thought of four walls stifled him, and at last, unable to find Garry, he rode Tar Baby out of town and made a miserable camp by the creek.

Morning brought a breeze rich with the tang of spring, and Nye climbed a hillside. He knew Garry would be coming out the

Paintbrush road if he returned to the ranch where they had been pitching hay, and he waited up on these slopes all day for sight of the boy.

It was early afternoon when the rider appeared on the winding road. Half a dozen men, with Sheriff Means in the lead, that uplifted tension of a marked man in his high, square shoulders. Nye got on his horse, drawn by some vague, nagging impulse to follow their line of direction, though he remained on the higher slopes.

Nye found himself looking at them from a bushwacker's position: how simple it would be for a hired killer from one of those bluffs below. It would not give him much head start, if the posse gave chase. But escape, somehow, did not seem to be the issue, any more than merely killing Means. That killing could have been accomplished any time. It was something else. Something tied up with Garry and Paintbrush Gap —

Then, as the knife slash of the Gap itself appeared in the hills ahead, a door seemed to open in Nye's mind. The knowledge it brought filled him with a sudden, nauseating fear, causing him to pull Tar Baby up sharply.

At the same instant, down in the valley, there was the cracking detonation of a distant gunshot. Means pitched off his horse. The posse began milling about the fallen man, some of them staring up at the bluffs which lay beneath Nye. And from the timber of these bluffs, a man appeared, fighting to mount a wheeling horse. Nye knew which way he would turn, long before the man battled his excited horse into the right direction. Up on the highlands, above the whole scene, Nye turned his own mare toward Paintbrush Gap.

He crossed the valley ahead of them and that would give him a few minutes. He pushed Tar Baby to her utmost, crashing recklessly into the first brush choking Paintbrush Gap. He reached the spot where he thought that cutoff should be, and could not see it. The posse would go right by, and within a quarter hour would be riding down the main cut into the hollow — the same hollow he now galloped for, hauling Tar Baby back onto her haunches when that sagging corral came into view. And there was the woman, jumping back from where she had been pinning something on a cottonwood bar.

He was off his horse, holding her arm in one brutal hand, tearing the note from her with the other. It was a short line, unsigned, asking Garry to wait for her half an hour, at least; she would explain later.

"Just long enough for the posse to find him, is that it?" Nye said, grasping her other elbow. "What drew Means out this way? A false lead on the Shane boys? And Benny, shooting him? So Benny comes down Paintbrush and ducks into that cutoff and the posse comes right on in here and finds Garry. Everybody knows Garry and Means quarreled over you, and it all adds up, with no strings on Kordes."

"Nye — " There was a plea in her voice, in her wide, fear-filled eyes.

It reached him with poignant shock how similar Debbie had looked in that last moment. Then he heard the horse. Not enough noise for the posse. And Benny would not be coming this far. So that had to be Garry — and he knew he couldn't tell Garry the facts. It would take too much time, even if he could convince the boy. There was one way, then —

Pony fought him as he pulled her in. She felt hot and rich in his arms. He wanted to spit on her; he mashed his lips against hers till they brought a muffled sound of pain from the woman.

They were that way when Garry rode into the clearing. When Nye released Pony, the boy was already off his horse, the blank, shocked surprise of his face rapidly swept away before a concentrated rage.

Nye could not stop himself, in that last moment, holding out his hand, and saying the name, in a strangled, incoherent way.

"Garry — "

"You bastard," Garry said.

His first blow knocked Nye against the corral fence. Nye blocked the impulse to raise the hands in defense. Garry beat him till he hung like a sack of wheat over the bars. Then he stepped back and let Nye slide onto the ground.

Nye lay on his face for a measureless space of time. His one poignant hope was that the boy should leave Paintbrush Gap, in the other direction. It was a logical hope. There was no reason for Garry to go back to town. And when Nye finally found strength to raise his head, Garry was gone, and Pony, and he was looking up into the brutal, avenging faces of the possemen.

For a week there was talk of lynching in Buffalo Bow. But not enough connection could be established between Kordes and the prisoner. On the third day, Garry came back. It was evening, and most of the restless groups that had been stirring aimlessly around outside the jail were gone, when Quintin Cameron brought the boy back.

"I'll give you fifteen minutes," he said, looking at Nye with that same puzzled, studying attitude he had maintained from the first. He had never evinced the anger shown by the rest of the posse. In fact, he had never showed much of any emotion, as if reserving something not yet resolved within himself. "Don't try to hatch up anything crazy," he said. "You're safer inside this jail than outside with the feeling in town right now."

His shoulders as he turned back down the hall, seemed held upward slightly, in some tension. It reminded Nye of Means. Then that was gone, and it was just Garry, staring at Nye.

"What can I say?" the boy murmured, finally.

"Say you'll forget it, and I'll do the same," Nye told him.

"I can't forget it — that easily. After what I called you, what I did." He gazed at Nye, shaking his head. "You did it deliberately, didn't you, Dad? Knowing I was coming, knowing that I was liable to do — "

"Hoping what you'd do — and get the hell out of there," grinned Nye. "You're a fool to come back now, Garry. I'm surprised Cameron didn't slap you right in jail."

"I used my last four bucks on a lawyer

in Rocker Junction," said Garry. "He told me he'd pull me out on a habeas corpus if they jailed me. I told that to Cameron, and it must hold water, because he didn't bother to book me. Apparently they're satisfied with you. I was fifty miles out in the Owl Creeks when some high-line rider dropped word what was happening down here. I killed my horse getting back."

He grabbed the bars, something strained entering his voice. "Pony was hooked up with Kordes, then?"

"We're the only ones who know it," said Nye. "Kordes had this built hogtight. They had to get rid of Means and they had to have a goat that would divert the blame from Kordes. Your rivalry with the sheriff over Pony made it a perfect setup. Even having it switched from you to me didn't throw it off the track enough. They figure I was seeking revenge for my son or something."

"I'm getting you out, Dad." The boy's voice was hardly audible.

"Don't be a fool, Garry. If you get in trouble now, what I did would be completely in vain, can't you see that?"

"But you aren't just going to sit here and wait for them to — to — "

"Hang me?" said Nye quietly.

"There isn't a chance of anything less, is there?"

Nye turned to pace across the cell, staring out the window at the night sky. "You weaken me, Garry," he said softly.

"You *haven't* given up yet, then." Tingling hope was in the boy's voice.

Nye wheeled in a swift decision, coming back to the bars. "Just getting out wouldn't solve anything, Garry. You wouldn't want a murderer for your saddlemate."

"But you're not — "

"In the eyes of the law, in the eyes of everyone we'd meet, I'd be a murderer," said Nye.

The boy stared at him a long time, the rapport between them a quivering, vibrating thing, so that Nye did not have to speak what was in his mind, but just watch the comprehension fill the boy's eyes.

"Kordes," whispered Garry, at last.

"It's the only way, Garry," said Nye.

Garry shook his head in a tortured way. "How, Nye? You said yourself he had it sewed up hog-tight. There isn't a string on him. Not one of those notes Pony wrote was signed. There isn't a person in town who knows Pony and Bob Kordes are connected."

"There must be someone," said Nye. "The

note-writing was only for you. Kordes wouldn't take that chance with himself. There must be a go-between."

"Benny?"

"It must have been," said Nye. He turned away once more, pacing to the window, trying to piece it together. Finally, lips pinched with the effort of thought, he faced back to his son. "Can you make love, Garry?"

A slow, wry smile spread the boy's lips. "If I can, it's inherited."

"You've got to see Pony," said Nye. "More than once. Not a word of accusation. Maybe you can convince her you're glad to get me off of your neck. But the main thing is, make love."

Garry swallowed. "All right, Dad."

"It will get back to Kordes," said Nye. "And he'll want to know what's going on. I think he'll want to know it from her personally, if I'm any judge of Kordes. That's where Benny comes in. When you're not with Pony, you watch him. When Benny goes to Pony, that's the time I want out of here."

"And when that time comes?"

Nye grinned wryly. "Be sure Quintin Cameron is on duty. Come about an hour before you think I should be out. And bring a bottle. The biggest, fullest bottle in Buffalo Bow."

After that, it was the waiting. Word came that the circuit judge was in Laramie. Then in Rocker Junction. The townspeople still gathered in knots outside the jail. Summer heat made the cell a sticky, suffocating chamber of torture for Nye. He could not sleep well at night, and he found himself looking at his tense, corded hands, and wondering if he would be in shape to do anything if he did get out. It was three days before Garry showed up again, Cameron allowing him the usual fifteen minutes.

"It was hard," the boy told Nye. "But she finally invited me up to her apartment behind the Alley Cat for dinner last night."

"I hope the waiter interrupted a tender little love scene."

"I saw that he did," grinned Garry.

"That'll get to Kordes quick enough," Nye nodded soberly.

"It's funny how different people look when you can see things clearly," said Garry. "I owe it to you that I didn't have to find out about Pony the way you found out about — Mom." They were silent a moment, then the boy touched his hat brim in an attempt at jaunty farewell. "Next time I come back, let's hope it's with the bottle."

The next day Cameron brought word that Judge Bailey had finished his cases in Rocker

Junction and would be in Buffalo Bow on the morning stage. Nye sweated the rest of that afternoon out in a cell so small the walls seemed to crush him.

Evening was sultry, with a deep haze filtering the moonlight until about nine, when it came through bright and yellow as new paint. The stragglers had finally left the front of the jail, and the only sound was the intermittent scratch of Cameron's spurs, as he moved restlessly about the front office.

Listening to that, Nye wondered if he had judged the man's weakness right. Cameron was strong enough in some ways — it surely took guts to work with Means that long. But if he had taken to drink as an escape from the tension of merely working with the man, what would it bring to be put in Means's shoes?

The creak of the outer door brought Nye up off his cot. Then Cameron's voice rang down the corridor.

"I thought you'd let Dad have this, being it's his last night and all," came Garry's response.

"If Judge Bailey found it out he'd have my job," said Cameron. "You can see your dad if you want, but you'll have to leave that here."

In a moment, the officious clang of key

and lock filled the corridor, and then Garry was coming down the cement floor with that quick, light tap of his heels. His face was gaunt and strained, dark hollows under his eyes from lack of sleep.

"I've stuck so close to Benny I'm starting to smell like molasses," he said, his face close up to the bars. "It's finally happened. There's a back stairs to Pony's apartment. He went up this evening about nine. He was there ten minutes. Do you think it'll be tonight?"

"It's got to, with the judge coming in on the morning stage," said Nye. "Forget to pick up that bottle on your way out. Give Cameron about an hour with it. Then come back. Whatever happens, don't render him incapable of coming with us."

After Garry left, Nye sat on a mattress sodden with his sweat, listening in an agony of tension to the sounds. There was the scrape of those spurs again. The rattle of paper. Cameron clearing his throat. *For God's sake,* Nye thought, *the hour's almost up.* Then, faintly, so low he could hardly be sure, came the clink of glass on glass —

After that, he realized the first space of waiting must have been but a few minutes, really, and that the bulk of the hour was still left, and that eternity was actually a very short measurement of time. Finally he heard the song, vague, muttered, as friendly and drunken as it had been that first night:

"My mother she's dead in a lonely grave,
My father he ran away,
My sister she married a gambling man — "

"And this gun in my hand ain't hay," Garry Hackett finished, in a soft, dangerous tone, from that outer room.

There was a moment devoid of sound. Then a fumbling, uncertain rattle of Cameron's spurs.

"Don't be silly, boy, put that gun down. One man in this town see you takin' your dad out of here and you'll have a lynching on your han's."

"That's why you're going with us," said Garry. "And if anybody asks, you say you're taking Nye down to Rocker Junction under orders. The plans have been changed and Judge Bailey's sitting on the case down there to avoid any trouble from the people around here."

"I wish I wasn't so drunk," complained Cameron; "I could think of something to do."

Nye Hackett had ridden from Texas to Montana, but the ride out of Buffalo Bow was the longest he had ever experienced.

They took back streets, on horses Garry had waiting behind the jail, but there were still idlers gathered before a rotgut saloon on a nameless corner, or a night watchman going to work. Cameron must have recited his little piece half a dozen times before they passed the last building.

Then it was the Paintbrush road, and the same slope Nye had watched from that first time. They dismounted and eased saddle girths and stood with the wind beating softly against them. Cameron was losing his glow, now.

"You're a damn fool," he kept telling Nye. "I don't know what you're up to, but if there was any chance of you getting off that hangrope, it's sure gone now."

"How can you be sure it'll be Paintbrush road, Dad?" asked Garry, ignoring the deputy.

"It's the chance we'll have to take," said Nye. "Kordes won't meet her in town. Of the two roads out of Buffalo Bow, this is the one I'd choose. Isn't there something about a thief returning to the scene of his crime?"

The movement on the road below stopped their talk. They were obscured by timber up here, but a summer moon illumined the road with searching detail, shining softly on the coat of the horse down there, till it glistened like wet blood. Nye tightened his girth, and stepped aboard.

"Aren't you waiting for Kordes, Dad?"

"He'll be along. Step aboard, Cameron. We're going to a little show."

They trailed Pony till she turned into Paintbrush Gap, and gave her a few minutes, and then plunged into the brush after her. Nye kept an eye out for that cutoff, and saw where Benny's horse had left sign that first time, turning off onto it. Nye led them into the mouth of the cutoff and waited again, hidden once more.

In ten minutes, there was a crashing passage of more than one horse out in the main gap. When they were by, Nye dismounted.

It was not a long walk to where the gap itself widened out, and those old corrals stood. Long before they came in sight of the people, they heard Kordes's voice rising steadily in increasing anger.

"I don't care about that, Pony, all I want to know is why you are seeing Garry Hackett."

"Maybe it amuses me." That was the sultry, veiled mockery of Pony's voice.

"Will it amuse you," asked Kordes, "to hear that you're not seeing him again?"

Nye and Garry and Cameron were at the fringe of brush now, and they could see it.

The pool of moonlight filled the glade with color so rich it looked viscid, bringing Pony's face into sharp, angry relief where she stood before Bob Kordes, by the corrals. Benny had pulled a few yards away toward the other side of the clearing, presumably in an attempt to give them privacy, and was holding their two horses.

"Maybe I want to see Garry again," pouted Pony.

Kordes grabbed her by the arms. "You're not falling for that saddle bum."

Her face twisted with the effort of breaking free. "What if I am? I'm tired of all this hiding and running and seeing only who you choose. Maybe I want an affair of my own once in a while."

"The only affair you'll have is with me!"

"Fine affair. Meeting out in the brush and not even looking at you on the streets — "

"It's worked out, hasn't it? Nobody connects me with that killing. It worked out just like I told you — "

"Like getting the old man in jail instead of his son?"

"That wasn't my fault," said Kordes savagely. "What's the difference? They've got their killer, haven't they?" He retained his grip on Pony's arms, but softened his voice. "Listen, Pony, when this blows over, you can come out in the open, it'll be just like I told you, we'll own the town, I'll be the king and you'll be the queen — "

There was more, but Nye didn't hear it. He was pulling Cameron's gun from his belt and handing it to the man. Cameron stared at him, shaking his head from side to side in some undefined wonder.

"Would you like the honor of stopping the show?" asked Nye in a whisper.

"I think it's due you," said Cameron with that sudden, impish smile Nye had seen the first time they met.

Kordes was still talking when Nye stepped into the open. He saw Pony's eyes widen, looking over his shoulder, and he wheeled. His swinish lips parted in shock.

"Benny," he bleated; then, "Benny!"

Nye was getting out his gun, as the horses reared up in a whinneying, whirling motion, with the violence of Benny's effort to get his weapon free. Then Garry's shot rocked Nye's head. Benny threw up his arms with a cry and pitched out of the saddle. Nye was still running forward, and he did not try to pull his gun out any farther, with Kordes ahead of him.

"Go ahead now, Bob," he shouted. "There isn't anybody else to do it for you."

Vicious, brilliant little lights flashed in

Kordes's eyes as he threw the girl free of him. He bent forward in a grotesque, hunching way, so that his lapel sagged, and his hand darted under his coat there. Running on into him, Nye let him get the little ivory-handled pepperbox just clear enough so that he could knock it aside in a sweeping, vicious swing of his hand.

I'm not Halloran, I'm not unarmed, and my back isn't turned. Nye hit him for that, in the heavy belly. Then he hit him for a boy beating his father till he hung on these very corral poles like a sack of wheat. Then he hit him just because he wanted to hit him.

After that Kordes lay on the ground, making small, ugly, retching sounds. Pony was gripping one of the corral uprights, and her eyes were wide now, turned on Garry in naked plea. Garry met it squarely, and her gaze fluttered, finally, and dropped, before the blank, unrelating indifference in his raw, wind-burned features. Cameron came back from Benny with a bleak look to his face.

"He's dead," he said. "Do you think we've got enough to stick it on Kordes?"

"You'll make an awful good witness," Nye told him. "Stay sober and they might even make you sheriff for it."

"You can't," gasped Kordes, trying to sit up. "Just the word of one man. It won't

360

go, Cameron, I'll break you, if you do. I'll — "

"Kill me, like you did Means?" said Cameron acridly. "You don't have Benny to do that now, Kordes."

"It'll be more than the word of one man," said Nye, staring at Pony. "Isn't there something they call state's evidence, that they give a witness leniency for turning?"

Pony's eyes flashed upward again, filled with that momentary, desperate plea. She turned her face away, trying to hide it, but Nye had seen it, and he knew what it meant.

"You're cooked, Bob," he said. "A woman you wouldn't even look at on the street will sew you up good." He turned to Garry. "Shall we help the deputy take them in, son?"

"You know," said Cameron, staring at them. "If I didn't know you were father and son, I'd swear you were brothers."

"Not brothers," smiled Garry, moving over to put his hand on Nye's shoulder. "Saddle-mates."

Bibliography of Books

BY LES SAVAGE, JR.

WESTERN NOVELS

Treasure of the Brasada. New York: Simon & Schuster, 1947.

The Doctor at Coffin Gap. New York: Doubleday, 1949.

The Hide Rustlers. New York: Doubleday, 1950.

The Wild Horse. Greenwich, Conn.: Fawcett Gold Medal, 1950.

Shadow Riders of the Yellowstone. New York: Doubleday, 1951.

Land of the Lawless. New York: Doubleday, 1951.

The White Squaw, as by Larabie Sutter. Greenwich, Conn.: Fawcett Gold Medal, 1952.

Outlaw Thickets. New York: Doubleday, 1952.

Teresa. New York: Dell, 1954.

Last of the Breed. New York: Dell, 1954.

Return to Warbow. New York: Dell, 1955.

362

Once a Fighter. New York: Pocket Books, 1956.

Hangtown. New York: Ballantine, 1956.

Beyond Wind River. New York: Doubleday, 1958.

Gun Shy (completed by Dudley Dean). Greenwich, Conn.: Fawcett Gold Medal, 1959.

Western Novels as by Logan Stewart:

War Bonnett Pass. Greenwich, Conn.: Fawcett Gold Medal, 1950.

They Died Healthy. Greenwich, Conn.: Fawcett Gold Medal, 1951.

The Trail. Greenwich, Conn.: Fawcett Gold Medal, 1951.

The Secret Rider. Greenwich, Conn.: Fawcett Gold Medal, 1952.

Savage Stronghold. Greenwich, Conn.: Fawcett Gold Medal, 1953.

Rails West. Greenwich, Conn.: Fawcett Gold Medal, 1954.

Historical Novels:

Silver Street Woman. New York: Hanover House, 1954.

The Royal City. New York: Hanover House, 1956.

Doniphan's Ride. New York: Doubleday, 1959.

Juvenile Novel:

The Phantom Stallion. New York: Dodd, Mead, 1956.

A Note about the Author

Although he died tragically young, Les Savage, Jr. was a prolific writer of Western and historical fiction, publishing 24 novels and well over 100 short stories, novelettes and novellas in his sixteen-year career. Even more remarkable than his output is the consistently high level of quality he attained, whether in the novel length or in the shorter forms.

Savage's fiction is highly atmospheric, assiduously accurate as to period, and vividly evoked. He was meticulous about plot, inventive, innovative, and loved to experiment. His painstaking research is apparent in all that he wrote, as is his intimate grasp of the terrain wherever a story would be set, his vital familiarity with the characteristics of flora in the changing seasons, and the ways of horses, mules, and men.

The Best Western Stories of Les Savage, Jr. collects nine of his most accomplished short stories and novelettes from such forties and fifties magazines as *Argosy, Dime Western, .44 Western, Lariat Story Magazine,* and *Zane*

Grey's Western Magazine. The settings here are widely varied, from Texas and New Mexico to Montana to the Far North; and the characters — soldiers, mountain men, frontier women, Indians, engineers, camp cooks, Mounties — are anything but typical stock figures that populate most Western fiction of the period. Like the novels of Les Savage, Jr., these stories are the work of an extraordinary popular-fiction talent.

Les Savage, Jr. was an extremely gifted writer who was born in Alhambra, California, but grew up in Los Angeles. His second published story was "Bullets and Bullwhips" accepted by the prestigious Smith and Street's WESTERN STORY. Almost ninety more magazine stories all set on the American frontier followed, many of them published in Fiction House magazines such as FRONTIER STORIES and LARIAT STORY MAGAZINE where Savage became a superstar with his name on many covers. His first novel, TREASURE OF THE BRASADA, appeared in 1947, the first of twenty-four published novels to appear in the next decade. Due to his preference for historical accuracy, Savage often ran into problems with book editors in the 1950s who were concerned about marriages between his protagonists and women of different races — a commonplace on the real frontier but not in much Western fiction in that decade. As a result of the censorship imposed on many of his works, only now have they been fully restored by returning to the author's original manuscripts. TABLE ROCK, Savage's last book, was even suppressed by his agent in part because of its depiction of Chinese on the frontier. It has now been published as he wrote it by Walker and Company in the United States and Robert Hale, Ltd. in the United Kingdom.

Savage died young, at thirty-five, from complications arising out of hereditary diabetes and elevated cholesterol. However, his considerable legacy lives after him, there to reach a new generation of readers. His reputation as one of the finest authors of Western and frontier fiction continues and is winning new legions of admirers, both in the United States and abroad. Such noteworthy titles as OUTLAW THICKETS, RETURN TO WARBOW, THE TRAIL, and BEYOND WIND RIVER have become classics of Western fiction. RETURN TO WARBOW is one of four of his novels so far to have appeared as a major motion picture.